DUTY, HONOUR, TRUTH, VALOUR

The tenets of the Knights of Champagne
will be sorely tested in this
exciting Medieval mini-series by

Carol Townend

The pounding of hooves, the cold snap of air,
a knight's colours flying high across the roaring
crowd—nothing rivals a tourney.
The chance to prove his worth is
at the beating heart of any knight.

And tournaments bring other dangers too.
Scoundrels, thieves, murderers and worse are
all drawn towards a town bursting with deep
pockets, flowing wine and wanton women.

Only these three knights stand in their way.
But what of the women who stand beside them?

Find out in
Carol Townend's

Knights of Champagne
Three Swordsmen for Three Ladies

LADY ISOBEL'S CHAMPION
and
UNVEILING LADY CLARE
already available

and
LORD GAWAIN'S FORBIDDEN MISTRESS
available now

AUTHOR NOTE

Arthurian myths and legends have been popular for hundreds of years. Dashing knights worship beautiful ladies, fight for honour—and sometimes *lose* honour! Some of the earliest versions of these stories were written in the twelfth century by an influential poet called Chrétien de Troyes. Troyes was the walled city in the county of Champagne where Chrétien lived and worked. His patron, Countess Marie of Champagne, was a princess—daughter of King Louis of France and the legendary Eleanor of Aquitaine. Countess Marie's splendid artistic court in Troyes rivalled Queen Eleanor's in Poitiers.

The books in my *Knights of Champagne* mini-series are not an attempt to rework the Arthurian myths and legends. They are original romances set around the Troyes court. I wanted to tell the stories of some of the lords and ladies who might have inspired Chrétien—and I was keen to give the ladies a more active role, since Chrétien's ladies tend to be too passive for today's reader.

Apart from Count Henry and Countess Marie, of whom we have brief glances, my characters are all fictional. I have used the layout of the medieval city to create my Troyes, but these books are first and foremost fictional.

LORD GAWAIN'S FORBIDDEN MISTRESS

Carol Townend

First published in Great Britain 2015
by Mills & Boon, an imprint of Harlequin (UK) Limited,
Large Print edition 2015
Harlequin (UK) Limited, Eton House, 18-24 Paradise Road,
Richmond, Surrey TW9 1SR

© 2015 Carol Townend

ISBN: 978-0-263-25555-3

Carol Townend was born in England and went to a convent school in the wilds of Yorkshire. Captivated by the Medieval period, Carol read History at London University. She loves to travel, drawing inspiration for her novels from places as diverse as Winchester in England, Istanbul in Turkey and Troyes in France. A writer of both fiction and non-fiction, Carol lives in London with her husband and daughter. Visit her website at caroltownend.co.uk

Visit the author profile page at millsandboon.co.uk

To Melanie with love and thanks
for always being there.
(I won't embarrass us both
by counting the years in public!)

Chapter One

August 1174—an encampment outside Troyes in the County of Champagne

Troyes was bursting at the seams—the summer market was at its height and every inn and boarding house was packed to the rafters with merchants and housewives. Tumblers and singers jostled for the best spots in the market squares. Mercenaries and cutpurses roamed the narrow streets, searching for the shortest route to an easy profit. Indeed, so many people had descended on the town that a temporary campsite had been set up in a field outside the city walls. The encampment was known as Strangers' City, and line after line of dusty tents filled every inch of the field.

One tent stood out from the rest. Slightly larger than the others, more of a pavilion than a tent, the canvas was dyed purple and painted with silver stars.

Inside the purple pavilion, Elise was sitting on a stool next to Pearl's cradle, gently waving a cloth back and forth in front of her daughter's face. It was noon and even for August it was unusually hot. Elise wriggled her shoulders. Her gown was sticking to her and it seemed she had sat there for hours. Thankfully, Pearl's eyelids were finally drooping.

Voices outside had Elise narrowing her gaze at the entrance to the pavilion. André was back, she could hear him talking to Vivienne, who was nursing baby Bruno in the shade of the awning.

Elise waited, gently fanning Pearl. If André had news, he would soon tell her. Sure enough, a moment later André pushed through the tent flap.

'Elise, I've done it!' he said, eyes shining. He put his lute on his bedroll. 'Blanchefleur le Fay has been booked to sing at the palace. At the Harvest Banquet.'

'The palace? You got a booking at the palace already? Heavens, that was quick.' Elise bit her lip. 'I only hope I'm ready.'

'Of course you're ready. I've never heard you in better voice. Count Henry's steward was thrilled to learn Blanchefleur is in town. The Champagne court will love you.'

'It's been a while since I performed—I was afraid that I might already have been forgotten.'

'Forgotten? Blanchefleur le Fay? That's hardly likely. Elise, it's the booking of a lifetime. I can't think of a better setting for Blanchefleur to step back on stage.'

Elise glanced at Pearl. Asleep. Carefully, she folded the cloth she'd been using as a fan and smiled to hide her disquiet. 'You did well, André. Thank you.'

'You might look a little happier,' André said, watching her. 'You're nervous about singing in Champagne.'

'Nonsense!' Elise said, although there was a grain of truth in André's remark. 'But I mustn't disappoint them.'

'You're afraid you'll see him.'

Her chin lifted. 'Him?'

'Pearl's father, of course. Elise, you don't need to worry, Lord Gawain's not in Troyes. He left to claim his inheritance.'

'You've been listening to the gossip.'

'Haven't you?'

Elise grimaced, but it would be futile to deny it. Maybe she shouldn't have listened, but where

Gawain Steward was concerned that seemed impossible. His image never left her; even now it was bright and clear, a powerful knight with a shock of fair hair and a pair of smouldering dark eyes. 'It's odd to think of him as the Count of Meaux,' she murmured. 'He had no expectations of inheriting.'

'Oh?'

'I gather there was bad blood between him and his uncle. I know no more than that.'

André shrugged. 'Well, he's count now, so they must have resolved their differences.'

'It would seem so.'

Elise was pleased for Gawain's good fortune. In truth, she was pleased for herself. Gawain's inheritance was her good fortune too. Blanchefleur le Fay had wanted to sing at the famous court in Champagne for years. Even the difficulties of her last visit here hadn't killed that ambition.

After Pearl's birth, when Elise had realised that Blanchefleur must make a truly spectacular return or risk fading into obscurity, she'd been inspired with the thought that she might stage her comeback at the palace in Troyes. It would be something of a coup to sing before Countess Marie herself. The daughter of the King of France, no less!

There had been a few ghosts to fight before

Elise had been able to return to Champagne. She would never forget that her sister, Morwenna, had died near Troyes. However, nothing Elise could do would bring Morwenna back. In any case, if Morwenna had been alive she would be the first to agree that the Troyes court was the ideal place for Blanchefleur le Fay's triumphant return.

And then there was Gawain, and the fear that she might run into him. What would she say to him? *He is the father of my child and he doesn't know...*

But then Elise had heard that Gawain had become Count of Meaux and that obstacle at least had been removed. Gawain was miles away, claiming his inheritance in the Ile-de-France. The coast was clear.

'What's he like?' André asked.

'Hmm?'

'Lord Gawain.'

Lord Gawain. 'He was a plain knight when I knew him. Striking. A warrior. But he was also kind. Protective.'

Last year, Elise had been both surprised and flattered to have been the object of Gawain's interest. It was even more astonishing when one stopped to consider that not once had she used

Blanchefleur le Fay's wiles on him. No, she'd simply been the shy and retiring maidservant, Elise.

'Yet you fear him. You were anxious not to meet him.'

Elise glanced at Pearl, biting her lip. 'I'm not afraid of Lord Gawain. I just wanted to avoid any…complications.'

'Complications?'

'André, Pearl's father is a count. I have no idea how he might react when he learns he has a daughter.'

'You'd prefer that he didn't find out.'

'Frankly, yes. The fact that Gawain is a count will not change his character. He is a dutiful man, a man of honour. I befriended him as a means of entering Ravenshold.'

André frowned. 'What about Lady Isobel? I thought you'd become her maid to get into Ravenshold.'

'So I did, but my friendship with Lady Isobel was untried. There was a strong possibility it might come to nothing.'

'So you kept Lord Gawain in reserve.' Eyes shocked, André looked at Pearl. 'I thought— knowing you—he'd be more than that.'

'I like the man, of course,' Elise said hastily. In truth, she had more than liked him. She might have befriended Gawain out of desperation, but she hadn't had to feign the attraction. Passion had flared up between them without any effort on her part. Sparks had been flying from the first. 'I'm not certain he will forgive me. You see, I did deceive him.'

Elise bit her lip. Deceiving Gawain had been both the hardest and the easiest thing she had ever done. She had flirted with a man—she'd never felt comfortable flirting, but it had been astonishingly easy with Gawain. It had been fun, of all things. Initially, she'd done it hoping to discover how her sister had died. Before she had come to know Gawain, she had told herself that uncovering the truth about Morwenna's death was all that mattered. But she had quickly realised that she'd been deceiving herself as much as Gawain. The liking between them had been strong. Too strong. They had ended up as passionate lovers even though she'd come to mistrust everything she felt for him. Was it really possible to feel so much for a man, and so quickly?

'It's a relief to know I won't see him,' she said. 'Particularly since he is the grand Count of Meaux. André, he lives in a different world.'

'The world of the court.'

'Just so. We might entertain there, but it is not

our world. But for you to have secured a booking so soon! It's wonderful.' She grimaced. 'Except for one thing.'

'Oh?'

'Blanchefleur's gowns.' Elise gestured at her stomach and tried to push Pearl's father to the back of her mind. 'Last time I tried them, they were still a little tight.'

'Rot! You're as slim as you were before Pearl came along.'

'You, sir, are a flatterer. Those gowns aren't decent and Blanchefleur wouldn't dream of appearing in a loosely laced gown. Remember, the world at large likes to think of her as innocent. They believe she's been on retreat in a convent. The gowns—'

'Try them on again, Elise, I am sure they'll fit. What about buying new ribbons?'

Butterflies were dancing in Elise's stomach. Nervous, excited butterflies. She drew in a breath. She had dreamed about performing at the Champagne court for years, and she'd be mad to let a few nerves spoil her chance of singing at the palace. Reaching for André's hand, she gave it a gentle squeeze. 'Very well,' she said, brightly. 'New ribbons it shall be. Will you keep an eye on Pearl for me while I go to the market?'

André looked regretfully at her. 'I'm sorry, Elise, you'll have to ask Vivienne. I'm meeting friends at the ale tent. We'll be going back into town.'

'Don't worry, that's fine,' Elise said.

Vivienne was Pearl's wet-nurse. Deciding to ask Vivienne if she would feed Pearl had been one of the most difficult decisions Elise had ever made. But it was unavoidable if she was to continue singing, because Elise's *alter ego*, Blanchefleur le Fay, couldn't possibly be a nursing mother. Blanchefleur never looked at men. The personification of innocence, she kept them at arm's length. Blanchefleur was aloof and pure. Untouchable. She didn't have a heart; she broke them.

Elise hadn't actually chosen Blanchefleur le Fay for her stage name. Extraordinarily, the name had evolved, possibly helped by the fact that she wore a white enamel pendant shaped like a daisy. Blanchefleur was mysterious. She was otherworldly and exotic. Famed throughout the land, Blanchefleur was fêted like a princess in the great houses of the south. Blanchefleur would die before she did anything as down to earth, as sinful, as having a child out of wedlock.

Briefly, Elise had thought about taking on another persona, one that would allow her to be more open about being a mother, but Blanchefleur had been good to her. Blanchefleur was a good earner and Elise was reluctant to let her fade into obscurity. Real ladies—noblewomen—had wet-nurses, so why shouldn't she?

But there was no escaping that it had hurt to give up feeding Pearl herself. It felt like a betrayal and her whole being ached—even now, several weeks after the birth. She hadn't expected to feel so bad.

Vivienne had been the obvious choice for Pearl's wet-nurse. Vivienne had joined their troupe back in the days when Elise's father, Ronan, had been alive. Vivienne wasn't a singer and she hated performing, so she cooked and cleaned and helped them pack up when they moved from town to town. She acted as Blanchefleur's maid.

The three of them, Elise, André and Vivienne, had lived together for years and recently—as recently as last winter when Elise had been away in Champagne—Vivienne and André had become lovers. Crucially they also had a newborn—baby Bruno was only a few days older than Pearl. Elise was lucky to have Vivienne as Pearl's wet-nurse. Without her, earning a living for her and Pearl would be doubly difficult.

* * *

Winding the cherry-coloured ribbon neatly round her fingers, Elise tucked it into her purse and smiled at the stallholder. 'Thank you, I love the colour.'

'It's silk, *ma demoiselle.*'

'I can see that.'

The ribbon was perfect. It was strong enough to act as a new lacing, and it was only slightly longer than the old one. It would seem André had been right when he'd said she had regained her former figure. Elise could get into both Blanchefleur's gowns, and the cherry-coloured ribbon would be perfect with the silver silk of her favourite one.

Flicking her veil over her shoulder, Elise grimaced as she pushed through the crowd. The heat in the market square was unbearable. It was like an oven in town, far hotter than in the campsite at Strangers' City. The rows of narrow wooden houses trapped the warm air. Elise felt smothered. She couldn't wait to get back to the pavilion and take off her veil.

She elbowed her way clear of the press round the stalls and had almost reached the shade beneath the Madeleine Gate when she heard hoofbeats.

'Stand back,' a man in front muttered. 'Horses coming through.'

It was a knight and his squire. The knight was not wearing his chain mail. He was wearing a cream-coloured tunic edged with red-and-gold braid. None the less, there was no mistaking him as a knight. Only a knight would sit so confidently on so large a horse. He was turned the other way, laughing at something his squire had said.

Elise's breath stopped. The knight had fair hair, just like Gawain's. His horse—an ugly black-stockinged bay—seemed familiar. And the knight's squire—her heart seemed to shift in her chest—that red tunic, that golden griffin emblazoned across it, there was something different about that griffin, but…

The knight turned his head. *Gawain.* Her heart turned over. It couldn't be, but it was. Elise jerked back and peered through the screen of people in front of her. *Gawain.*

Her mind raced. Gawain wasn't supposed to be in Troyes! Elise wouldn't have dreamed of coming back if she'd known he was in town. Why was he here?

Everyone knew that Gawain's uncle, the Count of Meaux, had died and that Gawain had inherited. Gawain was supposed to be safely in the Ile-de-France, settling into his new county. This could be very awkward. *That man gave me a daughter and I never told him. Lord, what shall I do?*

Elise watched him ride through the arch, a strange cramp in her belly. Gawain's hair was fairer than it had been last winter. Sun-bleached. His face was bronzed and more handsome than she remembered. The cramp intensified. She hadn't wanted to see him.

He's supposed to be in Meaux.

How could Blanchefleur le Fay perform with Gawain in town? If he came to the palace when she was singing, he'd be bound to recognise her. And then the questions would start. And the re-criminations. He would find out about Pearl, and then...

Briefly, Elise closed her eyes. She really didn't want to face him. And it wasn't just because last year when they had met she'd parried most of his questions about her life as a singer. She'd told him as little as possible. She wasn't sure how he would react when he learned that Pearl was his. What if he wanted to take Pearl from her? He wouldn't do that, surely?

The new Count of Meaux and his squire turned away from her, the crowd parting to let their horses through. Elise stared at Gawain's back, at his wide shoulders, and wondered whether he was the type of man who would want to bring up his child. If only she knew him better. Most knights would gladly wash their hands of any responsibility for their illegitimate children. She looked through the crowd at his fair head, heart beating like a drum. A count might do anything he wished.

Dear Heaven, Gawain—here in Troyes. This changed everything.

Lord, he was looking over his shoulder. Her heart leaped into her throat. He was looking right at her! Shrinking back, she trod on someone's foot.

A woman scowled at her. 'Watch it!'

'My apologies,' Elise muttered.

Turning away, she stumbled into the Rue du Bois.

Her mind was in chaos, but one thought dominated. Gawain Steward, Count of Meaux, was in Troyes, and he had seen her. Heart pumping, she kept her head down and pushed her way through a group of merchants talking by the entrance to one of the cloth halls.

'Excuse me. My pardon, sir.'

'Elise? *Elise!*'

Gawain was about twenty yards behind her and the air was full of noise—the braying of a mule, the honking of a goose—yet she heard the jingle of harness. Hoof beats. She stopped dead in her tracks, eyes fixed on a small girl clinging to her mother's skirts. What was the point? She couldn't outrun him. True, the street was busy and she might dive into an alley, but there were children here and that brute of a horse was trained to barrel its way through anything. Someone might get hurt.

Drawing in a deep breath, she turned. Her mind was a complete blank. She didn't have the first idea how she would greet him. *Lord Gawain, what a pleasant surprise. I trust you are in good health. By the by, I had a baby. I am hoping she will have your eyes.* Heavens, she couldn't say that. She didn't want to tell him about Pearl. She needed time to think, but it didn't look as though she was going to get it.

'Elise? Elise Chantier?'

Elise stood quite still as he approached, steeling herself not to back away from that great bay. The animal might look ungovernable, but Gawain could control him. She craned her neck to look up at him.

'Lord Gawain!' She dropped him a curtsy. 'What a pleasant surprise.'

There was a creak of leather as he dismounted

and gestured at his squire to take the reins. He offered Elise his arm. 'Walk with me.'

Elise tipped her head on one side and managed a smile. 'Is that a command, my lord?'

He was taller than she had remembered. Larger. The sound and colour of the busy street faded as she looked at him. At those deep brown eyes— how could she have forgotten those grey flecks? Or those long eyelashes? And his nose, that aquiline shape was so distinctive. Elise had loved his nose. She had liked to run her finger down it as a prelude to a kiss. His mouth… As her gaze skimmed over it, she felt her smile freeze. His mouth was tight. He looked…not angry, exactly. He looked weary. How strange. He didn't look like a man who had just inherited a vast estate.

'Walk with me, Elise.'

'Yes, my lord.'

Gawain glanced at his squire. 'Meet me in half an hour, Aubin. Outside the castle gatehouse.'

'Yes, *mon seigneur.*'

When Elise put her hand lightly on his sleeve, Gawain, Count of Meaux, let out a relieved sigh. Gawain had been looking for Elise and he was pleased—far more pleased than he ought to be— to have found her. He set off in the direction of the

Preize Gate. 'It will be quieter once we get clear of the streets round the market,' he said.

Elise smiled and nodded and pushed her veil over her shoulder. Her cheeks were flushed. It was too warm for a cloak and Gawain could see the rise and fall of her breasts beneath her gown. He frowned. There was something different about her. Her eyes were the same, and her face...but something was different.

'I didn't expect to see you, my lord. I thought you were in the Ile-de-France.'

'You heard about my uncle.'

She nodded and looked away. 'I expect you will be leaving again soon.'

Something about her tone grated. Gawain frowned thoughtfully at her profile. 'That would please you?'

Her colour deepened to crimson and he imagined he saw a flash of guilt. What could she have to feel guilty about? Last winter she had enjoyed their time together as much as he had. There was no question of that. He couldn't have misread her so badly. *She is hiding something.*

'Not at all, my lord,' she murmured. 'It is good to see you.'

Gawain decided not to probe. If she wanted to keep things from him, that was up to her. There was, after all, no real connection between them. Once he had reassured himself that all was well with her, he could forget all about her. He had his own life to lead. He was about to meet his betrothed, Lady Rowena de Sainte-Colombe. 'You found the ribbon you were looking for?'

She shot him a startled glance. 'You've been to the pavilion.'

Elise was walking discreetly at his side. There were several inches between them and Gawain didn't like it. He was taken with the impulse to wind his hand round her waist and bring her closer. Instead, he gave her a curt nod. 'A friend mentioned seeing you in Strangers' City.'

She was silent for a space. 'A Guardian Knight, I assume. I've seen their patrols.'

He nodded. 'When I found your tent, the woman who lives with you told me you'd gone to buy ribbon.' Gawain put his hand on her arm. 'Elise, how have you been? Is all well with you?'

'I am very well, my lord.'

'That is good to hear. Did you find the success you were after?'

'My lord?'

'Your ambitions as a *chanteuse*.'

The colour went from her cheeks. 'I...I haven't done as much singing as I thought I would.'

'Oh?' Gawain watched her whilst he waited for her answer. It struck him that they were addressing one another as though they'd only just met. A potter hurried past leading a donkey laden with pots. The man would never suspect that they'd been lovers. Elise hadn't answered and Gawain leaned in. The scent of her—a heady combination of musk and ambergris and warm woman—hit him like a blow to his stomach. He almost groaned out loud. *Elise.* She had been the perfect bedmate.

'You left without warning,' Gawain heard himself say. The words were out before he could stop them.

Dark eyes watched him. Large and unfathomable. She'd never been an easy woman to read. Except when they were in bed. She'd been a rare joy in bed. And not only that—she'd had enough experience to know which herbs to take to stop her conceiving. Yes, a rare joy indeed. But this woman staring up at him was unfathomable. 'I had to leave.' Slender shoulders lifted. 'My time in Champagne was over.'

'Because you'd found everything you needed to know about your sister?'

'Yes, my lord. Once it was clear that Morwenna's death had been an accident, I had no reason to stay.' She smiled. 'I had to get back to my singing. And my friends expected me to return. My life is with them.'

'So you had no reason to stay.'

Those unfathomable eyes didn't as much as blink. 'Sir—my lord—what are you saying?'

Gawain took Elise's slender wrist and tugged her off the street and under the eaves of one of the houses. A peculiar tightness was centred in his chest. He couldn't account for it, although he suspected it had something to do with Elise.

'There was nothing lasting between us,' he muttered.

'Gawain, why are you looking at me like that?'

'God forgive me,' he said, pulling her close. One arm slid round her waist and the moment her body was aligned with his, Gawain's tension eased. Better. He caught her by the chin and tilted her face up—her mouth lay a mere inch away. He breathed in the subtle fragrance of musk and ambergris. Better still. Did she taste the same as she had done last winter? She'd been sweet as honey. His eyes fixed on her lips.

'Gawain?'

His mouth met hers in a whisper of a kiss. There'd been nothing between them, yet he hadn't wanted her to leave. And until this moment he hadn't realised how strongly he'd missed her. How much he'd enjoyed his time with her.

'Elise,' Gawain muttered, as he came up briefly for air. She tasted just as sweet. Enchanting. And then he was kissing her again. Hungrily. Eagerly. She was more of an armful—more womanly—than she had been last winter. He liked the difference. A thrill shot through him as their tongues touched. It felt as it had always felt with Elise, that she had been made for him.

He slid his hand down the curve of her buttock and lifted his head with some reluctance. '*Mon Dieu*, Elise. I know we made no vows to each other, but you didn't even say goodbye. I worried about you.'

She was breathless and it was pleasing to see the roses back in her cheeks. She wasn't unmoved. He hadn't liked to think that she'd found it easy to walk away without as much as a backward glance.

'I…I am sorry, my lord.' She eased back, fingering her mouth, which was flushed from his kiss. 'Was…was that a farewell kiss?'

As Gawain released her, he noted with surprise that it went very much against the grain to do so. Lord, this woman was a trial to him. She had been from the beginning. A quiet shy woman who had him in knots without even trying. He would have liked to continue kissing her, but of course he shouldn't have kissed her in the first place. It hadn't helped. It had made him long for more, which was impossible. He must think about his future. He was going to marry Lady Rowena de Sainte-Colombe. However, it was hard to think about Lady Rowena, whom he had never met, when Elise was looking up at him with that dark, hard-to-read look in her eyes. She fascinated him.

He leaned his hip against the corner of the house. 'You may call it a farewell kiss if you wish. Elise, I came to find you because I need to know you are well. That woman you live with—'

'Vivienne. She's a good friend.'

'You've known her for long? Is she a *chanteuse*?'

'I've known Vivienne long enough and, no, she's not a *chanteuse*.'

'What of her husband, then? Is he a good man?'

'Vivienne isn't married.'

Gawain's gut tightened. 'You're not telling me that you and Vivienne are living unprotected in a tent in Strangers' City?'

'Of course not. André lives with us.'

'Who the devil is André?'

'Vivienne's lover.'

'The father of the twins?'

'Twins?' For a moment her face was quite blank. Then she gave a bright smile. 'Oh, yes. The twins.'

'Is André a good man?' Gawain asked. Was it his imagination or was her smile a shade too bright? And why was she avoiding his gaze? 'Tell me about him.'

Her face softened. 'I am very fond of him.'

'He's a singer?'

'André plays the lute. We perform together.'

Gawain swallowed a sigh. Her answers were very brief. She was being evasive, and what she had said about her living arrangements wasn't re-assuring.

Had her ambitions as a singer led her into bad company? Vivienne had seemed nice enough, but he would have to meet this André before he'd feel happy about Elise sharing the man's tent with his woman and children. And even if André was perfectly honest, was he capable of defending Elise in a crisis? Gawain didn't number any lute-players among his friends. In the event of a robbery or worse, was André strong enough to protect her? And even if he was, he had his woman and children to look out for. Could he look after Elise too? If Gawain met the man he could judge for himself. Clearly, Elise had the will to pursue her ambitions as a singer, but she needed someone strong at her side.

'So you're happy in your life as a singer?'

'Singing is very fulfilling.'

'I am glad you find it so.' He pushed away from the corner of the house. 'You are on your way back to the camp?'

'Yes.'

'Allow me to accompany you.' With luck, by the time they got back to the pavilion, André the lute-player would have returned. You could tell a lot from a man by looking him in the eye.

She backed hastily away. 'My lord, I can manage without your escort.'

Elise was looking at him in complete horror. How could this be? When he'd kissed her just now, her tongue had touched his. 'Elise, what's wrong?'

'Nothing's wrong, my lord. I can find my way back to the pavilion without your assistance.'

Gawain's heart sank. She was trying to get rid of him. Why? What was she hiding?

At a recent visit to the Black Boar, Gawain's friend Raphael, Captain of the Guardian Knights, had mentioned being concerned that counterfeiters had come to Troyes. Raphael seemed convinced they were hiding out in Strangers' City.

Gawain couldn't believe Elise would have connections with counterfeiters, but it was possible. She was acting very oddly and he intended to find out why. 'Elise, I'm coming with you.'

Chapter Two

Elise's mind seemed to freeze as they walked towards the castle gatehouse to meet Gawain's squire. Gawain couldn't come back to the pavilion! She had no idea what Vivienne had said to him, but thankfully she didn't appear to have given the game away. Gawain had mentioned twins—he must have seen both babies and assumed that they were Vivienne's.

He had no idea that he had fathered a child. As far as Elise was concerned that was all to the good. What would be gained by telling him?

He was talking as they walked along. She struggled to pay attention.

'So, Elise, you have done some performing since we last met?'

'Yes, my lord.' It was true, Elise had sung. A little. She had sung until she could no longer squeeze into Blanchefleur le Fay's gowns and had been forced into retreat at Fontevraud Abbey.

'Where did you sing—at Poitiers?'

Elise gave the innocuous answers Gawain seemed to want. When they reached the castle, she was feeling decidedly panicky. What if he found out about Pearl? How would he react?

Gawain's squire was waiting by the gatehouse.

'My thanks, Aubin,' Gawain said, taking the reins and swinging easily into the saddle. He offered her his hand.

Elise stepped back. 'My lord? You expect me to ride with you?'

Gawain lifted an eyebrow. 'You've already had me walking far more than I ought to have done. I'm a count, I'm expected to ride everywhere. What will it do to my reputation if you have me walking all the way to Strangers' City?'

Since when had Gawain cared what people thought of him? In any case, Strangers' City wasn't far. He was teasing, wasn't he? A pang shot through her. One never quite knew with Gawain, but they used to tease each other a lot. She'd missed it. She put a hand on her hip. 'And what about my reputation, my lord?' The great horse's nickname came back to her. 'What do you suppose it will do to my reputation if I arrive at the pavilion on the back of The Beast?'

He grinned. 'Not on The Beast's back, sweet. I'll have you before me.'

Before Elise had time to blink, Gawain was leaning out of the saddle at a crazy angle, taking hold of her around her ribcage. She heard herself squeak as her body thumped against the horse's shoulder. It wasn't seemly being pulled on to a destrier. Such a thing would never happen to Blanchefleur le Fay. No one would dream of treating her in such a way.

'You make it harder on yourself if you struggle,' he said, lips twitching. 'Give in, Elise.'

Something tugged on her veil, her skirts fluttered about her knees, her free arm tangled in the destrier's reins before she found purchase, and then—another ungainly thump—somehow she was sitting sideways in front of him, gasping for breath.

Dark eyes looked down at her. His lips curved.

'Put me down, my lord, everyone is staring. This is most unseemly.' Face hot, she pushed at her skirts.

His arm tightened about her waist. 'You needn't fear. I won't drop you.'

'I am not comfortable, and I am sure your horse is not. I am practically sitting on his neck!'

'The Beast has carried worse burdens.'

'My lord, please put me down. If you must accompany me back to the pavilion, I am perfectly capable of walking beside you.'

His thumb shifted against her ribs in an ambiguous movement that might or might not have been a caress. 'Later.'

Spurs jangled as he kicked his destrier's flanks and they lurched into motion.

Blessed Mother, Elise prayed. *Don't let him discover that he is Pearl's father.*

'Relax,' Gawain murmured, as they rode through the Preize Gate.

There were smiles and raised eyebrows from the guards as they went under the arch, but to Elise's amazement no ribald remarks. At least none that she heard. The guards were probably too clever to risk saying anything disrespectful before the Count of Meaux. Elise glanced up at him through her eyelashes and wondered what the men would say once they'd ridden out of earshot.

The horse walked on. Elise put an arm about Gawain's waist and clung to his belt. He brushed back her veil.

'Wretch,' she muttered. However, she was grateful the horse was walking. It would be even more embarrassing if she had to try to stay on when he was trotting. Gawain's arm was firm about her body. Secure. She was grateful for that too. His arm felt strong. Last year, she'd taken comfort in his strength. How could she have forgotten?

With a start, she realised that she was enjoying being in Gawain's arms; she was enjoying being able to look up at him like this. Which wasn't good because being close to him was distracting her from planning what to say when they reached the pavilion. She kept her gaze fixed rigidly on the forest of tents in the distance.

His thumb moved again. It was a caress, she was sure of it. A caress.

His white linen tunic had an open neck. His skin was bronzed, his chest broad. The temptation to rest her head against that chest was overwhelming.

She frowned.

'Elise?'

'This is a bad idea. A very bad idea.'

He studied her. 'If you dislike it that much, you may walk alongside.'

Her fingers curled round his belt. She shrugged

and gave a tragic sigh. 'It's too late. My lord, we are almost at the camp. My reputation is already in tatters.'

There was a little awkwardness when they first arrived back at the pavilion.

The babies were asleep under the awning and Vivienne was fanning them. She looked up when she heard the hoofbeats and slowly came to her feet.

'It's all right, Vivienne,' Elise said, as Gawain helped her down. 'You have already met Lord Gawain, I believe.'

Vivienne nodded.

Gawain walked over to the babies and stared down at them. 'Twins,' he murmured, lifting an eyebrow. 'I expect they will be something of a handful.'

Vivienne looked helplessly at Elise. It was clear she didn't know what to say.

Elise's heart was in her mouth. She really couldn't cope with Gawain discovering that Pearl was his daughter. It was far too complicated. She had to get him away from the babies before she or Vivienne said something that would give the game away. And she had to do it quickly. Acting on instinct, she took his hand and pulled him into the tent.

Gawain was so tall that his fair hair grazed the canvas. He looked about with interest, gaze running over the three bedrolls, the babies' cots, the travelling chests. 'So this is how you live.' He smiled. She didn't think he had noticed, but he still had hold of her hand. 'There's not much room.'

'That's true.'

'What's it like in winter?'

'When it freezes, we often take lodgings.'

Just then Vivienne coughed and stuck her head through the flap. 'My apologies for the interruption. This will only take a moment and then I shall leave you in peace.' With a grimace, Vivienne gestured at one of the travelling chests. 'It's urgent. Bruno needs fresh linens.'

Vivienne went to her chest, flung back the lid and burrowed inside. She threw a number of other things on to her bedroll, grabbed an armful of linens and went back to the entrance. As she lifted the door flap the pavilion brightened. 'Thank you, I'll leave you in peace.'

Elise watched her go, biting her lip. She was racking her brains for something to say—anything that would distract him from thinking about the babies.

Absently, Gawain rubbed the back of Elise's knuckles as the flicker of disquiet he'd felt earlier hardened into a quiet certainty. Elise was uneasy about something, and it wasn't just that she'd not expected to see him in Troyes. Was it the counterfeiters his friend Raphael had mentioned? He couldn't think what else it might be.

'When will André be back?' he asked.

'I've no idea. We shall have to ask Vivienne. Sometimes he—' Elise broke off, frowning.

Gawain followed her gaze and then he was frowning too. A sword lay on the bed, half-obscured by gowns and baby linens. A sword? Vivienne must have unearthed it from the bowels of her trunk and in her haste she hadn't put it away.

'Whatever's that doing here?' Elise freed her hand and picked it up.

The sword had a leather scabbard that was black with age. It made a scraping sound as she drew it. The sword looked old. Antique. The blade was dull, but a large red stone flashed in the pommel of the hilt.

'It's very heavy,' she added, looking at him. 'Heavier than yours.'

Gawain's stomach tightened. After the All

Hallows Tournament she had expressed an interest in his arms and he remembered explaining how damascened swords were forged. It shouldn't please him that she remembered too, but it did. Sad to say, the pleasure of that memory was pushed aside by his growing disquiet. What the devil was this sword doing in Elise's pavilion?

There was a slight scrape as she pushed it back into its scabbard. With a shrug, she dropped it back on to the bedroll. 'André told me he'd met up with a troupe of players,' she said. 'Old friends, apparently. They must have left it behind.'

Mind working, Gawain grunted. He was trying to remember exactly what Raphael had told him in the Black Boar. A man had been arrested for attempting to trade a fake relic. No, not a relic, a crown. Raphael had also mentioned rumours of someone making a replica of Excalibur. They were thought to be attempting to pass it off as having once belonged to the legendary King Arthur. The idea had seemed so unlikely, Gawain had hardly heard him.

Could this be that sword?

If someone was about to fool some idiot into parting with good money for a counterfeit sword, Raphael would have to be told. Gawain couldn't keep something like this from the Captain of the Guardian Knights, not when he knew Count Henry had asked the Guardians to watch out for suspicious goings-on in Strangers' City.

'I'd like to look at that,' he said, holding out his hand.

With a shrug, Elise retrieved it and passed it over.

Gawain's brows shot up as he drew the sword and tested the weight for himself. 'You're right, it is heavy. Clumsy.' He ran his thumb along the edge—it was startlingly keen. 'It has a surprisingly good edge.'

Brown eyes found his. 'Gawain, what's bothering you?'

He continued examining the sword. Trying the weight, shifting back to give it a swing. He looked at the pommel. Lord, that yellow metal looked very like gold. And the stone...

'It's a garnet,' he said. He could hear the surprise in his voice. 'A genuine garnet.'

A crease formed on her brow. 'It's not real, Gawain. It can't be.'

'It belongs to some players, you say?'

'André said he saw the players shortly after we arrived in Troyes. I can't think where else it might have come from.'

Gawain stared at the garnet in the pommel with a heavy heart. The more he looked at the sword, the more uneasy he became. He couldn't keep this to himself. It might well belong to a troupe of players, but Raphael would have to be told about it. He didn't want to believe that Elise was involved with counterfeiters, but it was beginning to look as though her friends might be. 'This sword doesn't feel right,' he said. 'The balance is skewed and the blade is a horror, but because of the hilt and the gem it's worth a fair bit.'

Her eyes widened. 'It can't be! It's a stage sword—just a prop.'

He gave her a direct look. 'A man might kill for the garnet alone. And if the hilt is gold...' Gawain let the silence stretch out, well aware that what he was about to do would damn him in her eyes. Which was a pity. He liked Elise and he wanted her to think well of him when they parted. He shoved the sword back into the scabbard with a snap. 'Ask Vivienne to step inside, would you? I need to speak to her.'

Elise blinked. Gawain's voice had changed. It was clipped and curt. Military. Thankfully he was distracted from Pearl, but he looked so serious. 'Gawain, what's the matter?'

'I need to speak to Vivienne.'

Elise searched his face. It was closed. Unreceptive. 'Vivienne, would you come in for a moment?'

Vivienne came in with the babies. Pearl was whimpering so Elise took her and draped her over her shoulder. Gawain looked so stern that despite the heat of the day, a chill ran through her.

Vivienne glanced at the sword in Gawain's hand. She bobbed into a curtsy, deposited Bruno into his cot and stepped forward with her hand out. 'I'll put that away, shall I, my lord?'

Slowly Gawain shook his head. 'I'll hang on to it, thank you,' he said, voice like ice.

'But, my lord—'

Elise rubbed Pearl's back.

Gawain took a deep breath. He hadn't taken his eyes off Vivienne. 'I'd like you to tell me what a sword like this is doing in your belongings. A sword the hilt of which is, if I am not mistaken, pure gold.' An eyebrow lifted as he touched the garnet. 'And this gemstone is genuine. The setting is really very good.'

Vivienne's mouth worked. 'I don't know much about it, *mon seigneur*. It belongs to a friend of André's. I think he wants to sell it.'

'And the name of this friend, if you please?'

Vivienne stood there, opening and shutting her

mouth. Elise put her hand on Gawain's sleeve. 'Gawain, there's no need to bark at Vivienne. You're frightening her.'

He looked at her, eyes stony. 'I'm merely asking questions.'

'You're frightening her.'

'If she has done nothing wrong, she has nothing to fear.' He turned back to Vivienne. 'The name of your friend, *madame*?'

'I…I've forgotten.'

'How convenient. Do you think André might know?'

Vivienne made a little moaning noise. Or it could have been Bruno, Elise wasn't sure. Bruno was definitely stirring. A little fist was moving about in his cot.

Gawain's frown scored heavy lines in his brow. 'What does André call himself when he's performing?'

'André de Poitiers.'

'Do you think he will recall the name of the friend to whom this belongs?'

'Most likely, my lord.' Bruno started to wail. Vivienne looked distractedly at him.

'Please continue, *madame*.'

Vivienne made a helpless gesture. '*Mon seigneur*, n-no one here is bearing arms, so I don't think we've broken any laws. I think André's friend is hoping to sell the sword.'

Gawain stared at her. 'You are selling this sword for him?'

'No, my lord. André's friend is going to sell it. André is simply keeping it for a time. He put it in my coffer. To be honest, I forgot it was there.'

Gawain made a sound of exasperation. Elise's stomach was churning. She wasn't sure what was happening, but it was clear Gawain suspected either Vivienne or André of some sort of wrongdoing.

'Lord Gawain?' Vivienne stepped forward, eyes anxious. 'We haven't done anything against the law, have we? All we are doing is holding a sword for someone who is going to sell it.'

'Vivienne, this sword is extremely valuable.'

'My lord, if it's valuable, then André's friend will get a good price for it.' Vivienne looked questioningly at Gawain. 'Where's the harm in that?'

Vivienne looked so confused that Elise felt herself relax. Whatever the reasons for the sword being in her coffer, Vivienne was clearly innocent of any wrongdoing. Gawain would surely see this.

'There is no harm,' Gawain went on, voice stern, 'provided the buyer is not misled as to the sword's true provenance.'

'My lord?'

'Someone might be tempted to pay more for a sword if they had been led to believe—for example—that it once belonged to King Arthur.'

'The legendary Excalibur,' Elise murmured, staring at the golden hilt. The garnet flashed blood-red, like the eye of a dragon. 'Those tales are just stories. They're not real.'

'My point exactly.'

Bruno let out a full-throated wail and Vivienne picked him up. Rocking him from side to side, she looked at Gawain with large, innocent eyes. 'My lord, I know nothing about any legendary sword.'

Gawain looked at her. The silence was broken by a wasp buzzing in and then out of the tent.

'Truly, my lord, I don't know what you're talking about.'

Elise found she was holding her breath. Gawain's expression was so serious, she hardly recognised him. And when his brown eyes fixed on her, she actually shivered.

'When's the lute-player coming back?'

'André? I've no idea.'

Vivienne shifted. 'He'll be back at suppertime, *mon seigneur*.'

'Not before then?'

'No, my lord.'

'Very well.' Gawain towered over Vivienne. 'Is my squire still outside?'

'Yes, my lord.'

He strode to the door flap and flung it back. 'Aubin! In here, if you please.'

Aubin hurried into the tent and nodded awkwardly at Elise. Elise gave him a weak smile and listened as Gawain rattled off a series of commands.

'Aubin, go straight to the Troyes garrison. Speak to Sir Raphael and to no one else. Tell him—' He broke off, frowning thoughtfully at Elise. 'No, that won't do. Elise, you understand the Guardian Knights will have to be told about this?'

'Will they?'

'Of course. Vivienne will have to accompany me to Troyes Castle. The Captain of the Guard will want to question her about this sword.'

Vivienne gasped and went white.

'She can't do that,' Elise said. Stomach twisting in apprehension, she stared at the sword. 'I have no idea why this is in our tent, but I'm convinced that Vivienne is not at fault.' She frowned at Gawain. 'I'm even more convinced that you can't take her to the garrison. She's a nursing mother. What about the babies? The Troyes garrison is no place for babies and she can't leave them behind. They need feeding at all hours.'

Vivienne swallowed. 'Are…are you arresting me, my lord?'

'No, I'm not arresting you. But I cannot pretend I have not seen this sword. You'll have to explain it to Sir Raphael.'

'Gawain, you can't take her to the garrison, not with the babies.'

Gawain looked at her.

'Gawain, the garrison really is no place for a nursing mother.'

'Very well.'

Elise let out a sigh. 'Thank you.'

'However, I shall have to take Vivienne into safekeeping.'

'Safekeeping?'

'She shall accompany me to my manor.'

Elise's eyes went wide. 'As your prisoner?'

'As my guest. Le Manoir des Rosières is only a few miles away. Sir Raphael can interview her there just as well as at the garrison.' He looked at Vivienne. 'Will that be preferable, *madame*?'

'Thank you, my lord,' Vivienne said, in a small voice. She looked so distraught that Elise's heart went out to her.

'Gawain, you can't do that!' Elise hugged Pearl

to her. If Gawain took Vivienne to his manor, Pearl would have to go too. And if Pearl went so would Elise. She swallowed. She wouldn't be parted from Pearl.

'I think you will see that I can. Aubin?' Gawain tapped the strange sword against his thigh. The garnet seemed to wink balefully.

'My lord?'

'Go back to the manor and tell Sir Bertran I need half a dozen horse soldiers to be at the ready.' He measured Vivienne's travelling chest and the two cots with his eye. 'And ask him to organise a cart for tomorrow. Vivienne, do you ride?'

'Not well, my lord. We have a cart. I usually travel in that.'

'Pity. We need to be discreet today, so we can't use your cart. We'll have to get you and the babies as far as the Preize Gate. The rest of your belongings can wait until later.' Gawain shot Elise a look. 'After I have spoken to Raphael and André.'

Gawain went on issuing commands. Something about borrowing a cart and a couple of guards from the garrison. Elise didn't hear much of it, her mind was in turmoil. She held Pearl to her and all she could think was that Gawain was about to take Pearl from her. Heart pumping, she stroked

Pearl's hair. Somehow, she must stop him. Whatever happened, she was not going to be separated from her baby.

'Yes, my lord.' Aubin was repeating his orders. 'I am to take a cart and some guards to the Preize Gate, where they will wait. Then I am to come back here and escort Vivienne to the cart on foot. With the babies.'

Saints, Gawain was taking Pearl away and she could think of no way of stopping him. Elise's head began to pound. For the first time it really hit home that since Gawain was the Count of Meaux, he could do anything. Against him, she was defenceless.

She found herself clutching at the flimsiest of straws. 'Gawain, you can't take Vivienne back to your manor. She acts as my maid.'

Dark eyes bored into her. 'Are you telling me you cannot manage without her?'

Her cheeks warmed. 'Naturally I can manage, but this is Vivienne's home. You can't simply uproot her.'

'Watch me.' He glanced at Vivienne, who was frantically rocking Bruno from side to side, and his voice softened. 'Elise, you must see that I cannot let this slide.'

Unfortunately, Elise did see. Gawain, as an honourable knight—as a count—was bound to uphold the law. However, there was also André to consider. What would he do when he got back this evening and found Vivienne and Bruno gone? And what exactly was the nature of his involvement with the sword? 'André might be completely innocent.'

The fair head nodded. 'For your sake, I hope that he is.'

Elise bit her lip and shot Vivienne a look. Was she entirely innocent? She must be. There was no way that Vivienne would be involved in anything underhand. But she was not certain she could say the same about André. The previous autumn, Elise hadn't been able to rest until she'd found out how her sister had met her untimely death. She hadn't wanted to leave André and Vivienne to fend for themselves, but it had been obvious she couldn't take them with her. She'd hoped that leaving them to manage without her would encourage André to grow up. And when she had rejoined them at the turn of the year, she'd been pleasantly surprised to see how well they had coped.

But what if they hadn't coped? Recently, André had actually had plenty of money, whereas before he'd always been short. Where had it come from? Had he fallen in with felons in his efforts to provide for Vivienne? She stared at Vivienne, heart like lead, and prayed that neither of her friends had done anything wrong.

'If you're taking Vivienne to your manor, you will have to make room for me too,' Elise said. Yes, that would answer very well. She need not be separated from Pearl. She would go with them to Gawain's manor.

Gawain's eyebrows lifted. When he simply looked at her, tension balled in her stomach.

I will not be parted from Pearl. Clutching Pearl to her, Elise rushed on. 'Vivienne can't go on her own, she…she'll need help with the babies.' This wasn't true, Vivienne was a wonder with the babies, but Elise couldn't stomach the idea of Vivienne being thrust into a strange environment where there would be no familiar faces. Vivienne might have become used to the wandering life, but for years she'd always had either Elise or André with her. *We are a family.*

Not that she could expect a man like Gawain— a loner—to understand that.

Gawain nodded a dismissal at his squire. 'Thank you, Aubin. Carry on.'

'Very well, my lord.' Aubin ducked out of the pavilion.

Elise stared at the father of her child and bit her

lip. Gawain Steward, Count of Meaux, was ignoring her. He had taken Vivienne into custody and she wasn't sure he was going to take her to his manor. Heaven help them.

She drew in some air. He must take her with him! 'My lord, I insist on accompanying Vivienne and the babies back to the manor.'

He looked sharply at her. 'You *insist*?'

'Yes, my lord, I insist.'

Vivienne shifted. Her eyes were huge with concern. 'Be careful, Elise.' Muttering under her breath, she took Bruno outside.

'Gaw…Lord Gawain.' Elise turned to face him squarely. 'I am sorry if this inconveniences you, but I feel most strongly about this. Vivienne needs me with her. If you insist on taking Vivienne to your manor, I shall have to come too.'

'I understand.' Gawain grimaced. 'In your shoes I would feel the same. However, much as I would personally enjoy offering you hospitality at the manor, I have to tell you that I cannot entertain you there.'

Her jaw dropped. 'You would offer space for Vivienne and the babies, but have none for me?'

'I'm afraid not. My circumstances have changed since your last visit to Troyes, and I suspect you don't know the full extent of the changes.'

Her brow puckered. 'Enlighten me.'

'After my uncle's death I left Troyes—this was a few weeks ago. I have returned to meet my betrothed.'

She caught her breath. 'You're to be married? You're right, I hadn't heard. Congratulations, Lord Gawain.' A cold stone lodged in her chest.

'My thanks. The marriage is a political one, to the daughter of an old ally of my uncle. It has the blessing of the King of France.'

Elise nodded. She bent over Pearl to hide her expression. Heavens, could matters get any worse? If he was going to be married there was no way he would want her at his manor! 'May I enquire the name of the lady you are to marry?'

'Lady Rowena de Sainte-Colombe. Her father has estates near Provins.'

'I wish you both well, Gaw—my lord. Now I understand why my presence at the manor might be awkward.'

He gave her a mocking bow, tapping the sword against his thigh. 'I thank you for your understanding.'

Her jaw worked. Her mouth was dry. 'None the less, I will not be separated from the babies.'

'Don't be difficult, Elise.'

'I'm not being difficult! I am merely telling you that I will not be separated from the babies.'

He shoved his hand through his hair. 'Elise, for God's sake—'

'Gawain, Pearl is my daughter!'

Gawain's face went blank. He stared at Pearl. 'Your daughter? Are you telling me that this baby—Pearl—is yours?'

'Aye.' Elise closed her eyes. When she opened them again, Gawain was looking at Pearl as though she'd dropped from the sky.

'Elise...' He cleared his throat. 'This cannot be.'

'Pearl is my daughter. I won't be parted from her.'

Gold gleamed as he dropped the sword on to a bedroll. He reached a hand towards Pearl and let it fall back. 'I thought both babies were Vivienne's. You let me think they were twins.'

Chapter Three

Elise's heart banged against her chest, she couldn't bring herself to answer. Outside, Bruno was gurgling, the sound seemed to be coming from a far distance. Elise could hear her breath, and Gawain's. And the chink of a metal spoon in a cauldron. She could feel the rise and fall of Pearl's chest. She could see Gawain's mind working. Calculating. His gaze did not shift from Pearl.

'Pearl is your daughter. Yours...' he paused '...and mine?'

'Yes, my lord.'

'You told me you were safe.'

'Safe?' Elise swallowed. 'So I believed. As you see, the herbs the apothecary gave me did not work.'

His nostrils flared. He held out his hands for Pearl. 'May I?'

His face was unreadable as Elise settled Pearl in the crook of his arm. As he stared at his child, a lock of bright hair fell across his forehead. Elise steeled herself not to brush it back. She wasn't sure how she had expected Gawain to react. He seemed to be taking the news better than she had dared hope. So far.

'How small she is,' he murmured. 'How very delicate.'

As he stood, a tall golden-haired knight taking his first real look at his daughter, Elise felt her eyelids prickle.

Gawain cleared his throat. His eyes were suspiciously moist. 'My daughter.' Then he blinked and lifted his head. '*Our* daughter.' He gave Elise one of those smiles that she remembered from last winter and her heart contracted. 'She is healthy?'

'Very much so.'

'And you?' His skin darkened. 'Your confinement? The birth?'

'I am fine, my lord. Vivienne is feeding Pearl in order that I may focus on my singing. I can't be at Pearl's beck and call when I am performing.'

'I see.' He resumed his study of Pearl, gently stroking her hair. When he lifted her to rub his nose against his daughter's cheek, Elise had to bite her knuckle to contain the tears. 'So this is why you haven't done much singing?'

'Yes.' Chest tight, Elise watched him swallow. She saw the moment his face went hard.

'You weren't going to tell me. If I hadn't seen you at the gate today—'

'I hadn't thought to find you in Troyes, my lord.'

His eyes narrowed. 'You were going to send word to Meaux?'

Guilt shivered through her. She hadn't intended to tell him. She hadn't thought to find him here. In truth, she had been doing her best not to think about him at all. She'd been relieved to hear that he'd gone to claim his county. And now here he was in front of her, holding Pearl to his heart, and the realisation of all that she had walked away from at the turn of the year slammed into her. Gawain was a kind man. He was strong enough to be gentle. He was loving. Gawain had offered her not one word of love and yet love—and care—had shown in his every action. But she must remember, he was not hers. He never would be. Gawain was Count of Meaux and she was a nobody.

'I feel dreadful,' she murmured.

Their gazes locked.

'So you should.'

Elise lifted her chin. 'But now you will under-

stand why I cannot allow you to take Vivienne—
and Pearl—to your manor. I won't be parted from
her.'

Pearl shifted in his arms, distracting him. Her
eyes opened. 'Blue,' he said softly.

'Most babies have blue eyes when they are
small.' Elise let her hand rest gently on Pearl's
chest. 'Given that you and I both have dark eyes,
it seems likely that hers will change.'

'Most likely.' He shook his head thoughtfully.
'What a miracle she is.'

'Gawain, you won't separate us.'

'Of course not.'

Elise went weak with relief. As Gawain went on
staring at Pearl it struck her that it was Gawain
who was the miracle. He had accepted Pearl as
his child without a murmur. A lesser man might
have tried to bluff his way out of admitting fa-
therhood. He could have accused Elise of sleeping
with someone else. Not Gawain. He was angry
with her for not telling him sooner, but he simply
believed her.

Gawain held the small bundle that was his
daughter to his chest and struggled to take command of his thoughts. It wasn't easy. This revela-
tion—he had a daughter!—had left him reeling.
She was so small. So perfect. He had a daughter.

'When was she born?'

'A month since, she was a little early.'

He lifted an eyebrow. 'That apothecary must have given you the wrong herbs.'

Elise's hand shifted. She gripped his arm. 'My lord, you need not fear I shall make demands on you in the future. I am able to care for Pearl.'

Gawain looked at the small fingers on his arm and held back a sigh. 'You will rely on your singing, I suppose.'

The hand was removed and Elise's eyes sparked. 'I am quite able to provide for her.'

He let his gaze wander pointedly round the purple pavilion. 'I never thought a child of mine would be forced to live in a tent.'

Her cheeks went crimson and her chin inched up. 'Not forced, my lord. I live here by choice.'

'You love this life.'

'Love it?' She looked startled. 'It is what I am.'

It was a statement that might mean anything. Elise could well love this life. She'd certainly been eager enough to get back to it at the end of last year. Her hasty departure had shown more clearly than words ever could what she thought of him. They had enjoyed each other's company for a time, but singing was everything to her. Of course, she might also mean that she considered this mendicant life was the only life to which she was suited. A statement that he would have questioned most vigorously last year had she stayed and given the slightest sign that she might one day come to feel something for him.

Gawain's thoughts were confused. In truth, they had been confused since last winter when he'd found her crying in the palace chapel. Crying over the death of a young man she had only just met. Elise might not know it, but from the first she had commanded Gawain's loyalty. It was a pity she didn't feel the same for him. Particularly since loyalty would bind them for eternity. They had a daughter.

'You have given me a daughter,' he murmured, heart twisting as he stared at the baby in his arms. Lord, why did this have to happen now of all times? He was no longer free.

He wanted to help them. It was his duty as a father to help them. But this went beyond duty. He wanted to be part of Pearl's life. He didn't want Elise or Pearl to vanish in the way Elise had done at the turn of the year.

Yet what could he do? What about Lady Rowena?

'You weren't going to tell me,' Gawain said again.

Elise's heart ached. Gawain had never looked at

her in quite this way, his eyes looked so strange. She could see anger there, held firmly in check. Confusion. Shock and hurt. 'No.'

She studied him as his dark gaze returned to Pearl. A slight frown creased his brow. Once again she had to check the impulse to touch him.

Taking Pearl from him, Elise fought to keep her voice even. 'I should like to explain about last winter, my lord.' She drew in a deep breath, half-expecting him to interrupt. When he said nothing, she continued. 'As you know by now, I came to Troyes to discover what had happened to my sister.'

Dark eyes watched her. 'You deceived me then too. You let me think you were simply Countess Isobel's maidservant.'

'Have you no brothers, my lord? No sisters?' Even as Elise asked the question it struck her how little she knew about Gawain. They'd been strangers when they had become lovers. They were strangers today.

'None.' He gave a slight smile of acknowledgement. 'However, I confess that if I did, I might have acted in the same way.'

She nodded vigorously. 'You would have wanted to know what had happened to them. You would have needed to know if there had been some in-justice, a wrong that needed righting.'

'Aye.'

'So it was with me, my lord. Gaw...Lord Ga-wain, the channels you might use—connections, influence—were not open to me. I am truly sorry that I deceived you.'

'You wanted to gain entry to Ravenshold.'

'My lord, I am not nobly born. I am not power-ful.' She stared at his belt buckle. 'I was desper-ate, my lord.' She lifted her eyes and hoped that he could see that she was telling the truth. 'What I am trying to say is that I didn't come to Troyes with the intention of deceiving you.'

His mouth was wry. 'You had no plans for se-ducing one of Count Lucien's household knights?'

'The thought never entered my head.'

'But that is in fact what happened.'

'Not by design, my lord.' She found herself star-ing at his belt buckle again. 'I...I don't know how that happened exactly.'

He stepped closer. Dark eyes held her immobile. 'Allow me to remind you. The evening after the tournament, I heard crying in the palace chapel.'

A warm hand reached out and gently, as gently as it had done then on All Hallows Eve, touched her arm. 'Geoffrey's death upset you.'

She nodded. 'There was so much blood, so much. And the suddenness of it—the injustice. One moment Sir Geoffrey had been vital, alive. He'd been looking forward to taking part in the tourney. And the next...' Her voice cracked. 'He was so young, just a boy really.'

Gawain's chest heaved. 'Geoffrey's death pointed out the futility of it all. The pointlessness of life.'

She frowned, wondering if that was what he really thought. 'That is very cynical.'

'That is life. We have to make of it what we can.' He brought his head closer. 'Geoffrey's death touched you because of your sister. Her death too was untimely and unjust.'

Elise went still as his deep voice washed over her, confirming that he was not entirely a stranger. Last winter she had seen his compassionate side. She was seeing it again today. This man was more than a warrior. His sensitivity had reached her after the All Hallows Tourney, and it reached her now.

She pressed her lips to Pearl's forehead. *Your father is a good man.*

'My lord, what happened between us—well, I cannot deny that I was sorry to mislead you. I hadn't known the countess for long and she could have dismissed me at any moment. As one of Count Lucien's household knights you were ideally placed to help me find my way into Ravenshold.' Her cheeks scorched. 'The attraction between us was strong. I...I didn't mislead you about that, my lord. I could not have become your lover without it. I was strongly drawn to you.' Elise bit her lip before she confessed that she still was drawn to him—witness that kiss in the town. It was probably just as well Gawain was betrothed to Lady Rowena, because even without his betrothal there could be nothing lasting between them. Elise loved her life as a singer. She would never marry.

He cleared his throat and she saw him glance briefly at her mouth. 'As I was to you.'

She eased back, and her heart missed a beat— the way he was looking at her mouth! Saints, this was the most awkward conversation of her life. 'My lord, however it came about, we became lovers. We were intimate with each other several times.'

The fair head dipped, his mouth quirked up at the edges. 'I have a memory, Elise.'

She felt herself flush and looked away. 'Gawain, I truly thought I would not conceive. The apothecary swore the herbs he gave me would prevent it. When I knew I was with child I was as surprised as you are.'

'I very much doubt it.'

His dry tone had her gaze snapping back to meet his. 'Gawain, you...you wouldn't try to take her away?'

'Peace, Elise. I have no intention of separating you from Pearl.'

'You swear it?'

'On my father's soul, I swear it.'

Elise's shoulders relaxed and she let out a shuddering sigh. Gawain grimaced. Had she really thought he would take Pearl from her? Every word she uttered condemned him. She didn't trust him. Last year she hadn't trusted him enough to bid him farewell, and if he hadn't returned to Troyes to meet Lady Rowena he doubted she would ever have told him about Pearl.

'Elise, I shan't take Pearl from you. However, I would like to acknowledge her.'

Her dark eyes were puzzled. 'Is that wise? Lady Rowena will surely take exception. And if the marriage has the blessing of the King—you can't put that at risk.'

'Lady Rowena must accept it. I will not shirk

my responsibility to Pearl. Or to you for that matter.' Gently, he touched her cheek.

Gawain felt as though he was being torn to shreds. He owed duty to Lady Rowena. He must honour the wishes of his late uncle, who with his aunt, Lady Una, had promoted the betrothal. The match was a good one. Lady Rowena was the King's goddaughter.

However, that was not the reason why the match was important to Gawain. The match was important because he and his uncle had been estranged for years before his uncle's death. It had happened during Gawain's first, ill-fated betrothal to his cousin, Lunette. Tragically, Lunette had died. His uncle had blamed Gawain for Lunette's death, and the ensuing estrangement had caused a rift in the family. It was a tragedy that had given Gawain many sleepless nights.

Which was why he had jumped at the chance to make amends—he could finally please his widowed aunt by marrying Lady Rowena. He owed it to the family.

And now he was a father, he had a duty to Pearl too. Never mind what he felt for Elise. He ran his fingertips gently over her cheek. So soft. So beguiling. Would she have married him if he were free?

'*Mon Dieu*, I wish you had told me sooner. Where was she born? Here in the tent?'

Elise took a step back. 'That is none of your business, my lord.'

'Is it not?' Hurt stabbed like a knife in his guts. She didn't trust him and he had to admit that was largely his fault. Their loving had been so sweet and tender—it had meant much to him, but he'd been taken aback by the speed at which she'd had him enthralled. He'd mistrusted his own feelings. He hadn't understood them at the time, save to acknowledge that he couldn't get enough of her.

He should have told Elise how much he valued her. It had been his fault. Ever since Lunette's death—he and Lunette had been inseparable as children—Gawain had kept his feelings to himself and women at arm's length. And sadly, thanks to his recent betrothal, he could say nothing of this today. He was no longer free. He could never tell Elise how important she was to him. Nor could he say that she had been so even before she became the mother of his child. His heart felt as though it had turned to lead.

His gaze fell to the sword on the bedroll and he straightened his shoulders. Torn he might be, but one duty was plain. 'Elise, you have my word I shall not separate you from Pearl. Equally, I cannot ignore the finding of this sword. Sir Raphael must be told about it. In the meantime I want you and our daughter safely away from here. If you won't think of yourself, think of Pearl. Is she safe here?'

'Until now I've never had reason to believe otherwise,' Elise said, frowning at the sword. 'Gawain, I cannot believe Vivienne is guilty of wrongdoing.'

He leaned in and the scent of ambergris tugged at his senses. 'Can you say the same of André?' She hesitated and he made an impatient sound. 'I thought not.'

'Gawain, André is very young. There's no malice in him and I find it hard to believe he's broken the law, but—'

'You could not swear to it.'

She remained silent, biting her lip.

'Elise, I have to inform Sir Raphael.'

'I know.' Dark eyes held his. 'I just wish…'

'What?'

'Couldn't you speak to André before you speak to Sir Raphael? Please, Gawain.'

What it was to be a man of influence, Elise thought. An hour had passed with a flurry of messages winging back and forth between her pavilion and the garrison. Poor Aubin must be worn out with all the toing and froing. But the upshot of the messages was that Gawain had apparently secured lodgings for Vivienne and the babies—not in his nearby manor, but in a house in the Rue du Cloître.

It seemed there would be space there for Elise too. Since Gawain had explained that he was betrothed, his reluctance to have her lodging in his manor was entirely understandable. However, knowing why he refused to entertain her there hadn't made Elise feel any better. She felt sick to her core, but it was obvious that ensconcing his former lover and his love child in the family manor would not endear him to his future wife.

Elise wondered whether she would be able to stand living in town—she was bound to feel confined. However, stand it she must if she and Pearl were to stay together.

Thus it was that Gawain and Elise returned to Troyes, to the Rue du Cloître.

Mouth dry, Elise found herself standing in the street gazing at a small house. It was the only stone-built house in the street. A Romanesque arch was filled with a heavy wooden door. Rather ominously, it was studded and banded with iron.

A large key was produced and they went in. Despite the afternoon heat—the town was sweltering—it was cool inside. Cool and dark. Gawain flung back a shutter and hinges groaned. A spider scuttled across the floor and on to the hearth. It vanished into a crack in the plaster. There were bars on the windows. Elise took a shaky breath. There was also dust on the floor, enough for her to draw a circle in it with her foot. Her nose wrinkled. 'What is this place?'

'It's been empty for some time. I believe Count Henry uses it as a storeroom from time to time.'

She eyed the bars. 'Are you sure it isn't a prison?'

'Quite sure.' Gawain dragged his hand through his hair. 'Elise, we were lucky it was free. The town is bursting at the seams because of the fair.'

'I know. Thank you for securing it for us. I really didn't want to be kept from Pearl.' She made her voice bright. 'And it's not very dirty—nothing a broom and a few pails of water won't fix.'

A narrow stairway led to an upper chamber. The window there—it was also barred—looked out over the Rue du Cloître. Elise could see the top of the cathedral over the roofs of the houses. She would be able to hear the cathedral bells mark out the hours. She sighed. There would be rules here in Troyes, and they would be almost as stringent as the Rule at the convent. She thought she had escaped all that. She thought wistfully of the freedoms of Strangers' City. 'I wish you'd let us stay in the pavilion.'

'You'll be safer here.'

Elise nodded. What Gawain wasn't saying was that the Guardian Knights could keep more of an eye on them here. It was close to the garrison. And however much he denied it, the barred windows put her in mind of a prison rather than a storeroom. At least there was plenty of room. Their pallets and the babies' cribs would easily fit in. The upper chamber even had a fireplace.

'Not that we will need a fire upstairs at this time of year,' she said, thinking aloud as they made their way back downstairs.

'It's acceptable?'

'Thank you, yes.' Understanding that he was doing his best for them, she forced a smile. 'Given you insist on tearing us away from the encampment, I really am grateful not to be separated from Pearl.'

He was looking at her mouth and her heart stuttered. It hadn't been easy for her seeing him again—telling him about Pearl; fighting not to be separated from her. But it wasn't easy for him either. Gawain's expression was tense—there was a tightness about his lips that she'd never seen before. She was responsible for it. Seeing her again, learning about Pearl just as he was about to meet Lady Rowena. *I hope that woman appreciates her good fortune.*

'My lord, I am truly sorry to put you to all this trouble.'

'It is no trouble,' he said, turning for the great oak door. 'My sergeant will see the house is swept out, and then Aubin and the men can shift your belongings over here. It shouldn't take long to settle in.'

The sky was streaked with crimson and gold, the light was going. Swifts were screeching through the air over the tents and pavilions of Strangers' City. Pennons hung limp, as though they too were wilting in the heat.

Gawain glanced at Aubin. Their horses were stabled back at the garrison and he and his squire were sitting on cross-framed canvas stools outside the ale tent. They were trying to look as though they belonged there, so their tunics bore no insignia. Gawain had ordered Aubin to wear a short sword.

Gawain kept his gaze trained on the purple

pavilion. No one had gone near it. André de Poitiers had yet to return.

'He's late,' Gawain murmured. Aubin nodded, but said nothing. Gawain had told the boy not to address him by his title and he suspected he was afraid to open his mouth.

The swifts hurled themselves through the sunset. Campfires flickered into life, the glow of the fires warring with the violet twilight.

Once again, Gawain glanced towards Elise's pavilion. He swore under his breath.

Aubin looked at him.

'No fire,' Gawain muttered. 'With Elise and Vivienne in the Rue du Cloître, their fire isn't lit. If the lute-player notices, he might become suspicious. Especially if he has something to hide.'

For the women's sake, Gawain hoped his fears regarding André de Poitiers were unfounded. Sadly, his instincts were telling him otherwise— André de Poitiers was up to his neck in trouble. Captain Raphael had come to the same conclusion and consequently the Guardian Knights were out in force. Every half an hour or so, the chink of harness and the plod of hoofs alerted Gawain— and everyone within earshot—that they were on patrol.

'They're far too conspicuous.' Gawain grimaced. 'I'm convinced a more covert approach is called for.'

He was sipping his ale—watery as it was, it was welcome in the heat—when Aubin dug him in the ribs. 'Over there.' His squire spoke quietly. 'At the end of the line.'

Between the lines of tents, a woman was striding through the dusk. As she passed a fire, the glow silhouetted her shape—her gut-wrenchingly pretty and familiar shape. Elise!

Gawain gripped his ale pot. 'What the blazes is she doing here?' She should be making herself at home in the Rue du Cloître. 'Blast the woman.'

Elise paused by the ropes of a makeshift paddock that was full of mules and donkeys. Gesturing for a groom, she slipped something into his hand. Gawain felt himself tense. What was that all about? Vivienne had mentioned travelling in a cart. If they had a cart, they probably kept a mule. His tension eased. Likely Elise was ensuring the animal was cared for in her absence.

He saw her pat the boy on the shoulder and tracked her progress as she made her way to the purple pavilion, now almost lost in the gathering dark. He was on the point of rising when the shadow that was Elise bent to pick something up. She went to the nearest campfire, where another woman was crouched over a cooking pot. Then she was back at the pavilion, a light in hand.

The cooking fire. She was lighting the fire so André would assume everything was as it should be. Gawain couldn't fault her for that. None the less, her presence in the camp disturbed him. Undoubtedly she'd come back to keep an eye on André. She would never admit it, but she must suspect him of wrongdoing.

A patrol went by. Gawain studiously avoided looking at the lead rider as they passed the ale tent, but he did note that they rode by the purple pavilion without giving it more than a cursory glance. Thank the Lord, Captain Raphael had some sense.

The patrol moved on. Elise went into the pavilion as a group of drunks stumbled up to the ale tent. To judge by their gait, they had already emptied several barrels in town. They staggered to a bench, clamouring for wine and ale. One man lurched half-heartedly at the serving girl. She evaded him neatly and a roar of laughter went up.

Gawain watched the drunks, a crease in his brow. Did Elise find herself fending off men like these on a regular basis? The thought wasn't pleasant. And neither was it any of his business. He was here to make sure that the lute-player hadn't involved her in anything underhand. He would find a way to help her and then he must leave her to her own devices. He would shortly be a married man. The thought left him with a bitter taste in his mouth that had nothing to do with ale and everything to do with Elise. She had made him a father. Gawain stared abstractedly at the glow outside the purple pavilion. A father owed a duty of care to his children, and whilst Pearl had come unexpectedly into his life he couldn't simply forget her. Yet what could he do? How could he fulfil his duties to Pearl when he'd sworn to marry Lady Rowena and finally heal the family rift?

Chapter Four

Elise sat on her pallet inside the pavilion with her chin on her hand and stared through the entrance towards the ale tent opposite. Gawain was out there. His hair gleamed like gold in the sunset—he'd been impossible to miss. He had his squire with him. No doubt they thought to leap on André the moment he appeared.

The crimson streaks slowly faded from the western sky and the bats took flight—dark flecks flitting silently overhead.

Every now and then Elise slipped out to feed the fire. She tried not to look too obviously towards the ale tent, but she knew Gawain and Aubin hadn't moved. Each time she returned to her pallet in the pavilion, it was harder keeping her gaze from straying their way. On one foray outside she lit a lamp and brought it back inside with her.

As she shifted on the pallet, another patrol

clopped by. There was no André. Above the background murmur of the camp a man laughed. It was a deep, full-throated sound that in Elise's nervous state sounded impossibly happy. Impossibly carefree. Where was André? With every breath she took, her tension increased. Where was he? Why hadn't he returned?

Something thudded against the back wall of the tent. She stiffened and went cold.

There was a ripping sound. A silver crescent—a knife—was slicing its way through the canvas. Light from the lamp reflected on the blade. Holding her breath, Elise watched as another slash was made. The silver crescent vanished. A hand appeared. A foot.

Heart sinking, she froze. It might not be André. Unfortunately, she feared it was. She felt oddly detached. It was as though she was an observer and she was watching her own reactions. It must be because she wasn't truly afraid.

'André?' she whispered. 'Is that you?' She heard scuffling. A grunt.

André's head poked through the opening. 'You're alone?'

Nodding, Elise reached behind her to close the tent flap. The shadows edged in on them. 'What are you doing? André, where have you been?'

André pushed into the tent. He wasn't carrying his lute and his breath smelt of wine.

'Where's Vivienne?'

'She's safe. Staying in the town.'

'What?' Swearing under his breath, André turned to where Vivienne's coffer had been and drew up sharply. 'Where is it?'

Elise watched him cast about for the sword, a cold lump in her belly. 'The sword—if that's what you're looking for—is in the castle garrison.'

'Hell, what happened? What have you done?'

'That's the question I should be asking of you. What have *you* done?'

'Why has the sword gone?'

Elise stared at him, mind working. It was impossible to forget that Gawain and Aubin were sitting on those canvas stools outside the ale tent. They were bound to have seen her and Gawain could take it in his head to come over and check on her at any time. She was pulled two ways. She hated the idea of doing something that might alienate Pearl's father. On the other hand, what would happen to André if he was taken into custody?

Whatever André had done, at heart he was a good person. Elise would never forget the countless evenings André had sat with her, patiently giving her the confidence to use her full voice;

patiently playing for her, over and over until it was impossible for her to hit the wrong note. Blanchefleur le Fay owed her existence to André. Gawain didn't know him as she did. Gawain didn't realise that to put someone like André under lock and key…

It would destroy him. She couldn't let that happen. André had become a father and Elise could see that he found his new responsibilities daunting. To be arrested would be the last straw, and it certainly wouldn't help Vivienne and Bruno, who depended on him.

André's eyes glittered. 'I've not hurt anyone.'

'No? What were you going to do with that sword? And why cut open the side of our pavilion? So underhand.' André must have a guilty conscience; why else would he damage their tent?

André looked at her. 'I was tipped off that the Guardian Knights had been showing an interest in the pavilion. I thought I'd better be careful.'

'You were going to sell that sword for more than it is worth.'

'I'm not selling it. Someone else is going to do that.'

'Saints, André, it makes little difference who actually does the selling. If you are involved and that sword is passed off as—'

'Elise, how do you think we've been living all these months? How do you suppose we are going to live in the winter when pickings are slim?'

Wine fumes hung about him. He was swaying slightly.

'You're drunk.'

'How clever of you to notice.' Wearily, he scrubbed his face. The shadows made his face grey. He looked twice his age. 'Lord, Elise, I've had all I can take. I've made mistakes, I admit it. I didn't want to get involved. But last winter when you left, I worried. I worried about Vivienne. About what might happen if you never returned.' His mouth twisted. 'My earnings have always been better when Blanchefleur le Fay is with me. And then you came back.'

'I told you I would.'

'Aye, but you were sick all the time, you couldn't perform. And then you got large, you couldn't perform.' Again he scrubbed his face. 'I worried. I still do.'

A clunk outside had his head turning sharply. 'You say Vivienne is in town?'

'In the Rue du Cloître.'

His brow creased. 'Why?'

'Lord Gawain. He–'

'Lord Gawain's in Troyes and you brought him

here?' André looked appalled. 'So it's your fault the Guardians have the sword. Why bring him here? In heaven's name, why?'

'I had no idea he was in town. He's shortly to be married and he returned to meet his betrothed. André, we ran into each other by accident. He insisted on bringing me back here.'

André looked at her, shaking his head. 'It was he who took the sword?'

'Yes. André, I'm sorry it happened, truly.'

'What the hell am I going to do? I'm supposed to pass it on.'

Elise hesitated. She had no clear idea what André was mixed up in, but she was wondering whether to suggest he made a clean breast of it with Gawain. Gawain might be able to help him. The Count of Meaux would have influence. However, André was still swaying slightly and she wasn't sure he could be reasoned with until he had sobered up. 'Gawain might speak for you.'

Impatiently, he shook his head. 'Not likely. Vivienne is in the Rue du Cloître, you say? Where, exactly?'

'Look for the stone-built house. You can't miss it. There's only one. I'm told that Count Henry uses it as a storeroom.'

'The babies are with her?'

Elise nodded.

'Tell her…tell her I love her. And that I'll be back.' André's expression was tortured. 'I've done wrong, Elise, and I'm sorry that you and Vivienne have been dragged into it. I shall put things right and then I'll be back.'

He reached for the slash in the canvas and looked at her, eyes luminous in the lamplight. His mouth tightened. 'By the way, this could mean that Blanchefleur le Fay will have to find another lute-player to accompany her when she sings at the palace.' Glancing at the entrance, he grimaced. 'Someone's coming.'

With that, André slipped through the rip in the canvas and was gone.

Elise stared frantically at the pavilion entrance, pulse racing. Was Gawain out there? With luck, André would be out of Gawain's line of sight, running down the back of the tents. She wasn't confident that the Guardian Knights—or Gawain for that matter—would give him the benefit of the doubt.

A distraction was needed. Noise, plenty of noise. Well, that was no problem for Blanchefleur. Elise took a deep breath and began to scream. She really put her heart in it.

* * *

The scream turned Gawain's blood to ice.

'Aubin, with me.' Snatching out his sword, he sprinted to the pavilion. Lord, what a voice, it cut like a knife.

Elise was holding on to the central tent post, staring at a gaping hole in the back of the canvas. The instant Gawain stepped inside, the screaming stopped. Dark eyes looked at him.

'You're hurt?' Puzzled, Gawain ran his gaze over her. He couldn't read her, but she didn't look hurt. The lantern gave enough light for him to see that her hair was neatly braided. Her clothing hadn't been disordered in any way. She looked fine. Slightly flushed, perhaps, but it was a warm night. Otherwise, she looked fine. 'Elise, what happened?'

She opened her mouth as Aubin raced in, panting.

'Aubin, take a look outside. Round the back.'

'Yes, my lord.'

When Elise touched Gawain's arm, the temptation to cover her hand with his was strong. When she bit her lip, the temptation to kiss her on the mouth was stronger still.

'Gaw—my lord, you will think me such a fool.'

Gawain looked speculatively at her. 'What happened?'

'A knife.' She gestured at the tear in the canvas. 'I was waiting for André. I...I didn't expect to see a knife cut through the back of the pavilion.'

'Did you see who it was?'

Her hesitation was brief, but Gawain marked it. 'It could have been whoever forged that sword,' he said, slowly. 'But I don't think it was. It was your lute-player, wasn't it?'

She lowered her gaze, seeming to speak to the ground. 'I...I am sorry, my lord. I think my scream scared him away.'

'Don't lie to me. You warned him,' Gawain said in a cold voice. Sliding his sword back into its scabbard, he took her by the wrist. 'Your lute-player must have noticed the extra patrols and thought he'd be clever. And you, Elise, you warned him. You weren't the least bit afraid, were you?'

She swallowed and kept her gaze on the ground.

'Elise?'

She looked up, eyes fierce. 'Yes, I warned him. You would have had him arrested!'

'Not necessarily. I merely want to question him.'

Grip firm on her wrist, Gawain pulled her closer, close enough for him to catch the faint scent of ambergris. 'Did he stay long enough for you to speak to him?' Her lips tightened. 'Well?'

'I… Yes!'

'And…?' Her mouth worked. She was frowning at her wrist. Gawain eased his grip. 'Elise?'

'*Mon seigneur*, André knows he has done wrong and he is sorry. He says he will try to put things right. He will come back when he has done so.'

Gawain clenched his teeth. He hated the way she had addressed him as *mon seigneur*. 'You expect me to leave it at that? Elise, the lute-player—'

'His name is André.'

'André appears to have dealings with people suspected of trading counterfeit arms. Fraudsters. Criminals. He must be questioned.' Gawain huffed out a breath. 'You do yourself no service by preventing that from happening.'

'What do you mean?'

'I had hoped to discover that you were not involved. But you have just admitted that you warned the man away.' He frowned. 'Elise, what am I to think but that you too are involved?'

'Do you really think that?'

'I would be failing in my duty if I did not consider it.' Tightening his hold, he brought her close. 'Elise, what have you done?'

'Nothing, I've done nothing! All I want is for you to leave us alone.'

He shook his head. 'I wish I could, but I can't. Elise, what happened between us last year—'

'Was a mistake.'

Gawain felt a muscle flicker in his jaw. 'I hadn't thought so. What I was going to say was that it had consequences. Pearl. Her very existence binds me to you.'

At her sides, Elise's fists clenched. 'I don't see why, I'm not asking for help. You can forget all about us.' She gave him a strange look. 'Gawain, you can marry Lady Rowena with a clear conscience. If you are concerned that one day Pearl and I shall turn up at your gate begging for alms, don't be. I wouldn't embarrass you like that.'

A cold fist formed in Gawain's belly. She dismissed their loving as though it had been of no account. It hadn't been of no account, not to him. And she dismissed him as a father too, which was worse. However, he had to be honest, with his forthcoming marriage he wasn't in a position to offer her much. He felt his frown deepen. She was distracting him, making him forget what he was trying to say.

'Elise, this is no longer personal, it's no longer just about Pearl. The discovery of that sword has turned it into something else entirely. It's about the trafficking in counterfeit regalia. It's about trickery and deceit. It's about honest people being gulled into buying dross.'

'Gawain—'

'Elise, when I saw you by the market I thought simply to return you to your pavilion. You must see that has changed. I find myself embroiled in— in what, exactly? Are you and your little troupe part of a larger ring of counterfeiters? Is this how you really make your living? I need you to answer me honestly. What is the exact nature of your involvement with the counterfeiters?'

Her jaw fell open. 'None. I have no involvement with counterfeiters whatsoever. How can you think it?'

He leaned in, caught the scent of ambergris and straightened quickly. 'I don't know you. I thought I did, but I don't. You might be involved in anything.'

'Well, I'm not.'

'So I believed, so I hoped. But you must see that letting André get away does not put you in a good light.'

'He's gone to make amends! I told you.'

'You believe that?'

She nodded vigorously. 'André has a good heart.

I've known him for years and he has a sweet, loving nature. I think that learning he was to be a father pushed him off course for a while, but I believe him when he says he will sort things out. He will. You'll see.'

'*Mon Dieu*, I almost wish I'd not seen you at the market,' Gawain muttered. He didn't mean it. Despite all that had happened—Pearl; the finding of the sword—it had been a relief to see Elise looking so well. As to her involvement with the fakers—he didn't know what to think. She had always struck him as fundamentally honest.

Yet he knew she was capable of evasion. When he'd met her last year, she'd not mentioned her sister, Morwenna—he'd only learned of the connection between Elise and the late Countess d'Aveyron after Elise had fled Champagne. Elise had kept him in the dark about her need to gain entry to Ravenshold, just as she had kept Lady Isobel in the dark. It was hard to look into her eyes, now turned so earnestly to his, and think her capable of serious deceit. Would she lie for her friend André? It was possible.

'If I could, I would wash my hands of you,' he said. 'But I don't think you would like it if I did.'

'How so?'

'When I approached Sir Raphael about the

sword, he made it clear that because we are old friends he is staying his hand. You wouldn't like it if I withdrew. You and Vivienne are likely to end up in the castle lock-up while your lute-player does whatever he deems necessary to make amends. And as you yourself say, the castle prison is no place for babies.'

Elise felt the fight drain out of her. Gawain was right, Sir Raphael would want to make sure of them. As Captain of the Guardian Knights he would be bound to hold Vivienne as a surety of André's return. And in the meantime, Bruno and Pearl would be incarcerated alongside her. And since Elise would not desert them, so would she.

Quick footsteps heralded Aubin's return. He ducked into the tent. 'I found nothing, my lord. I went as far as the Madeleine Gate and asked everyone I saw. No one will admit to seeing anything unusual.'

'My thanks, Aubin. If you wouldn't mind waiting by the fire?'

'Mon seigneur.' Bowing, Aubin went back outside.

Gawain looked down at her, blond hair shining in the lamplight. 'I shall give you the benefit of the doubt,' he said. 'For the moment, I think it best if you remain my responsibility, don't you agree?'

'Thank you, my lord.'

Gawain gave her a tight smile and took her hand. He hooked her arm around his. It was a familiar gesture, a possessive gesture. Elise was irritated to discover that it was also a comforting gesture.

'I shall escort you back to La Rue du Cloître,' he said. His smile twisted. 'It's a pleasant evening for a walk.'

'Walking, my lord, again? Where's The Beast?'

'Back at the barracks. Elise, I give you fair warning, my men will be watching the house at all times. I'd hoped to spare you that, but after to-night you must see that I cannot shirk my respon-sibilities.' He sighed. 'It has to be better than the castle dungeon.'

Elise stared at him and saw in her mind the bars on those windows. It would seem they were to be prisoners after all. Still, she had to agree it was better to be hemmed in by Gawain in La Rue du Cloître than to be tossed in the castle dungeon. 'I understand, my lord,' she heard herself say. Even though, in her heart, she wished it was otherwise.

The shutter was open. It had been an airless, tiresome night. Elise had hoped a breath of wind would find its way into their bedchamber, but she had hoped in vain. Ever since dusk, Bruno and

Pearl had taken it in turns to be fretful. No sooner had Elise shut her eyes than it seemed Pearl was crying again—and Pearl's crying was surely loud enough to be heard in Paris. Sighing, Elise heaved herself up on an elbow.

Vivienne was sitting in a shaft of dawn light, feeding Bruno. Shoving her hair out of her eyes, Elise yawned. 'I'll bring Pearl over.'

Nodding, Vivienne bent over Bruno, but not before Elise saw the glitter of tears. 'Vivienne?'

Vivienne sniffed. A tear splashed on to Bruno's cheek. Vivienne's face was pale, her eyes shadowed.

'You're thinking about André.'

Vivienne's throat worked. 'It's been three days.' Her voice was thick with emotion. 'Three days since we last saw him and there hasn't been a word. Where is he, Elise? Where?' Another tear landed on Bruno's cheek.

'We must have faith in him. He's not stupid. He told me—'

'That he would put matters right. I remember what you said.' Vivienne swiped her eyes with the back of her hand. 'But how is he going to manage it? If he has truly been dealing with counterfeiters, do you think they'll take kindly to him confessing that he's lost that sword?'

Picking Pearl up, Elise came to the window and searched Vivienne's face. 'You know more than you have told me.'

'No, I don't. Truly. But I've been thinking. Elise, these past three days I've done nothing but think and if André's friends—the players he told us about—if the players are the counterfeiters, what will they do when they learn the sword has fallen into the hands of the Guardians? They might hurt him.'

'I don't think they will.' Elise spoke firmly, even though the thought had occurred to her too. When she had seen André in the pavilion she hadn't imagined that three days would pass without a word. Three days. No message, nothing. Just a silence as ominous and oppressive as the August heat.

'It's possible he tried to get a message to us,' Elise murmured. Pearl squirmed in her arms. 'But with Lord Gawain's men posted in the street to watch our every move, he might have been afraid to come near.'

Vivienne looked at her, eyes watery. 'They're still out there?'

Elise peered into the grey morning light. 'Two men are leaning against the house opposite. And though I can't see from here, I'm guessing that two more will be stationed either side of the door as they were yesterday. I think there will be four of them.'

She sighed, Gawain was nothing if not thorough and Elise didn't like it. She really did feel as though she had been imprisoned. It didn't help that every hour she had to listen to the tolling of the cathedral bells—every horrible note brought back the convent. Trapped. Trapped. Trapped. The bells, the rigid routine... She thought she'd escaped all that.

'I suppose we should be grateful we're not locked in,' Vivienne said. 'What shall we do?'

Pearl let out a wail. Elise handed her to Vivienne and waited until she had settled before she spoke again. 'I'm going back to Strangers' City.'

Vivienne jerked her head meaningfully in the direction of the guards in the street. 'Will they permit it?'

Outside, Gawain's men stood as still and solid as carved wooden pillars. Their expressions didn't betray the slightest hint of fatigue even though they'd been there all night.

Elise pursed her lips. 'Lord Gawain didn't actually forbid me to return.'

'No, but two of his men accompanied you when you went to buy bread yesterday.'

'That's true.' Elise squared her shoulders. She wished things were easier between her and Gawain. If only she could trust him. No, that wasn't right, she could trust him. Gawain would do the right thing. He always did the right thing. And that was exactly the problem. Elise wasn't sure what André had done and she wanted him to have a chance to make things better. But the instinct to ask for Gawain's help was strong. 'It must be resisted,' she murmured.

'What's that?' Vivienne asked.

'My pardon, I was thinking aloud. I'm going to the tents.'

'Despite Lord Gawain's wishes?'

'Lord Gawain's men can come with me if they must. After all, he knows I am a singer. He knows I have to practise. I must have space or I will go mad. Since André hasn't returned I am forced to make other arrangements.'

Elise wasn't going to admit how worried she was. She was worried about André, but it was more than that. His disappearance had put her very future at risk. And since Pearl's arrival it wasn't just Blanchefleur's future that was at risk. Vivienne's and Bruno's were too. If André couldn't perform, what would they live on? What if André didn't return in time to accompany her at the banquet? They should be finalising the programme. Rehearsing. So many songs. So many lute solos. Without André, Elise's little troupe faced a bleak future. Like it or not, Elise needed to plan. What would she do if André never came back?

Elise had nursed the dream of performing at Count Henry's palace in Troyes for years, but whenever she'd imagined it, André had been at her side. She liked performing with André. She loved him. Of course there were other lute-players she could call on, but André was familiar. He'd been with her from the beginning and he gave her confidence. Confidence she would need if she was to sing before the daughter of the King of France and Queen Eleanor of England.

I must succeed in this. Before André's disappearance, Blanchefleur's success as a *chanteuse* had been vital for her and Pearl. Elise looked at Vivienne and Bruno and tried to keep the anxiety from her expression. Without André, her success was doubly important.

Vivienne patted Pearl's head and looked up. 'You'll have to be careful if the count's men are with you.'

'Don't worry, I won't do anything rash.' Reaching her gown down from a hook on the wall, Elise dragged it on and rummaged about for her comb.

'Did you know Baderon de Lyon is in the camp this summer?'

'The lute-player who used to perform at the Poitiers court?'

'That's the one.' Deftly plaiting her hair into a single braid, Elise grabbed her veil and turned for the stairway. 'I need to practise. Perhaps he will play for me.'

'Be careful, Elise.'

'Try not to worry.' Elise laughed. 'Gawain knows I am a *chanteuse*. He knows I have performances to give. He cannot expect me not to rehearse.'

Chapter Five

'She's where?' Dismounting outside the house in the Rue du Cloître, Gawain looked at his sergeant in disbelief.

The sergeant took a hasty step backwards. 'She said she was going to Strangers' City, my lord. She…she's not on her own. Two men have gone with her. She said she's going to work.'

'Work?'

'My lord, you didn't say she was to be confined.'

'No.' Gawain knew he was frowning and he couldn't help it. Lord, what was she up to? He hadn't wanted to come here this morning. He'd told himself it wasn't necessary and that he had no business visiting Elise, not when he was in Troyes to meet his betrothed. But what she had said about being imprisoned had preyed on his mind, and so he was here. He'd been hoping to see her, hoping she understood that he had confined her in La Rue du Cloître in order to prevent worse imprisonment at the castle prison. Hoping she realised that he was involved now not because he wanted to interfere in her life, but to stop the Guardians dealing harshly with Vivienne, who was currently employed as his daughter's wet-nurse. He still found it hard to credit. He had a daughter.

'And the babies—where are they?' He couldn't help but ask.

'The infants are still in the house, *mon seigneur.*'

'Good.' Gawain hadn't told his men that one of them was his. They didn't need to know. However, he had made sure that whatever happened, the men knew they must ensure the safety of the babies.

Disappointment sat cold in his gut—Elise wasn't here. Lord, what a trial she was. He hadn't actually forbidden her to return to Strangers' City, but she must know he didn't want her near the place. With the sword in Sir Raphael's hands, she might find the camp more dangerous than before.

'When did she leave?'

'About two hours ago, my lord.'

Gawain stared blindly at the Romanesque arch over the door. What was she doing? Was she really singing, or was that an excuse to cover up a meeting with this André de Poitiers? Or worse, with the counterfeiters?

A prickle of unease ran through him. For the first time Gawain considered the real possibility that Elise herself might be involved in the sale of counterfeit regalia. He shook his head. Not Elise. However, he couldn't turn a blind eye to her returning to the encampment. Sir Raphael had only agreed that the women might be housed in the Rue du Cloître on the understanding that Gawain was responsible for their good behaviour. And Gawain, fool that he was, had agreed. He even remembered telling Raphael that a singer and a wet-nurse could hardly pose much of a threat to the County of Champagne.

'Stay here, Gaston. Watch those infants.'

'Yes, my lord.'

'And if Elise Chantier returns before I do, keep her here. I want to speak to her.'

Gaston saluted. *'Mon seigneur.'*

Muttering under his breath, Gawain took The Beast's reins from Aubin and set his foot in the stirrup.

As Gawain had expected the purple pavilion was empty but Elise wasn't hard to find. A woman was singing nearby. *Elise.* Her voice had a haunting quality. It was otherworldly. Magical. Even though Gawain had only heard her sing a few times, he would know her voice among a thousand others. He followed the tantalising thread of sound to a tent the colour of dark moss. His men were stationed outside.

Gawain nodded briefly at them. 'Aubin, wait here.'

Someone was accompanying her, Gawain could hear a lute. Stiffening, he broke step by the entrance flap. Was she with André de Poitiers? His fingers formed a fist. If she was meeting her lute-player and she hadn't told him… Heavy-browed, he pushed inside. The flow of singing cut off.

Elise looked at him. 'Lord Gawain!'

The lute-player was sitting on a camping stool. He was slower to react to Gawain's entrance—a last ripple of notes hung in the air and then faded before he rose to his feet. He was older than Gawain had expected. His brown hair had a trace of grey at the temples. Gawain looked him in the eye. 'You, I take it, are André de Poitiers.'

Elise made a sharp movement. 'No, my lord, you have it wrong. This isn't André.'

'No?'

'This is Baderon, my lord, Baderon de Lyon.

Baderon, allow me to present Gawain Steward, Count of Meaux.'

The relief—she had not gone behind his back, she really had come to practise her repertoire—was so intense Gawain felt a smile forming. He lifted an eyebrow. 'Baderon de Lyon,' he murmured. The name was familiar. Gawain knew little about Elise's world—the world of the troubadour was not his—yet even he had heard of Baderon de Lyon. 'My apologies for interrupting.' Giving the man a distracted smile, he took Elise's arm and steered her outside.

His men jumped to attention. 'Stay here,' he told them. Walking down the avenue between the tents, he led Elise towards one of the ale tents. 'Singing is thirsty work, I imagine?'

Dark eyes wary, she nodded and took a place at one of the trestles. Gawain ordered ale and fixed her with a look. 'So that's not André.'

'No.'

'Had you arranged to meet him here?'

Her mouth set in stubborn lines. 'No. I would have been happy to see him though. Vivienne is out of her mind with worry.'

Gawain studied her. 'You are worried too I imagine.' She nodded and he saw her swallow.

'Elise, I am not your keeper, but it concerns me to find you wandering about Strangers' City.'

'I wasn't on my own.' She gestured back down the rows of tents. 'Your men came with me.'

The girl arrived with the ale. As she set the mugs down, froth spilled on to the trestle.

'Be that as it may,' Gawain continued, 'I think you should avoid seeing your André. Until this business is resolved, I would prefer it if you didn't come here.'

He could see objections forming in her mind and before he knew it he'd put his finger to her mouth to stop them emerging. The desire to trace the shape of her lips with his fingertip caught him off guard. Checking the impulse, he pulled his hand away. 'With the sword at the castle, there may be dangers for you here. Elise, you put yourself at risk and if you aren't concerned for your safety, I implore you to think of Pearl. How would she fare if she lost her mother?'

She looked swiftly away, biting her lip.

'You came to find André.'

She lifted her shoulders. 'Naturally, I hoped to see him, but I really do need to practise. I am a professional. I have audiences to consider. Singing is my life!'

'Oh?' Gawain sipped his ale.

Her chin lifted. It was a determined chin. Then she gave him one of her shy, heart-melting smiles and he ached inside. 'I shall be performing for Count Henry himself while I am in Troyes.'

She looked so pleased there was no question but that she was speaking the truth. Well, he knew about her ambitions and he was glad for her. He was impressed. But as to the rest—could he take her at her word? Could she be relied upon not to meddle in this underworld business? He wanted her to be safe.

'Have you found anything more about your friend André?' A strand of dark hair was winding down her temple in the most entrancing way. It shone in the sun and trembled every time she moved. Gawain was on the point of stroking it back behind her ear when he realised the way his thoughts were tending and stopped himself touching her. Again. Lord, what a trial she was. He gripped his ale mug.

'No, my lord.'

'Would you tell me if you had, I wonder?'

'Mon seigneur?'

His mouth curved. 'Don't flutter those eyelashes at me, my girl. Elise, must you come here to rehearse?' He paused, tapping his ale mug. Fiddling with his mug helped keep his mind off what he really wanted to do, which was to test whether that shining strand of hair was as soft as he remembered. 'Should I hear anything concerning Monsieur de Poitiers I will tell you. I understand that you and Vivienne must be worried sick.'

'And my singing, my lord? How am I to practise if I cannot meet up with Baderon?'

'There's nothing to stop Baderon coming to the house in La Rue du Cloître. I should think you could practise there just as well. Better. Baderon's tent is far too small. I shall have a word with him.'

'Thank you, my lord.'

He smiled at her. 'You sounded very good, by the way. Beautiful.' Before he had time to check himself, Gawain covered her hand with his. Her hand was warm, the skin smooth. 'You have an entrancing voice.'

Her eyes danced. 'Why, thank you, my lord. How kind.'

'When do you sing before Count Henry?'

'At the Harvest Banquet.'

His breath caught. 'At the banquet itself? The one in the palace?' Naturally, Gawain was glad that she'd found somewhere prestigious to perform. Short of Poitiers or the Paris court there was nowhere more elevated than Count Henry's palace in Troyes. But the Harvest Banquet?

Lady Rowena would have arrived in Troyes by then and if all was well between them, he was expected to make a public announcement of his betrothal at that very feast. Elise knew of his coming marriage, yet for some odd reason it was deeply disturbing to think of her being present when he confirmed it. 'You are to sing at the palace?'

Dark eyes held his. 'What's the matter, my lord? Don't you think my voice is good enough?'

Gawain's mind reeled. The Harvest Banquet. Elise was to sing there on the very evening when he would announce the date of his marriage. It brought a bitter taste to his mouth. God have mercy!

Beneath his hand, small fingers shifted. Glancing down at the board, Gawain was shocked to find his fingers playing with hers. Hastily unlinking them, he dragged his hand clear. 'Not at all. No. Your voice is perfect.'

'Thank you, my lord.'

Her smile was warm. Gawain looked at her mouth, at the twist of brown hair at her temple, at the slender hand on the table, and his stomach clenched in a miserable flash of understanding. *I don't want Lady Rowena.* Once formed, the thought seemed to burn into his brain. Lady Rowena might be the most beautiful woman on earth, but he didn't care. He didn't want her, he never would. As the thought turned into certainty he picked up his mug and tossed back his ale. *Lady Rowena expects our marriage to take place. My uncle endorsed it and my aunt expects it. Not to mention that Lady Rowena's godfather—the King—supports the match.*

Mon Dieu. I want...

Gawain looked into Elise's mysterious brown eyes and pushed to his feet. She had not lost her allure in the months they had been apart and something told him that she never would. The word 'duty' jumped into his mind. Duty. It was such a heavy word. So cold. He felt as though there was a stone in his throat. He forced out some words. 'You've finished singing for today?'

She nodded and that glossy brown curl caught the light. 'Yes, my lord.'

'We can arrange for Baderon to come to the house and then I shall walk back with you to the Rue du Cloître.'

Dark eyes dancing, she put her hand to her breast. 'Even more walking? My lord, you do me much honour.'

Murmuring a response, Gawain looked towards Baderon's tent. It was tempting to call for one of his men to bring him his horse. If he had his way, he would be riding back to the Rue du Cloître with Elise sat before him on The Beast. He longed to feel her body settling against his again.

Best not. He sighed. He mustn't touch her. He mustn't even think about touching her, not when it was the King's wish that he should marry Lady Rowena de Sainte-Colombe. Duty. Lord.

He had no idea a man could feel so trapped. And he wasn't even married.

The next day began with a small irritation. Gawain still couldn't stop thinking about Elise. As he rode towards Troyes Castle with his squire, he found he had to steel himself not to look in the direction of La Rue du Cloître. He told himself that there was no need for him to worry about Elise. He could forget all about her. She had made it perfectly clear she wanted him to have no involvement in her life. The fact that he desired her, ached to possess her again, was irrelevant. He was promised to Lady Rowena.

Gawain yawned. He had barely slept. Thinking about Elise had had him tossing and turning until the stars had begun to fade. However, the night had not been entirely fruitless. After finally achieving a few hours' rest he had woken with a decision made.

Gawain couldn't lie to himself. He still desired Elise. Seeing her again had made him understand that he had never stopped desiring her. No matter. He was no longer free. Yet he couldn't dismiss her completely, partly because of his fear that she was involved with this criminal gang, but mainly because of Pearl. His daughter. He simply could not neglect little Pearl.

The solution, when it finally came to him, was simple. He would give Elise a grant of land. It would be something for her to fall back on if her singing let her down. Gawain couldn't stomach the thought of Elise and Pearl reduced to penury. He was well aware that Lady Rowena might object to him giving Elise a grant of land. Did she have to be told? What he had done before meeting his betrothed could hardly be held against him. His past relations with Elise Chantier were nothing to do with Lady Rowena de Sainte-Colombe.

Until the deed was drawn up, his men would remain stationed at the house. They would keep an eye on Elise. Sergeant Gaston had been expressly ordered to send him a message should either of the women set foot outside the city walls. Sergeant Gaston would also watch out for André de Poitiers. With that straight in his mind, Gawain would surely be able to stop thinking about Elise.

'Aren't we going to the house, my lord?' Aubin asked, looking down La Rue du Cloître as they passed the head of the street.

Gawain looked firmly ahead. 'No, we're going to the garrison. I need to speak to Sir Raphael.'

By the time the castle walls were louring over them, Gawain was conscious of another twinge of irritation. Despite his decision to give Elise that gift of land, something that felt suspiciously like dread was curling in his guts. He wasn't looking forward to meeting Lady Rowena. It was ridiculous to dread meeting the woman whom fate had decreed he must marry. Ever since Gawain had won his spurs he had understood that in order to rise through the ranks he must make a sound marriage. And now he was a count this was even more important. But the idea of making a good dynastic alliance was hard to swallow today. He wanted Elise. He burned for her. She was the mother of his child. However, the brutal truth was that Elise wasn't the right woman. Marriage to Elise wouldn't reconcile him with his aunt. Nor would it bring him lands and the King's approval. In any case, Elise had made it plain that she had her own life to live.

He would give her the manor and then, knowing that she and Pearl were provided for, he would be able to stop thinking about her. He couldn't marry her, and he wasn't a man to marry one woman and conduct an affair with another. Even if—his mouth twisted—Elise were to agree. And that would be far from certain.

Sighing heavily, Gawain clattered into the bailey and guided The Beast towards the stable. Raphael was likely to be in the guard house or nearby.

Inside the guard house, a knot of soldiers stood in the light of the window embrasure. They were arguing about the whereabouts of Queen Eleanor of England. The Queen—she was still occasionally referred to as Eleanor of Aquitaine—had vanished mysteriously the previous spring and the Champenois were fascinated by her disappearance. They had good reason to be interested. Countess Marie of Champagne was her daughter from her first marriage to the King of France. Gawain caught a few phrases before the men turned his way.

'Queen Eleanor's in England.'

'That King Henry has locked her up. He—'

A sergeant noticed him. 'Can I help you, my lord?'

'Any sign of Captain Raphael?'

'He's off duty until this evening, *mon seigneur.*'

Nodding, Gawain turned on his heel, knowing exactly where Raphael would be. He was never really off duty. Gawain would shortly be leaving Troyes to meet Lady Rowena's father near Provins, and he didn't want to hear that in his absence Raphael had put Elise—or her friend Vivienne for that matter—under lock and key in the castle prison. Raphael must be made to understand that he would have to answer to Gawain if either woman was roughly handled.

Elise's character was not in question. Raphael must be made to understand that too. It was a pity Gawain couldn't vouch for André. Elise and Vivienne were worried about him and if Gawain were honest, so was he. For the women's sake, he would reserve judgement on André de Poitiers for as long as possible. Elise clearly loved her luteplayer and she might yet be proved right as to his character. The lad was young. Anything was possible.

In his own youth, Gawain remembered doing things he later regretted. Who didn't? But that didn't mean he would ask Raphael to stop his enquiries. The counterfeiters must be caught.

As Baderon shouldered his lute, Elise went to the door and reached for the latch.

'Thank you for coming here to play for me,' she said, smiling. 'It's a bit of a walk from Strangers' City.'

'It's no trouble. I like walking. And if truth be told, it's an honour to be playing for Blanchefleur le Fay.'

Elise shook her head. 'You are too modest. It's a greater honour for me. You are famed throughout Christendom.'

'My thanks.' With a grin, Baderon patted his purse. 'Did I mention that Lord Gawain made it worth my while to come and rehearse with you?'

Elise felt her smile fade. She almost choked. 'Lord Gawain paid you to come here?'

Baderon's grin widened. 'He slipped me a little *pourboire*.'

'When? I didn't notice.'

'Elise, it was just a tip to help you practise.' His grin turned sheepish. 'I would have come without it. It is a pleasure to play for someone with your voice. It is a gift we must all treasure.'

'You're too kind.'

As Elise closed the door behind Baderon her gaze rested briefly on the sharp eyes of Gawain's sergeant across the street. She'd learned his name was Gaston. She gave him a brief smile and closed the door with a snap.

Upstairs, one of the babies let out a piercing shriek. It was Pearl. Elise could tell from the tone. Pearl might be tiny, but she was bored. And when her daughter was bored, the world soon knew about it.

Since their arrival at La Rue du Cloître, both babies had been unsettled. Elise thought she knew why—Vivienne was miserable and tense and the babies sensed it.

Picking up her skirts, she went upstairs. Vivienne was bent over Pearl's crib, crooning softly.

'She won't settle?' Elise asked.

'No. Her linens are dry and I've fed her. She shouldn't need feeding again for at least a couple of hours.' Vivienne rubbed her brow. 'She should be tired.'

'It's possible she's fed up with staring at these four walls. I'll take her for a walk.' Elise reached for her shawl, tying it around her in such a way that she could carry Pearl sling-wise at her breast. Pearl liked being carried about in this way and usually gave her no trouble. She glanced meaningfully at Bruno's cot. 'Since Bruno's asleep, it will give you a chance to rest.'

'Bless you.'

Heat gusted into Elise's face the moment she stepped over the threshold. It was like walking out into an oven. She could hear the swifts screaming as they shot back and forth high over the castle. Nodding at Sergeant Gaston, she walked swiftly down the street.

Pearl stopped crying. The movement soothed her. As did being outside. Elise smiled. Perhaps Pearl shared her love of freedom. Wondering if Gawain's men had been ordered to shadow her again, Elise tried not to glance over her shoulder. It was up to them. Surely she could take her daughter out for a walk?

The weight of Pearl's body was comforting. A little warm in the heat perhaps, but definitely comforting. The streets were crowded. Most people were streaming in one direction, heading for the fair. Elise recognised where she was. She'd come this way with Lady Isobel on her last visit to Troyes.

She put her hand on Pearl's head. 'That was before I met your father,' she murmured.

Ahead of them, the street opened out into a small square. There was a tavern there, the Black Boar. Elise had been there too, again with Lady Isobel. Given the tavern's low reputation, Lady Isobel's insistence on going there had shocked her, but Lady Isobel had had questions and she'd known that she'd find answers at the Black Boar.

Nothing dreadful had happened to them then. *I wonder*...

Elise allowed herself to be swept along with the townsfolk and before she knew it, she found herself staring at the tavern, an idea taking shape in her mind.

The Black Boar was—putting it bluntly—more of a bawdy house than an inn. Elise wasn't surprised to see two pretty girls sitting, elegant in their dishevelment, on a bench by the door. Gaudy lacings were loosened. Generous expanses of flesh were on display. To one side, half a dozen horses—belonging doubtless to wealthy patrons—were sheltering in the shade of a makeshift awning. On account of the heat, the inn's shutters were wide. Smoke drifted into the square. There was so little wind a blue haze hung over the place.

Elise kept her gaze studiously on the inn door rather than the girls. For obvious reasons the place was popular with men from the castle garrison. But it wasn't only soldiers who came here. Merchants came here for lodgings. And hadn't André mentioned that his friends met here from time to time? It was something of a meeting place for men from all walks of life.

A cold shiver ran through her.

André. Where was he? What was he doing?

Someone inside might have heard something, and she owed it to Vivienne to try to find out.

Countess Isobel hadn't been afraid to do a little digging here, and neither would she. It was worth a try. Gawain would probably disapprove, but surely no one would harm her, not a mother carrying a baby.

Stiffening her spine, Elise held Pearl's head to her breast and marched to the door.

Chapter Six

In the tavern, in the gloom behind a roof beam, the Captain of the Guardian Knights, Sir Raphael of Reims, curled his hand round his wine cup. Gawain Steward, Count of Meaux, sat with him.

No one was near their table. None the less, Sir Raphael spoke quietly. 'In sum, you've heard absolutely nothing more about these fraudsters.'

Gawain grimaced and replied equally softly, 'Nothing you could take to Count Henry. I suspect a troupe of players are involved, though so far I have no proof. What about you? It seems likely the counterfeiters have a base somewhere in Champagne.'

It was Raphael's turn to grimace. 'Agreed. But I'm afraid I'm no further forward either. If you've no objections I'd like you to keep your eyes open for the next week or so. I take it your mistress is safely under watch in La Rue du Cloître?'

A pang of something that felt suspiciously like longing ripped through Gawain. 'She's not my mistress.' *More's the pity.* The question had wrong-footed him. It had planted images in his mind that had no right being there. Images he'd been trying to shift from his brain for weeks, no, months. Images of Elise lying soft and warm against him. Images of her... Lord, this must stop. He would soon be married. Gawain opened his mouth to tell Raphael that any help he gave him would have to be limited—he would shortly be leaving Troyes—but Raphael was speaking again.

'No? Then why are you so keen to protect her? Face it, Gawain, she must be involved. Damn it all, man, she's been sharing a tent with that lute-player for years. There can be no secrets between them. Both women must be involved. I don't want them making a run for it.'

'They won't do that.' Gawain felt himself frown. 'Those women are as innocent as the babes.'

'They must know something. By your own admission, their friend the lute-player went missing the moment we began our enquiries. The women must be involved.'

A knot formed in Gawain's stomach. Raphael could be as stubborn as a terrier. 'They hadn't seen that sword before. They are not involved. I'd stake my life on it.'

Raphael's lips curled into a cynical smile. 'That girl has you bewitched. She bewitched you last year and in my view the spell lingers. You're besotted.'

The knot twisted. 'That's not true. We were lovers for a time, that's all.' Even as the words slipped past Gawain's lips it occurred to him that he had no need to justify himself to Raphael. Worse, he was doing Elise a disservice. Thoughts—*longings*—flew through his brain. The phrase 'we were lovers' hardly did justice to the way Elise had felt in his arms, to the way she had felt beneath him. Nor, he thought wryly, was the glib phrase enough to explain the pain he'd felt after she left. And as for the way, even now, he lay awake at nights thinking about her. Wanting. Needing. No, not needing, definitely not needing. He couldn't explain it, save to say that Elise was the mother of his child. He couldn't stand the thought of her being taken to the castle for interrogation.

'Raphael, I'm glad I found you today. I will shortly be leaving Troyes and I'm asking you—whatever you find—to deal kindly with both women.'

Raphael's lips twitched. 'You've got it badly.'

Another knot formed in Gawain's belly. 'No. But I don't want to discover that the minute I leave town you've taken them to the castle. I swear they'll be safe enough in the Rue du Cloître.'

Raphael's eyebrow lifted and he leaned closer. 'They're involved.' He gave a short laugh. 'I can't turn a blind eye because one of them has you besotted.'

'They're innocent, I tell you.'

'Prove it. Bring me the counterfeiters. Help me smoke out the entire gang and then I'll believe you.'

Gawain heard himself sigh. 'I would if I could. Unfortunately, I'm leaving for Provins any day now.'

'Provins?' Raphael's eyes sharpened. 'You're going to discuss marriage settlements with Faramus de Sainte-Colombe.'

'Something of that nature.'

Raphael drummed his fingers on the table. 'Gawain, I can't swear not to interrogate those women. If nothing comes to light soon, I shall have no choice.'

Gawain hesitated. He should have no wish to prolong his association with Elise. It simply wasn't fitting that a man should be paying court to one woman while longing for another. And as far as he could see, the only way to forget Elise was to ensure that he never set eyes on her again. The feelings he had for her—the pangs of desire that kept sleep at bay—they would surely pass after he'd met Lady Rowena. Lord, now he came to think of it, he hadn't had a woman since Elise. He was no monk and denial seemed to be addling his wits. But all would be well, he was sure. Once he'd met Lady Rowena and married her, these longings for Elise would soon fade.

However, that didn't mean he wanted Raphael to put pressure on her. And there was Pearl to consider. The thought of his daughter, an innocent infant, being taken to the castle lock-up while her mother was being interrogated was not to be borne.

'Hell burn you, Raphael, I'd thought to proceed to Meaux once I've spoken to Lord Sainte-Colombe.'

'There is much there that needs your attention, I'm sure.'

'If you undertake not to act against Elise and Vivienne for…let's say a week, I'll return to Troyes after concluding my business with Lord Sainte-Colombe.'

Raphael's eyes lit up. 'You and your men will help me nail the fraudsters?'

'Provided you stay your hand with Elise.'

'My thanks, Gawain, I knew I could rely on you.'

Gawain gave his friend a jaundiced look. 'You drive a hard bargain.'

'I have to. What with the fair, the joust and the banquet, my men are stretched to the limit.' Raphael's gaze drifted towards a table by the serving hatch. One of the girls—Gawain seemed to recall she was Raphael's favourite—was flirting with a merchant. 'I knew I'd be able to twist your arm,' Raphael muttered, frowning. 'It's just a matter of knowing a man's weakness.'

Raphael's favourite planted a kiss on the merchant's cheek and a muscle twitched in Raphael's jaw. Gawain bit back a smile. It was just a matter of knowing a man's weakness, was it? 'That girl is uncommonly pretty for a whore,' he said, casually.

Raphael sent him a dark glance. 'Her name is Gabrielle, and she's not a whore.'

'No?'

Gawain was framing a teasing reply when the door opened and sunlight streamed across the floor. Elise walked in, swathed in a shawl. Elise? In the Black Boar?

Raphael stiffened and dug him in the ribs. 'Go on, ask her. Ask her if she's heard whether her lute-player's returned.'

Gawain hardly heard him. 'Quiet.' Elise's appearance in the Black Boar had caught him off guard. What the devil was she doing? Before Christmas, Count Lucien had mentioned Elise accompanying Lady Isobel to the Black Boar. At the time he'd not given it much thought, but he'd always wondered how it was that Lady Isobel, who had only then arrived in town, should have heard that the Black Boar was a good place to sniff things out. Of course, Lady Isobel could have just chanced on the place. Or…Elise might have friends here.

Elise walked to the serving hatch and gestured for Gabrielle.

'I told you Elise Chantier was involved.' Raphael's voice was knowing. He pushed back his bench and made to rise.

Gawain made a chopping motion with his hand. Sitting as they were in the shadows behind the roof post, Elise had yet to see them. 'Hold. You're too hasty, my friend. Watch. Wait.'

Raphael subsided. Both he and Gawain watched

as Gabrielle responded to whatever it was that Elise had said by approaching the serving hatch. The cook's red face and red hair appeared in the opening. More words were exchanged and Gabrielle turned back to Elise, shaking her head. A coin changed hands. Gabrielle smiled her thanks.

As Elise turned to leave, an unexpected sound reached the men in the shadows. The cry of a baby. Gawain stiffened. Pearl! Elise had Pearl hidden in her shawl.

Raphael snorted. 'It's not often you find a baby in the Black Boar.'

Gawain looked at Raphael and the words seemed to jam in his throat. *That is my daughter.* It was his innocent daughter and already she was being brought into a low tavern. Elise was a singer. He knew that, but he hadn't thought it through, not properly. What kind of life would Pearl lead in Elise's care? He would have to speak to her. He stood up abruptly.

Raphael moved to block his path. 'I'll do it,' he said.

Gawain looked blankly at him. 'Eh?'

'I'll speak to Gabrielle. She'll tell me what Elise had to say. If you don't mind.'

Gawain sank back, scrubbing his palm over his

face while Raphael wove between the tables. Sight of Elise in the tavern had Gawain's thoughts in disarray. He should cut loose from her, he really should. For the sake of Lady Rowena and his marriage. For the future of his county. But how could he? He must face this squarely. It was very likely that Pearl would become familiar with places that were far more disreputable than the Black Boar.

No. *No.* He couldn't accept it. He pushed to his feet.

He was halfway to the door when Raphael intercepted him. 'Thus far, it seems you are right in your judgement of Elise Chantier,' he said. 'Thus far.'

'Hmm?' Gawain bent to peer through a shutter. Elise was walking towards the Grain Market. If he hurried he could catch her.

'She was asking about the lute-player,' Raphael said. 'She really doesn't know where he is.'

'I told you—she and Vivienne are innocent.' Gawain gripped Raphael's arm. 'Look, I understand you must continue the hunt while I am away. I simply want you to swear you'll not distress the women in the Rue du Cloître.'

'You have my word.'

Gawain released Raphael. 'Did Gabrielle tell her anything?'

'Gabrielle knows nothing. Enquiries will be made, however, on Elise's behalf.'

Gawain lifted an eyebrow. 'Gabrielle will tell you what she discovers?'

Raphael's grin was confident. 'If Gabrielle hears as much as a whisper, you may be sure that I shall be the first to know.'

'Elise?'

Elise broke step, briefly closing her eyes. *Gawain.* Slowly, she turned. He was stalking towards her, a crease in his brow. She waited, foot tapping. She could no longer see his guard dogs. They'd trailed her to the tavern. She'd glimpsed them when she'd entered. Had he dismissed them?

When Gawain reached her, his dark eyes were glowering.

'There's no need to scowl,' she said. 'Your men know exactly where I have been. I don't know where they've gone, but they followed me across town.'

He reached out and twitched the shawl from Pearl's face. He stared down at her, shaking his head, and a lock of blond hair fell across his forehead. Elise looked quickly away. She could remember the texture of his hair, its softness, its warmth. She could remember the way the scent of bay from his soap lingered in those bright strands.

'I expect the men were distracted by the girls when they saw you going into the Black Boar,' he said.

'Gawain?' Elise bit her lip. His eyes were narrowed, but he was close enough for her to see the grey flecks in his eyes. She knew that look. He was angry. A large finger stroked Pearl's cheek and something cramped inside her. He was gentle even in his anger. In Elise's experience that was a rare quality in a man.

His dark gaze met hers and he made a sound of exasperation. 'What were you thinking, taking Pearl to the Black Boar?'

He was so tall, she resisted the urge to take a step backwards. 'It's just an inn.'

He shook his head. 'The Black Boar is more than just an inn, as I'm sure you know.'

She stared at him. 'It can't be that bad, my lord. Countess Isobel went there last winter. I know because I accompanied her there.'

'That's no excuse.' He shoved his hand through his hair and another lock fell out of place. 'To take our daughter into such a place...'

She searched his eyes. 'Gawain, Pearl's innocence protects her.' She shrugged. 'In any case, I was only there for a moment and she was wrapped up in the shawl the whole time.'

'It was more than a moment.'

'Oh?' Realisation crashed in on her. 'You were in there! Why didn't you make yourself known?'

Gawain flushed. Guilt? Shame? Her foot tapped. She laughed and even to her own ears it sounded bitter. 'What were you doing in the Black Boar, Gawain? Availing yourself of the local delights?'

'You are insolent.' Frown deepening, he threaded her arm firmly through his. She tried to tug free, but there was no denying him and she found herself being walked through the Paris Gate. 'Elise, I don't want to quarrel.'

'I am a free woman. You don't own me.' She was trying not to look at him and shot him a quick sideways glance. His expression was rueful.

'I know. I have no right to order your behaviour.' He caught her chin and made her look at him. 'Just as you have no right to question my motives for being in the Black Boar.'

'Very well.' She forced a smile and it really did feel forced. They had no claims on each other. Why then did the thought of Gawain going to the Black Boar to find a girl make her stomach churn? She felt positively ill.

Searching for a distraction, she glanced over her shoulder. 'You dismissed the men.'

He grunted. He was looking at Pearl again, expression unreadable. 'They are no longer necessary since I shall be accompanying you back to the house. You are happy to walk this way?'

'I suppose so. Pearl was restive at the house and I thought a walk might do her good.'

'You will permit me to accompany you. We shall take a turn around the city walls.' Gawain's lips curved and although she wasn't looking at him—*she wasn't*—Elise's heart gave a little jump. When he smiled at her like that he was well-nigh irresistible. A pang shot through her. *What had he been doing in the Black Boar?*

They crossed the moat—it was a dry moat, like a deep ditch—and strolled north on to the narrow road that encircled Troyes. On their right hand, the city walls rose up, solid and impregnable. A helmet gleamed on the battlements of one of the towers. A brace of horsemen trotted past, dust rising in their wake. Elise held her palm gently under Pearl's head and tried not to look at Gawain. She was trying not to do a lot of things and it wasn't easy. She was trying not to enjoy the feel of that strong arm beneath her other hand. And she was ignoring the unwelcome pang in her breast as she remembered the joy that had flooded through her when they had become lovers. What she had felt hadn't been love. She had no real belief in love. Just as she had no idea what had happened between them. *We were lovers. The desire between us was strong.* It wouldn't happen again. And there it was again—another pang of…something. Whatever it was, she wished she wasn't feeling it. It was painful.

It was ironic when you thought about it. Blanchefleur le Fay spent her days and her nights singing about love. Yearning and unrequited love were woven through the best of the songs—like gold and silver threads in a tapestry they brought them to life. But such passion had always eluded her. Except with Gawain. Gawain aside, Elise remained in control. What had happened with Gawain was passing strange. She was Blanchefleur and to her love was a mystery, except to say that everyone seemed to yearn for it. She had always hoped that one day she would understand it, but she was no longer so confident. Perhaps it didn't matter. Her singing didn't seem to have suffered. Love was unattainable. Everyone had unattainable dreams. That, she did understand. And that was what she sang about, the unattainable.

Gawain was getting married.

Gawain cleared his throat and gestured back to the city. 'My manor—Le Manoir des Rosières—lies past the wooded area to the east of the town.'

Elise nodded, half-listening as Gawain described his father's manor. She didn't know why he was bothering. It wasn't as though she was ever likely to see it. Lady Rowena, on the other hand...

Her jaw clenched.

Gawain was listing the improvements he'd made to the curtain wall when a rank smell caught in her nose. Something was rotting. Something dead.

Gawain broke off, nose wrinkling. 'What the devil?'

The source of the smell wasn't hard to find. Someone had tipped what looked like their entire household's refuse into the moat. A cloud of flies hung over it. Elise could see cabbage stalks; a broken clay pot; the mouldy heel of a loaf. And the source of that dreadful smell? Her stomach churned. There was a furry leg. A tail.

'Ugh!' Holding her nose, she turned away.

'Dead cat,' Gawain murmured, walking her swiftly past. 'I'll inform Raphael.'

'The Guardians have to be told about a dead cat?'

His lips twitched. Not that she was looking. 'It's not the cat so much, but the rubbish. If the moat fills up because it's choked with rubbish, it's no longer a defence. The Guardians are charged with keeping it clear. If Raphael discovers who is responsible, he will have them fined. It's not the first time the moat has been used as a midden and I dare say it won't be the last.'

Elise glanced at the ditch. This section, thankfully, was clear. 'I hadn't thought a knight would find himself clearing out the moat.'

'Raphael won't do it personally, but his men will.'

She pulled a face. 'I don't envy them. Does this happen a lot?'

'Aye. Sometimes it's worse. Cats aren't all that's dumped in the moat. Corpses have been found.'

'People?' Eyes wide, she stopped walking and scanned the length of the moat. First north, then south. She didn't know why it was, but she thought of André and shuddered. 'People?' An icy trickle ran down her spine and she gripped Gawain's sleeve. 'Gawain, do you have time to do an entire circuit of the town?'

Sombre dark eyes flickered towards the moat before returning to her. 'You're thinking about André.'

Pearl shifted. She tried to kick away her wrappings and let out a whimper that swiftly became a wail. Gawain touched Pearl's cheek and as he did so, he brushed Elise's fingers. The contact had been accidental. None the less, Elise's fingers tingled.

'Pearl is all right?' he asked.

'She's fine. She's hot, that's all. It won't be long before she's hungry. We'll have to hurry.' Eyes flickering back to the ditch, Elise took his hand. 'Gaw—my lord, you are right. I was thinking about André. I can't help thinking that he must have met with an accident after the loss of the sword. He might be in the moat even now.'

'You think he's been killed?'

'It's possible.' Her voice broke. 'He's never normally away for long.'

'So you really haven't heard from him?'

'Not a word. Gawain, if André was all right he would have sent a message. He's not cruel and he knows Vivienne will be worrying. Yet all we have is silence.'

Gawain looked thoughtfully at her. When Pearl let out another fretful wail, he turned them to face the way they had come. 'We can't walk round the entire city. It would take far too long. I'll get my sergeant to do it. Immediately after Pearl is back with Vivienne.'

* * *

Someone was pounding on the door. Elise stumbled out of bed and hurried downstairs. Even before she slid back the bolt, she knew Sergeant Gaston would be standing outside. Each morning since that walk with Gawain he'd come to report on the state of the moat.

'Good morning, *ma demoiselle*.' Sergeant Gaston inclined his head at her. He was invariably courteous.

'Sergeant?'

'Went on patrol again at dawn.' He lowered his voice. A perceptive man, Sergeant Gaston knew to keep his voice low so Vivienne wouldn't hear him. 'Thought you'd like to know the ditch at least is clear this morning.'

Elise let her breath out. 'Thank God! And thank you, Sergeant, I appreciate you checking again.' Gawain's sergeant was turning out to be a real boon. When Gawain had mentioned that he would get him to patrol the moat, she hadn't imagined that he would be doing it every morning. 'Thank you so much.'

'*Ma demoiselle*, you are very welcome.'

Elise closed the door and slid the shutters open. Two of Gawain's men-at-arms were standing directly outside. As she went to kneel by the fire to stir the embers into life—they needed warm water—she could hear them talking. Her stomach rumbled. She was looking forward to breaking her fast.

'She got here last night,' one of the men said. 'Hervé saw her entourage arrive at the palace.'

The other guard grunted. 'Is she as pretty as they say?'

Elise stiffened. Carefully, she hooked the kettle over the fire. Were they talking about Lady Rowena?

'Pretty? *Mon Dieu*, to hear Hervé talk you'd think she was an angel. She has hair like spun gold, eyes like sapphires and a waist a man could span with his hands. She's a bit on the skinny side apparently, though with such beauty that hardly signifies.'

'Lord Gawain's a lucky devil,' the second man said, pausing. 'How did he react when he saw her?'

'Lord Gawain wasn't at the palace. They'll meet at the tournament.'

Elise frowned into the fire, slowly feeding in more wood. She was no longer listening. She'd heard enough. The tournament was today. Gawain and Lady Rowena would meet today. This wasn't news that should affect her, but it did. A moment ago she'd been happy. Happy to learn that the moat was clear. And now? She felt out of sorts. She ought to hurry. She and Baderon had arranged a final rehearsal and he would be arriving very shortly. The banquet was being held tonight, after the tournament at the Field of the Birds and, since André still hadn't appeared, Baderon had agreed to play for her. Their performance must be perfect.

Elise was dreading the banquet now. Yes, that must be why she felt a trifle out of sorts. She was nervous. She'd waited so long for her chance to sing at Count Henry's palace. It wasn't a new feeling. Blanchefleur was often nervous. She didn't know a professional performer who wasn't. It was just that she did not usually feel quite so bad. She wrapped her arms about her stomach and wondered how she could have been thinking about breakfast when she felt so sick.

Gawain was meeting Lady Rowena that morning. At the tournament. She felt choked, utterly choked. She, who prided herself on her sangfroid.

There was another knock on the door. Baderon?

She went across and lifted the latch and it was indeed Baderon. She forced a smile as he came in. 'You're early.'

'I'm sorry.' Baderon's mouth was tight. 'Couldn't

sleep. I'll feel better when we've done the run-through.'

Elise grimaced. 'I understand. Come in, please.' Firmly, she told herself that she was nervous because of tonight's performance. Of course, her disquiet could in no way be connected to Gawain's meeting with his betrothed.

Baderon settled on a stool and set about tuning his lute. Cooings and stirrings from upstairs told Elise that the babies were waking. Vivienne would be down shortly. Baderon loosed an experimental ripple of sound and stilled it. He smiled up at her. 'It also occurred to me that you might be glad if we finished early.'

'Oh?'

He gave her a strange look. 'The tournament at the Field of the Birds—don't you want to see it?'

Elise bent to throw another log on to the fire and fiddled with the kettle. 'I won't be going.'

'You have friends who will be there. Countess Isobel.' Baderon's gaze bored into her shoulder blades. 'Count Gaw—'

'Leave it, Baderon. I'm *not* going to the tournament.'

Chapter Seven

A village of pavilions—or rather *two* villages— had mushroomed overnight in the Field of the Birds. The sun-bleached grass was bright with them—blue, green, yellow and black; plain and striped...

The pavilions and lance stands belonging to knights supporting Count Lucien d'Aveyron were sited at one end of the lists. The crimson pavilion of the Count of Meaux sat among these, its pennon slack in the summer heat, the golden griffin lost in the silken folds.

At the other end sat the pavilions belonging to guests of Count Henry of Champagne—the knights of his household; the Guardian Knights; his guests. A couple of the more wealthy merchants were also fielding knights and they too had joined Count Henry's team.

The townsfolk viewed the Harvest Tourney as

a battle between town and country, but Count Lucien d'Aveyron had made it clear that this tournament was not for the settling of grudges. Yes, the fighting would be hard and fierce, but there were to be no deaths. This was not a war; this was an exercise. It was also an entertainment. Ladies were present.

It was almost time for the review. By the crimson pavilion, Gawain was mounted. Helmet under his arm, he scowled down at his squire.

'You've a message from Lady Isobel? Lady Rowena has arrived safely?'

'Yes, my lord. Lady Rowena has taken a place on the ladies' stand next to Countess Isobel. Lady Isobel asked me to inform you that Lady Rowena would be pleased if you would accept her favour.'

Gawain's stomach sank and he narrowed his eyes on the ladies' stand. Lord, the woman expected him to pick her out in public when he'd never set eyes on her? What was this, some kind of a test? How was he to know which one she was? 'Lady Rowena expects me to greet her in public when I've not yet met her?'

The ladies' stand was little more than a raised wooden platform, but it was shaded by a blue awning, courtesy of Count Lucien. The shade would be most welcome in this heat. A handful of children were weaving in and out behind the barrier, amid bursts of laughter. Playing tag, he thought. Gawain could see Lucien's wife, Countess Isobel, sitting amid a bevy of ladies and maids. Which one was Lady Rowena? He could see a plump dark beauty, and a slender blonde. It must be the blonde. Except, hell burn it, there were at least *three* other blondes on that stand, and he had no clue which one was his fiancée. He would have to follow Isobel's lead.

Swearing under his breath, Gawain jammed on his helmet. This was nothing less than an ordeal. Four blondes. Lord. He started to mutter. 'It's all very well for the ladies. They know us by our colours.' The Beast's crimson caparison and the griffin on his shield put his identity in no doubt.

'Not to mention the herald's introduction,' Aubin said, hiding a grin.

Devil take the boy, he was enjoying Gawain's discomfiture. 'Be warned, Aubin, plenty of other lads are keen to step into your shoes.'

Aubin's grin widened. Gawain's threat was empty and he knew it. He knew Gawain liked him. A little impudence aside, he was the most devoted and diligent of squires.

'Yes, my lord. Good luck.'

As Gawain heeled The Beast into a walk and

took his place for the review, he wondered if Aubin was wishing him luck in his meeting with Lady Rowena or in the joust.

Elise pushed through the crowd at the side of the ladies' stand. She was trying to work her way round to the front. The sun was almost directly overhead and her heavy plaits and veil were making her hot. Irritably, Elise pulled her hair away from the back of her neck. She had a few minutes before the review began.

She wasn't here to see Gawain, she really wasn't. She was here because shortly after Baderon had left La Rue du Cloître it had dawned on her that she had no choice but to attend the Harvest Tourney. She wanted to see Lady Rowena de Sainte-Colombe before her performance at the palace. She *needed* to see her before the performance. And not because she was jealous of the woman—although she had the lowering feeling that she might indeed be jealous. No, she needed to see Lady Rowena in case first sight of her made her miss a note. Imagine if she lost the thread mid-song! She couldn't have that. Not when she was—at last—to sing at the Champagne court.

Her performance before Count Henry must be dazzling. And it would be. Provided she wasn't distracted by watching out for the woman who was to marry Gawain. Elise swallowed down a bitter taste. Jealousy. Was that what she was feeling? It felt pretty ugly.

Lady Rowena had better appreciate him. She had better be a good woman. Gawain deserved the best.

Elise paused in front of the ladies' stand, hand on the wooden railing. She was well aware that she didn't belong anywhere near the ladies sitting on these thickly cushioned benches. She looked at the bright silken gowns, at the delicate filmy ladies' veils, at the glitter of gold and silver circlets. She came from a very different world. True, she had put on one of Blanchefleur's gowns to come here, the silvery-grey damask with cherry-coloured ribbons. She knew it looked good. Blanchefleur had her own brand of glitter and shine, but she was still just playing a part. These ladies were the real thing.

Elise had a plan. She would pretend to be just passing by and hope that Lady Isobel would see her and acknowledge her. That ought to give her time to work out which noblewoman was Lady Rowena. Then there would be no shocks tonight, and her performance at the palace would be seamless.

A rosy-cheeked boy poked his head under the railing and grinned at her. *'Hôlà.'*

Elise smiled back. *'Hôlà.'* Lord, she was melting. She dragged one of her plaits forward and fiddled with a cherry-coloured ribbon. Lady Isobel was sat in the centre of the stand. Affecting to simply be walking past, Elise moved slowly on, eyes scanning the ladies. She'd heard that Lady Rowena de Sainte-Colombe was blonde but—

'Elise? Elise Chantier?' Lady Isobel was off the bench and at the barrier in the blink of an eye. Warm hands reached for her. 'Elise! How lovely to see you.' She gestured at the long, cushioned bench. 'You must join us at once!'

Elise's heart lurched. 'Oh, no, my lady, I couldn't.' Sit on the same stand as Lady Rowena? She really couldn't.

'Nonsense!' The countess tugged on her arm, she wouldn't take no for an answer. 'I have thought about you often. Come and tell me how you have been faring. You look well. Are you singing still?'

With a rustle of silks and brocades, the noble-women of Champagne and France shuffled along the bench to make room for her. Before she knew it, Elise was sitting on a plump cushion next to Countess Isobel. She felt out of place among these tightly laced, perfumed ladies. She didn't belong here! Feeling utterly trapped, she stared at the handrail in front of her and wondered how soon she could make her excuses. There were rules here, an etiquette that was likely to be as stringent as the Rule she had encountered at the convent. Elise had found it hard enough to follow convent rule, but here—she'd didn't have a clue. She would surely make a mistake and cause grave offence.

'You are singing, Elise?' Lady Isobel asked.

'Yes, my lady, I am singing.' Elise wasn't going to mention Pearl. She would say nothing about all the months she couldn't sing, months that must be made up for if they were to survive. There was no point, Countess Isobel couldn't be expected to understand a life that was so different from hers.

'Where are you staying, not in Strangers' City, I hope?'

Elise smiled sadly. The way the countess lowered her voice as she mentioned Strangers' City was yet more proof, if proof be needed, of the chasm that had grown up between them. Countess Isobel was never likely to set foot in a place like Strangers' City. Once, they had braved the Black Boar together—something like that would never happen again. Count d'Aveyron wouldn't stand for it.

'I was staying in Strangers' City.'

Several curious pairs of eyes fixed on her. Ladies were leaning close to hear her responses. Wide, avid eyes raked her up and down, assessing her gown, her veil. Elise lifted her chin and toyed with one of her plaits, twisting and untwisting the cherry-coloured ribbon. Thank goodness she had dressed with care. She had no real idea why she'd chosen the silvery damask. Instinct, she supposed. Pride. Even though she never dreamed Lady Isobel would invite her on to the ladies' stand, it had given her confidence to come to the Field of the Birds in a good gown.

Countess Isobel's eyebrows rose. 'Was?'

Elise's cheeks burned. 'I am in lodgings now.' She shot a sideways glance at one of the other ladies and wondered whether the woman would be shocked to learn that her lodgings had been found for her by Gawain Steward, Count of Meaux. What would these ladies make of that?

Trying not to be obvious, she studied them. Which one was Lady Rowena? The willowy one to the left? Or the child on Lady Isobel's right hand? She might even be the bosomy woman sitting slightly behind them…

'Your lodgings are in town?'

'Yes, my lady, in La Rue du Cloître.'

'Very nice.' Lady Isobel's eyebrows went up another notch. 'You are fortunate to have found them.'

'Indeed.' Another surreptitious glance had Elise coming to the conclusion that Lady Rowena couldn't be the child on Lady Isobel's right. She was far too young. No, Lady Rowena must be either the willowy lady in red or the woman behind her. Both of them were depressingly pretty. Not that it signified.

Elise touched the countess's arm. 'My lady, I thank you for inviting me up here. I hope you understand how sorry I was to leave Ravenshold at the turn of the year.'

'I was worried when you first vanished, but your message put my mind at rest.' Lady Isobel paused, smiling. 'However, it's good to see you in person. It was a hard time for me and I never thanked you for being such a support. I have missed you.'

'You are too kind.'

'No, truly.' The countess's eyes lost focus. 'Immediately after you left, the whole castle was in an uproar. Why I remember, Gaw—' A trumpet blast cut Lady Isobel off mid-flow, and everyone's gaze shifted to the field. 'We shall catch up with our news later,' she whispered. 'The review is about to begin.'

* * *

Count Lucien d'Aveyron was taking part in the preliminary jousts. Both he and Gawain were to lead their team as they paraded round the field.

Gawain hooked his helm over the pommel of his saddle and guided The Beast to Lucien's right hand. The Beast's red caparison fluttered like flame. The griffin on Gawain's shield glowed.

Lucien's standard—with its black raven on a blue ground—hung over the ladies' stand. When Gawain glanced towards it, he felt a distinct chill. Not long now. He would soon meet Lady Rowena. The cold feeling settled in his innards. It was odd how he'd never given marriage much thought before this. He had blithely assumed that marrying would be an easy matter. Once his bride had been decided upon by the King and his uncle, he had never thought to question their choice. He'd been pleased to hear about Lady Rowena's famed beauty. He'd been pleased he would be marrying an heiress with the right connections in France. Today that meant nothing. He simply didn't care. All he could think about was a pair of soulful dark eyes. He rolled his shoulders. He would do his duty, of course, but...

'Lucien Vernon, Count d'Aveyron,' the herald cried, as he read from the scroll listing Lucien's titles and honours. The crowd roared. Lucien had restored these tourneys to their former glory. Indeed, he had improved upon them so much they were even better than they'd been in his father's day. It had certainly made him popular. Given that Lucien was patron of the tournament, Gawain gave him precedence, restraining The Beast until the herald announced his own name.

'Gawain Steward, Count of Meaux, Lord of...'

This wasn't Gawain's demesne, but he had been steward of Ravenshold and his family had held Le Manoir des Rosières for generations. Gawain had a fair number of supporters in Champagne. The Beast surged forward amid a chorus of shouts and applause. His hoofbeats made a hollow sound—the field was as dry as bone.

The ladies' stand came into sharp focus and at a stroke, Gawain was deaf to the cries of his well-wishers and blind to all but the black raven on Lucien's standard. When he reined in, a grey dust cloud hung in the air. His throat felt as though half the grit in Champagne was lodged in it. He could do with a pot of ale to wash it away.

On his left, Lucien had his visor up. He was performing a circus trick that was a favourite with the ladies—his destrier was bowing a knee and lowering his head. It was a tricky manoeuvre for a horse, particularly when bearing a fully armed knight. The blue silk caparison rippled about the horse's legs. The ladies clapped and smiled and turned their gazes expectantly on Gawain. A little silence fell.

'Your turn,' Lucien murmured, with a grin.

'Hell fry you, Luc.' This was a challenge Gawain couldn't ignore, though for the first time in his life he felt like turning tail. It wasn't the thought of meeting his betrothed. It was the thought of all those women—noblewomen—watching him. He didn't like it, but it was clear there was no escape. He must equal Lucien's trick. His mouth went up at the side. He wouldn't equal Lucien's trick; he would better it. He clicked loudly with his tongue, leaned forward in the saddle, signalling with knees and hands and voice. 'Dance, Beast. Dance.'

Slowly, majestically, The Beast rose on his hindquarters and pirouetted around. The field seemed to shift and Gawain lost sight of the ladies. He could see the rooks flying over a stand of trees, he could see the far end of the lists, his red pavilion, the squires wheeling out the lance racks...

As the ladies came back into view he heard a sigh from the stand. The crowd roared approval. The Beast's forelegs thumped on to the baked earth and Gawain found himself looking at a pair of soulful dark eyes. His mind seized up.

Elise. He saw no one else. He shoved up his visor. What the devil—was his mind playing tricks?

No, there she was, idly playing with the cherry-coloured ribbon binding her hair. Gawain clenched his jaw and felt his cheeks scorch. Elise. Her gown was a subtle grey damask that wouldn't look out of place at the French court. Her veil was light as gossamer. She looked beautiful. Ladylike. He felt a frown form. Why was she here? Beautiful though she was, she really shouldn't be on this stand.

Lady Isobel must have invited her. Lord, was he to meet Lady Rowena with Elise watching his every move? Could this meeting get more difficult?

Lucien was still ahead of him. He had ridden up to the barrier and Countess Isobel was leaning over it, busily fastening a blue favour round her husband's arm. All too soon, Lucien backed away, abandoning him to his ordeal.

The countess gestured Gawain forward. Fixing his eyes on her, determined not to look at Elise again, Gawain approached the rail.

'Count Gawain.' Lady Isobel's gaze was resting on his face in a puzzled manner, her expression arrested. He saw her shoot a glance in Elise's direction. 'It is a pleasure to see you here today.'

'The pleasure is mine, my lady,' he murmured.

'My lord.' The countess made a gesture and the lady on her right hand rose from her seat. 'Permit me to introduce Lady Rowena de Sainte-Colombe.'

A child. Somehow Gawain kept his face steady. He was looking at a child tricked out in a crimson gown that matched the roses on her cheeks. Silk rustled as she moved. Her veil—a filmy blue affair—was held in place by a golden circlet. Red gems winked at him and a plain gold cross hung about her neck. The gold was real, no doubt of that, and the gems in the circlet had to be rubies. A curl of unease went through him. There was something staged about Lady Rowena's appearance. Both the gown and the ornaments had been carefully chosen to match his colours and he couldn't fault that. It was a courteous gesture. Yet…

Looking past the show, Gawain saw only a very young girl. She looked painfully nervous.

Lady Rowena is a child. A skinny child.

The child came forward and a tiny white hand was placed briefly in his. It trembled slightly.

Behind her, none of the ladies moved. Every-one seemed to be holding their breath, including Lady Rowena. Her blue eyes were wide and as she studied him, the roses seemed to leave her cheeks. Lord, could this get any worse? He doubted it. Lady Rowena was afraid. Of him? Of rejection? Gawain was glad he had his visor up. With luck it would make him less intimidating.

Gawain tried to ignore the unsettling thought that a pair of brown eyes were watching him. He put a smile in his voice. 'Lady Rowena, it is a great pleasure to meet you.'

'Th-thank you, my lord.' Her voice was pleas-ing—even though it was shaking almost as much as her hand.

'I hope you will do me the great honour of ac-companying me to the banquet tonight?' he said, gently.

Her hand jumped in his. Long eyelashes swept down, hiding her eyes from view. 'Yes, my lord. I...I look forward to it.'

This was the moment she should offer him her favour. When nothing happened, he pressed her fingers. 'Lady Rowena?'

'My lord?'

'Your favour?'

'Oh! Yes, yes, of course.' A crimson scarf appeared, the edge banded with gold. His colours again. Lady Rowena might be quivering with nerves, but she had been well schooled and everything had been carefully thought out. She fastened her scarf around his arm.

'Thank you, my lady. I will strive to do you honour.' Bowing his head at his betrothed, Gawain wheeled The Beast around, giving ground to the other knights lining up to pay their respects at Countess Isobel's stand.

The rest of the review passed in a blur. Gawain ought to be studying their challengers, but his mind wasn't on it. He checked the length of his stirrups. Changed his mind—twice—about which sword he would use and bawled at Aubin when he was slow. His concentration was broken. Several times he caught himself glancing in the direction of the ladies' stand, and several times he checked himself.

He mustn't allow himself to become distracted. Just because Elise—he swore and broke off the thought before it was formed and started afresh— just because Lady Rowena was sitting next to Countess Isobel there was no need for him to keep looking at that stand.

Beside him, Lucien's harness creaked. Lucien

cleared his throat and jerked his head towards the ladies. 'Well, what do you think? Pretty, isn't she?'

Gawain looked blankly at Lucien. He was trying not to think about any of the ladies on the stand and it took a while for the question to penetrate.

'Gawain, did you hear me?'

Gawain shook his head to clear it. 'She's stunning,' he managed. The crimson scarf on his arm seemed to shiver.

Lucien tipped his head to the side. Waited. Lifted an eyebrow. 'Is that all you have to say? You finally get to marry the heiress of your dreams, the heiress who looks like an angel, and all you can say is that she is stunning?'

Gawain set his mouth in a firm line. 'What else is there to say?' He frowned. 'She's a child!'

Lucien gave him an odd look. 'She's seventeen. Young, yes, but certainly old enough.'

'Seventeen?' Yes, Gawain seemed to recall being told as much. To his mind, she looked about twelve. 'She's a child.'

The review was almost over. The last of the knights on the Troyes team was approaching Countess Isobel's stand. Ladies were fluttering favours in the fellow's face but he ignored them all. The knight was staring at a quiet figure in a silver-grey gown. Gawain stiffened. He saw Lady

Isobel speak to the man, gesturing at the many favours before him. The knight shook his head. He was gazing at Elise as though bespelled. He must have asked for her, for the countess beckoned Elise to the rail.

A pulse began to thud in Gawain's temple. He was vaguely aware of Lucien talking to his squire, Joris. Something about the use of blunted lances at the beginning of the tourney. Gawain didn't catch much of it. He was too busy watching Elise as she smiled gently at the knight. She twitched the cherry-coloured ribbon from her hair and fastened it about his arm. Saluting, grinning from ear to ear, the knight retreated and went to take his place in the Troyenne team.

His shield was parti-coloured—black and red, with what appeared to be a white dove in the centre. Gawain couldn't place the colours. His guts were in a knot.

'Luc, who's that fellow?'

Lucien broke off and looked over. 'Hmm?'

Gawain pointed. 'The knight who has just joined the Troyennes? Who is he? His shield is parti-coloured, red and black. The device looks as though it's a silver boat.'

'That's Sir Olier of Les Landes.'

Elise was back on the bench beside the countess, and it seemed to Gawain her cheeks were flushed. The countess directed a remark at her and the flush intensified.

'Les Landes?' Gawain felt himself frown, observed that Lucien was regarding him altogether too thoughtfully and snapped his visor down. He didn't want Lucien to read too much into his interest. 'Never heard of him.'

'His holdings are in the south-west, in the Aquitaine, I believe. It's a large estate, though the land is pretty poor. Why?'

'No reason, just couldn't place him.' Gawain jerked his head at the lance stands. 'I hope we begin soon. The waiting's interminable.'

Lucien laughed. 'I couldn't agree more.'

This wasn't Elise's first tournament and she had mixed feelings about them. As she looked out at the lists, at the standards that had been set up along the fence, at the forest of brightly painted lances in the racks, she recalled the last time she'd been at the Field of the Birds. She'd been with Lady Isobel then too, but they'd not seen any jousting. One of Count Lucien's household knights had been murdered before events had got underway. Elise had seen the body. The poor boy—he'd been young for a knight—had been knifed. His blood had splashed on to Count Lucien's pavilion; blood every bit as bright as the crimson on Gawain's shield.

She bit her lip. Blood. Gawain's shield was the colour of blood. How odd, she'd always thought the red in Gawain's colours represented fire, but it could equally well be blood. He was a warrior. Heart in her mouth, she swallowed. *Holy Mary, don't let his blood be spilled today.* She wasn't sure she could control her reaction if he did get hurt.

'Elise, are you all right?' Lady Isobel asked, quietly. 'You look pale.'

Elise grimaced. 'I was recalling the last time we were here.'

'You are thinking of Sir Geoffrey.' The countess gave her a reassuring smile. 'That was tragic, but don't forget it was unrelated to the actual tourney. It was connected with the theft of that relic from Conques.'

'I remember.'

'I doubt there will be bloodshed today,' the countess continued. 'Lucien has decreed that lances will be blunted at the outset. They are merely training.'

Elise couldn't help but shudder. She found herself looking first at the colours of the Troyenne knights, and then at those of the knights mustering at Count Lucien's end of the lists. 'It's war they are training for, my lady. War.' She felt vaguely nauseous. What if Gawain were hurt? What if he won? Lord, she wasn't sure she could control her reactions either way. If he won a point she'd be hard pressed to remain in her seat. And if he were unhorsed...

I love him. I don't want him to be hurt. It occurred to her that the wife of a warrior like Gawain would have to get used to feeling like this. Of course, a wife might not care for him as much as she did. But if he did get hurt—ladies ought to be trained in the healing arts. Lady Rowena looked alarmingly young. Did she have the right skills?

The bench creaked as Elise craned her neck to see past the countess. She caught Lady Rowena's eye. 'Excuse me, my lady?'

Lady Rowena turned large blue eyes on her. 'Yes?'

'My congratulations on your betrothal,' Elise said. Her voice sounded strange. The words almost choked her.

'Thank you.'

'You have been waiting for this moment for a long time?' Elise could feel Lady Isobel looking curiously at her, but she couldn't stop herself. She had to know that if Gawain were hurt, Lady Rowena was competent to care for him.

Lady Rowena looked puzzled. 'Not so long, as it happens. My father signed the agreements with Count Gawain quite recently.'

'I see. But you must have been prepared for marriage in general,' Elise pressed. She knew that noblewomen were rigorously trained. The higher her status, the more a noblewoman would have to learn. Someone like Lady Rowena—the goddaughter of the King of France—must have been taught to manage several households; she would surely have learned how to organise the servants so that she and Gawain could move swiftly from one estate to the other; she would also have learned how to manage on her own when Gawain was away. And, most important, she would surely have learned everything there was to know about the healing arts.

Lady Rowena's blue eyes met hers. 'I have been trained in all aspects of managing a large estate.'

Elise kept a bright smile pinned to her face. At least she hoped it was bright. It felt rather forced. 'For myself, I have always had a particular interest in herbs and healing.'

Lady Rowena nodded politely. 'How interesting.'

Which told Elise precisely nothing. Conscious that Countess Isobel was taking in her every word, she leaned back with a sigh. She would have to leave it at that. If she said any more she might rouse suspicions, and the last thing she wanted to do was cause a rift in Gawain's marriage before it had even begun. Gawain was not hers and despite what she felt about him, despite that she had borne him a child, he never would be.

Elise shouldn't be on this stand, this wasn't her world and she didn't belong.

She touched Lady Isobel's arm. 'My lady, it was kind of you to invite me to sit with you, but I think I shall return to town.'

The countess was all concern. 'You are unwell?'

'Not unwell, no.' She touched her temple. 'I have a slight headache. It must be the heat.'

It had been a mistake to come. She loved Gawain. Love had crept up on her unawares. In truth, the thought—*I love him*—felt as familiar as an old friend. It seemed likely that she had loved him for a long time. Had she loved him last year? It was possible. He was a good man and deserving of any woman's love. Elise wished she had understood sooner that what she felt for him was love. She wouldn't have rushed off so quickly at the turn of the year. They might have had more time together.

'If you are thirsty, I could call for refreshments,' Lady Isobel said.

'No, thank you, my lady.' Elise lowered her voice to a confidential whisper. 'In truth, I am a little nervous.'

'Oh?'

'I am performing at the Harvest Banquet tonight and I need to prepare myself.'

The countess's face lit up. 'You're singing at the palace? Elise, that's wonderful. I shall look forward to hearing you.'

'Thank you. It will be good to know I have friends there.'

Lady Isobel squeezed her hand. 'You'll be fine.'

Elise's stomach cramped. She wasn't so sure. She would be singing in front of Gawain at his betrothal feast. She shook her head at herself. Such thoughts served no purpose. Rising, she curtsied to Countess Isobel. 'Thank you for your kindness, my lady. I really think it best that I return to town.' Elise never usually needed to rest before a performance, but she'd never felt quite so on edge.

When Lady Isobel slanted a knowing glance towards Gawain, preparing to ride on to the field, and murmured, 'Perhaps that is wise', Elise knew she had made the right decision.

Chapter Eight

Elise and Baderon were expected at the palace soon after Vespers. Baderon rapped on the door some time before the Vespers bell was due to ring.

'Good evening, Blanchefleur,' he said. Grinning, he gave her a flourishing bow.

Elise lifted her shawl from a hook and stepped into the street. It was far too hot for a cloak and though it would be late when she returned, it would still be warm.

Baderon looked her over, eyes widening. Lord Gawain's men-at-arms stared. Elise was wearing Blanchefleur's best gown. A rare and costly gold silk, the fabric was the most expensive she had ever owned. It shimmered and shone when she moved. The merchant she'd bought it from in Poitiers had sworn it came from Byzantium. Elise wasn't sure she believed him, but she knew a fine cloth when she saw one.

'Well?' She lifted her skirts and twirled around so the gown flared out about her. As Blanchefleur le Fay she was used to being stared at, she was used to appreciative glances. 'Good enough for the palace?'

Baderon sighed and reached out to touch the skirt. 'Gold silk? Lord, what a gown. Did you make it especially for tonight?'

She shook her head. 'I bought the fabric in the south nigh on two years ago.' Her lips curved. 'Blanchefleur insisted that I buy it.' Conscious that conversation was a distraction that would calm their nerves, Elise looped her arm companionably into Baderon's and they started down the street. They were only a stone's throw from the palace. 'Blanchefleur is much more extravagant than I. The fabric was breathtakingly expensive, and as it turns out she's hardly worn it. When Pearl came along, it soon got tight.'

Baderon paused to give her another courtly bow. 'Whatever you paid, it was worth it. Blanchefleur, you look like a princess.'

Elise put her hand on her heart. 'Why, thank you, kind sir.'

They had been told to ask for the steward in the porter's lodge next to the palace stable. A row of martins' nests ran under the eaves. While they waited for the steward to arrive, they stood in the yard listening to the martins twitter as they darted back and forth above them. The bells for Vespers started to toll. Elise shuddered.

Baderon touched her hand. 'Elise? What's the matter?'

She shrugged. 'An echo from the past. It is nothing.' Elise loved music. She took pleasure in almost any harmonious sound. Except the ringing of bells. It hadn't always been that way—as a child Elise had liked bells. However, her years at the convent had robbed her of that particular enjoyment. Today the cathedral bells served to remind her of her time at the convent, when every day had been a lost day—a day in prison. 'I'm fine, Baderon. Truly.'

'Good.' Baderon turned to look at an imposing building. 'That must be the great hall.'

Even though sunset was not yet upon them, light glowed through the long, traceried lancets. Inside, many candles would be lit. A wide flight of steps led up to the double door flanked by guards. The blue, white and gold surcoats over their armour marked them out as Count Henry's men. The doors were open and a burst of laughter floated through it. Elise heard the faint twang of a harp, followed by more laughter.

'That sounds promising,' Baderon said. 'Our performance will go more smoothly if people are already enjoying themselves.'

'Yes.' Elise nodded absently and shook out her gown. This performance would be a triumph. Her future depended on it. She would put her heart into her singing and pray that Gawain didn't distract her. She wouldn't let him. He would be in the great hall, on the dais no doubt, sitting alongside his peers. Lady Rowena would be at his side and...

She wouldn't let him distract her. Blanchefleur le Fay would sing her heart out, and after the performance the bookings would pour in.

'Baderon, are you happy to make note of any enquiries Blanchefleur may get as result of this evening?' Normally, taking note of enquiries was André's task. Since he was absent and Vivienne was caring for the babies, Elise hoped Baderon would take it on. Blanchefleur herself couldn't stoop to discuss terms. It was part of the myth of Blanchefleur le Fay that such matters were below her.

Baderon nodded easily. 'Of course.'

The steward—one of Count Henry's knights—bustled up, and they were ushered through a small door and into a shadowy corridor that ran along one side of the hall. The sounds of harp and laughter grew louder. The air was rich with scents—heady perfume and the more homely smells of fresh-baked bread and roasted meats; of rushes crushed underfoot. A stream of servants squeezed past and Elise glimpsed great platters of cheese and pastries; trays of cups and glasses. A dog snarled. Another yapped.

'You may wait in this chamber,' the steward said. 'You will be called just before it is your turn to perform.' He showed them into a tiny room that was simply furnished with a cross-framed chair and a side table. A jug, some cups and a candlestick sat on the side table. The steward waved at the wine jug. 'Help yourself to refreshments. Should you need more, ask one of the servants. They will be happy to help.'

'Thank you, sir. I never normally eat until after the performance, but Baderon might be hungry.'

'No, no, I'm fine, thank you.'

The steward left and Baderon followed him out, doubtless intending to listen to the other performers. They might have acrobats, dancers…Elise sank on to the cross-framed chair and looked at her hands. They were a little unsteady. It wasn't surprising. It had taken her years to get here. The nerves weren't unexpected; she'd known it would be hard. What she hadn't expected was that she would have to face an audience that comprised not only the Count of Champagne and half the nobles in France, but also the man she loved.

The thought—that she loved Gawain—was no longer surprising. In truth, she had probably been half in love with him at the turn of the year. It had been so unexpected that she'd been slow to recognise what it was. She'd taken it for a strong liking. For admiration. For lust. *I loved him all along and I never knew it.*

It had taken these past few days for her to see the truth. Gawain had been so kind. It must have been a great shock finding he was a father and yet he'd been so tender with Pearl. He'd been so thoughtful about André.

Gawain had never been hers, not even last year. When she and Gawain had been lovers, he had only been a knight, closer to her in rank than he was as the Count of Meaux. None the less, they came from different worlds. She'd known that from the start. Was that why she had not understood that what she had felt for him was love? It seemed likely. There was also the fact that last winter her heart had been set on learning how Morwenna had died—that had eclipsed all else.

No matter, Gawain was not for her. She loved

him, but he must never know it. He was marrying according to the dictates of his King and his family. The marriage would bring him lands and prestige. This banquet was his betrothal feast and she was the entertainment.

Gawain was courting Lady Rowena. She would have to turn a blind eye to that. She must sing— that was what she was being paid for. She simply had to sing.

There was a sharp pain in her chest. Absently, she rubbed her breastbone. She could do this. She would sing like a nightingale and no one, especially not Gawain, would have the slightest idea that her heart was breaking. She would sing for Gawain. It would be the most difficult performance of her life. It would require all the self-discipline that she had acquired over the years, but she knew she could do it. She had to. She gripped her hands in her lap and stared blindly at the window slit. She felt like screaming rather than singing, but screaming was out of the question. Screaming might strain her voice and she had to sing well.

For Gawain. For herself. And for Pearl. Her eyes prickled.

The door groaned. Baderon was back. He looked

across, brow troubled. 'Lord, Elise, you're not crying, are you? We are next up.'

Elise rose, shook out her golden skirts and gave him a bright smile. 'Certainly not, Blanchefleur le Fay *never* cries.'

Baderon gave her a look. 'Brace yourself, he's out there.'

Elise's chin inched up. 'Out there? Who?'

'Lord Gawain.'

Silk skirts rustling, Elise kept her smile on her face and crossed the chamber. 'I imagined he would be.' She paused, cheeks warming. 'Have you heard if he was successful in the tournament?'

'His team won.'

'Does he look all right? He wasn't hurt?'

Baderon squeezed her arm in reassurance as she moved past him and into the corridor. 'He looks well, which is more than I can say for another of your admirers.'

Elise looked back. 'Oh?'

'Sir Olier, I think his name is.' Baderon cocked an eyebrow at her. 'Vivienne mentioned that he has been courting you.'

Elise stiffened. 'Sir Olier is not courting me. He's amusing himself.'

'Not according to Vivienne. She told that when

you were in Poitiers last spring, Sir Olier asked for your hand in marriage.'

'Sir Olier wasn't serious. Baderon, knights don't marry troubadour's daughters.'

'Not even Blanchefleur le Fay?'

Elise gave a crooked smile. 'Blanchefleur le Fay doesn't exist.'

'Doesn't she? Vivienne is convinced Sir Olier's proposal is genuine.'

'Vivienne is wrong. Sir Olier doesn't mean it. It amuses him. It's a game.'

'Elise, Vivienne is adamant Sir Olier means it. She told me about the flowers he sends…the gifts…'

Elise frowned. 'Vivienne talks too much. Sir Olier is playing to the gallery. And I am most grateful to him. Refusing him merely adds to Blanchefleur's mystery. Baderon, he is not serious. I tell you, knights don't marry people like me.'

Baderon jerked his head at the door to the great hall. 'Sir Olier's wearing your favour tonight. I recognise the ribbon. I should warn you, he has a black eye and his face is one large bruise.'

'Oh, the poor man. What happened?'

Baderon's lips twitched. 'Lord Gawain unhorsed him.'

She went very still. '*Gawain* unhorsed him?'

'Went for him like a demon in the mêlée, apparently.' Baderon rolled his shoulders. 'I should have liked to have seen it. I'm told Lord Gawain was within an inch of getting himself disqualified for foul play.'

Elise stared at him for a moment longer, straightened her shoulders and set off towards the great hall and the performance of her life.

Gawain sat in the place of honour at Count Henry's high table, next to Lady Rowena.

The table was spread with a white damask cloth and in the traditional manner Gawain and his betrothed were sharing a goblet and a trencher. Gawain stared bleakly at a platter of baked crane. He didn't care for baked crane. Their goblet was silver gilt and encrusted with jewels—candle flames were reflected in the goblet's gleaming surface.

Overhead, the rafters were awash with knights' colours. Gold fringes shimmered in the firelight; silver embroidery glistened. Gawain's griffin blazed down from the hanging behind the dais. Silver and blue pennons—the colours of Sainte-Colombe—hung beside it.

The noise was astonishing. The clattering of

metal platters, the bursts of laughter, the bellowing across the tables, the twang of the harp…

'Would you care to choose a different wine, my lady?' Gawain asked, gesturing for a page. He stifled a sigh. Lady Rowena seemed determined to follow the protocols and he was resigned to a long evening of stiffness and formality.

'No, thank you, my lord. I would prefer you to choose it.'

The page came up. *'Mon seigneur?'*

'We'll have some more burgundy, if you please.' At least Count Henry knew a good wine.

'Of course, *mon seigneur.*'

When the boy had filled the goblet, Gawain gestured for Lady Rowena to try the wine. She shook her head. 'No, thank you, my lord.'

Gawain picked up the goblet. More of an ornament than a cup, it was so lavishly designed with its jewel-studded stem that it was difficult to handle. Gawain took a sip and tried not to grimace. Not only was the thing impossible to hold, but he preferred drinking from glass or clay. Silver gilt did odd things to the flavour of wine.

Lady Rowena looked shyly at him. 'Lord Gawain, if it's not to your taste, I am sure the boy will fetch another wine.'

Gawain shook his head. 'No point, there's nothing wrong with the wine.'

Their eyes met in sudden understanding. Lady Rowena's mouth curved and she leaned slightly towards him. She was rolling the edge of the white damask cloth between her fingers. She'd been doing it all evening. They'd been sitting side by side for hours—on show before every lord and lady in the land, and she was still afraid of him. 'It's the cup, isn't it?' she murmured. 'Everything tastes wrong.'

Nodding, Gawain looked thoughtfully at her. A trembling hand reached out, lightly touched his sleeve and quickly withdrew. Blink and you'd have missed it.

'Before you say anything else, my lord, I think you should know that the cup is a betrothal gift from my godfather.'

Gawain's eyebrows went up. 'It's a gift from the King?'

'Yes, my lord.' Her lips twitched. 'One mustn't be rude about the King's gift.'

'I wouldn't dream of it.' Gawain studied her. Lady Rowena might be too young for his taste, but she was doing her best to obey the wishes of her King and her father. He frowned and set the cup down.

'My lady.' He held out his hand. 'We have been sitting so long I feel I am turning to stone. I am sure no one would mind if we stretched our legs. The night is warm, and there's a small courtyard off the canal. Would you care to see it?'

Lowering her gaze, Lady Rowena murmured assent and placed her hand in his. 'Canal, my lord?'

'Troyes is full of them. Traders and merchants use them to shift goods about town.'

Gawain turned his back on the baked crane, conscious that all eyes were on them. The entertainers were using one corridor, so he took the other one. Briefly, he glanced back over his shoulder. Elise had mentioned she'd be singing tonight. Was she waiting out there? She had vanished early on in the tournament—not that he'd been looking her way—and he'd wondered why. He hoped she'd not heard anything untoward about the wretched André.

'We mustn't be long, a friend of mine is singing tonight,' he said, waving Lady Rowena through the door. 'I don't want to miss her performance.'

Gawain had to admit he was curious to hear Elise sing in public. She was such a shy, delicate creature; it was hard to imagine her singing before a hall full of people. However, she had clearly worked for her moment of glory and he wanted to witness it. He wanted to be there to applaud her.

Lady Rowena lifted her skirts in one hand as they stepped out into the courtyard. The sky was on fire with crimson and gold. Swifts arched overhead. 'You know Blanchefleur le Fay, my lord?'

'Blanchefleur le Fay?'

'You must have heard of her. The famous *chanteuse* from the south. I was told she's performing tonight.'

'I know little about the world of the troubadour, my lady.'

'That is understandable. You are a warrior.'

Gawain shrugged. 'Be that as it may, I believe my friend is less well-known.'

'You must point her out to me when she performs.'

'Certainly.'

The courtyard was small and already lit by flaring torches. There were steps leading down to the canal. Linking arms with Lady Rowena, Gawain walked her to the top of the steps. The water gleamed like polished jet. A bat flittered out of nowhere and vanished again. Spotting a stone bench, Gawain headed for it. Lady Rowena's skirts swished as they sat down.

He took a deep breath. 'My lady, I need to know your heart.'

'My lord?'

'Is our betrothal to your liking?'

'Why, of course.' She was looking at him as though he'd run mad. 'The King... My father—'

'Yes, yes, they endorse the match, but is it to *your* liking?' He drew in a breath. 'My lady, what I am trying to ask you is whether you think you could come to like me?'

'I already like you, Lord Gawain.'

'I am not sure you have caught my meaning.'

'My lord?'

Slowly, so as not to make her even more skittish, Gawain reached for her. 'I believe we should put it to the test.'

She didn't resist. Gawain started with a chaste peck on her cheek and drew his head back to study her reaction. She was sitting motionless on the bench, one hand curled round its edge as though for support. 'All right so far?'

'Ye...es.'

He shifted closer and managed a light peck on her lips. He lingered, but not for long. There was no touching of tongues. He was too conscious of that hand clinging to the bench. She was utterly rigid. A bundle of sticks would feel more welcoming. 'And that?'

'That's fine too.' Her eyes were screwed tightly shut, but she kept her head tilted towards him as though in anticipation of another kiss. Clearly, some attempt had been made to tutor her on what might be expected. Unfortunately, there was no question as to her response. She didn't like him, not in that way. Gawain told himself that she might warm to him in time. He wasn't confident that he would warm to her. He would give it one more try. He liked Lady Rowena, but he'd hoped for a little warmth in his marriage.

Gently, he ran his finger down her cheek. 'My lady, open your eyes.'

Wide, wary eyes fluttered open.

'Put your hand on my shoulder.' She didn't resist as he removed her hand from its death grip on the bench and placed it on his shoulder. Her other hand was clenched into a fist between them. Fearing she might make a bolt for it, he let her other hand alone. Taking her chin, he placed his lips on hers and immediately pulled back.

His stomach hollowed out. She was terrified—he could almost smell the fear. He wasn't used to women reacting to his advances in this way. It left him with a bitter taste in his mouth. Saints

preserve him. His uncle had wished for this alliance. The King approved the match. What was he
to do? Was a little warmth too much to expect?

'Relax, my lady. I will not hurt you.'

She hung her head and her veil trembled. Her
hand fell from his shoulder and she gripped the
cross at her neck. 'I have displeased you, Lord
Gawain, and I am sorry. I swear I will try to please
you in our marriage. I want to be a good wife.'

'I am sure you will be.' He smiled and sat back.
It was galling to see how she breathed more easily with him at a distance. 'My lady, if you are
planning to travel to your father's estate I should
be honoured to escort you. Count Faramus and I
have much to discuss.'

'Of course. Lord Gawain, if you are in agreement, I thought I might set out tomorrow.'

Gawain nodded. 'Tomorrow suits me well.'

Rising, he extended his hand to her. 'Come, let
us return to the hall.'

The hall was full of applause, so much that it
seemed the roof must surely be raised. A *chanteuse*
in a gold gown was taking up position in front
of the fire. The lute-player Baderon was already
seated on a stool to one side of the hearth.

Gawain checked again, almost tripping over the
rushes as he headed for the dais. *Baderon.*

It was Elise in the golden gown. Thank God he hadn't missed her performance. He blinked at her through a haze of candlelight. Her gown was dazzling. It set off her dark beauty to perfection. He ached to look at her. Gawain knew this ache. He'd felt it often with Elise. This was longing. The light from the fire behind silhouetted her beautiful, womanly shape—that slender waist, the soft curve of her hips. Lord, he wanted her. His lips twisted as he understood that the image of Elise standing before the hearth in Count Henry's palace would be burned into his memory for all time.

He told himself that it was the gold gown that made him feel this way. It was just the shimmer of her veil and gown. She looked ethereal, as though sprinkled with fairy dust. In it, she was utterly bewitching. He was not the only one to be so affected. About him, men and women alike were staring at her, mouths open, breath suspended. Lord, Queen Cleopatra of Egypt would have killed to own a gown like that.

Swallowing hard, Gawain reminded himself that he was not free and that he must not shame the King's goddaughter before half the nobility of Christendom. He must follow the protocols and do the right thing. Tearing his gaze from Elise, he caught Lady Rowena's arm, halting her progress towards the dais. 'My lady, there is the friend I mentioned earlier.'

Lady Rowena looked towards the fire and her brow wrinkled. 'The lady in gold?'

'Her name is Elise.'

'But my lord, that is the renowned *chanteuse* that the whole town is talking about. That is Blanchefleur le Fay.'

'Blanchefleur le Fay,' Gawain muttered, frowning at Lady Rowena's back as she proceeded ahead of him towards their places. The name didn't mean much to him. 'I didn't realise. This Blanchefleur is very well-known?'

She looked back. 'Blanchefleur le Fay is fêted throughout the southern territories. From Poitiers to Carcassonne lords have been known to fight to get her to perform for them. I understand Countess Marie has been eager to hear her for some time. Count Henry has been hoping she would sing here for years.'

'He has?' When they were both seated, Gawain looked across the tables towards the fire. Elise happened to be looking his way and their eyes met. Gawain was conscious of Lady Rowena chattering about the famous Blanchefleur le Fay, but he barely heard her. His mind was in ferment. Elise was renowned—so renowned that Count

Henry had wanted her to perform here for years. Dimly, he heard his betrothed telling him that Blanchefleur had performed before the Queen of England.

Elise never told me how famous she was. Gawain could understand her not confiding in him last year when she'd come to Champagne purely to learn how her sister had died, but she'd no reason not to mention it now. He liked to think that she had a fondness for him. Elise had always struck him as an intensely private person and he'd assumed that she would never have come to his bed unless she'd felt a strong passion for him. Warmth. The same warmth he wanted in his marriage. He scowled. He would swear there had been genuine warmth between him and Elise—but why had she never mentioned her fame?

'Of course,' Lady Rowena rattled on, 'when she vanished so mysteriously at the beginning of the year, this merely added to her mystique.'

Gawain forced himself to get a grip on what Lady Rowena was saying. 'When she vanished? Who? Who are you talking about? Are you referring to the Queen of England?'

Queen Eleanor had disappeared the previous year and word had only just got out that she had been kidnapped by her own husband. If the rumour was true, the Queen was presently confined in England.

'No, my lord, I'm talking about your friend Blanchefleur. It's clear you don't know her as well as you think. Blanchefleur vanished in the spring and her disappearance caused almost as many ripples as Queen Eleanor's. Some said that Blanchefleur had retired from singing. Others swore that she truly was a fairy and had been spirited off to another world.'

'That's ridiculous.' Gawain snorted even as Lady Rowena's words shivered through him. *It's clear you don't know her as well as you think.* He stared at the golden figure in front of the fire. How well did he know her? He'd thought she was shy and retiring, yet here she was about to sing before a hall packed with people. Secrets surrounded her—never mind her success as a singer, she'd been slow to tell him about Pearl, and then there was this business with the counterfeiters.

None the less, one thing was clear. Blanchefleur's so-called disappearance must have coincided with the time of her confinement. She would have had to stop singing for that. 'Blanchefleur le Fay is a real woman,' he said. 'She's flesh and blood.' *She has had a child, my child.*

Lady Rowena laughed. 'You can't have heard her sing.'

'Not before an audience.' Elise had sung privately for him though, and Gawain had to admit that although he was not a musical man, he had been moved.

'You will see, my lord. Blanchefleur le Fay is a heartbreaker. When she starts to sing, you will see.'

Chapter Nine

Elise stood before the hall fire. She was dizzy with the heat even though the fire was low—it had been lit to give light rather than warmth. Her pulse raced as she resisted the urge to move further into the great hall. This was where she had been told to stand, next to Baderon.

Perspiration beaded Elise's brow and her palms felt damp. Panicky chills ran down her back. Nerves. She smiled in the general direction of the dais. It was odd how minor discomforts became large before a performance. It happened every time. Her nerves were on edge because she must pour her soul, all of it, into her singing. It wasn't easy. She had to allow herself to feel and tonight there were too many feelings. Some of them were far from pretty. The hall was packed with people, yet she was conscious of only one man.

God help me.

Elise kept her gaze unfocused. It was a mercy that Baderon was experienced enough to lead her into the song without her having to look at the top table. Baderon would see Count Henry's signal. Count Henry was sitting too close to Gawain for Elise to risk looking in that direction again. She was afraid of what might happen. So many emotions were rolling about inside her, it was a struggle to hold them. Love. Anger and fear. Regret. Jealousy. Elise started to shake. These feelings were a gift, she told herself firmly, they must be contained. These feelings must be felt—she would need them when she sang.

A thousand butterflies were trapped in Elise's stomach, but she ignored them. She was holding a spray of wild roses to her breast. Deliberately, she pressed her thumb against a thorn. It was needle sharp. Elise allowed herself to fully absorb the tiny stab of the thorn—it would keep her mind on the songs. It would stop her attention drifting towards the handsome, fair-haired knight sitting on the dais.

She'd seen him slip back into the hall with Lady Rowena. Lady Rowena's cheeks had been as pink as the setting sun. There was no doubt in Elise's mind as to what they'd been doing—kissing. Composedly, Lady Rowena had taken her place at the board and now she was chattering away nineteen to the dozen while Gawain sat beside her, twirling a princely silver goblet round and round.

A hush fell. A bench creaked and the hush seemed to deepen. Elise drew in a deep breath and in a heartbeat she was no longer Elise, she was Blanchefleur.

Blanchefleur exchanged glances with her lute-player. She kept her thumb on the thorn. This was for Gawain. As the first notes led her into the song, her training took over. In order to give the impression she was singing for the Count and Countess of Champagne, she looked towards the griffin on the wall hanging behind the dais. The griffin was a blur.

As Blanchefleur, Elise sang about Tristan and Isolde and of love won and lost. She sang about betrayal. Emotion poured out of her in a great rush of feeling. She became the song. It was in her chest, in every bone of her body. Her voice rang round the hall, strong and true. When Blanchefleur sang the last note and lowered her gaze, the applause was deafening. If André had been beside her, he would have been grinning from ear to ear.

Elise's heart thundered in her chest and a new emotion was added to the others roiling about inside her. Triumph. Her first song was a triumph!

She wasn't given time to enjoy it. The applause died away and save for the crackling of the fire, there was silence. People had stopped eating—they were looking at her with bated breath, hungry for song instead of food. So she nodded at Baderon and he launched into an epic about Roland's last battle at Roncevaux. Elise smiled. She knew the menfolk loved songs about heroes.

Blanchefleur sang about life and death, about courage and cowardice. About the terrible and beautiful frailty that was humankind. Ladies clapped; soldiers drummed their heels on the floor. The rushes rustled; the dogs barked. Success was a heady feeling, stronger than wine.

Elise's blood thrummed in every vein. Then came that expectant hush and Elise gathered herself for the final, most testing song—the story of King Arthur and Queen Guinevere. She sang about forgiveness and aching loss. She sang of true love. Her heart felt as though it would burst. Every joy had its cost. She sang through the pain.

As the last plangent notes died away, Gawain found he had a lump in his throat the size of a gull's egg. Down the hall, the dazzle of gold that was Elise seemed momentarily lost in a fog. Blinking rapidly, Gawain cleared his throat. He would be the first to admit he didn't have a musical bone in his body, but even he could tell that Elise's voice was exceptional. Who would have thought she had the power to fill a hall this large with so wondrous a sound? Briefly, everyone at the feast had been transported: Cornwall, Roncevaux, Caerleon… And she'd made it seem easy.

Lady Rowena turned her head as the applause and drumming shook their table. Smiling shyly, she looked closely at him. 'I told you she was a heartbreaker. Even you are moved. Confess it.'

Gawain had lost the use of his tongue. He could only nod. And watch. The performance was clearly over and a stampede was taking place around the fireside.

Elise—*Blanchefleur le Fay*—was being mobbed by admirers, most of whom were male. Her eyes were bright and wild. She looked exhilarated by her performance. Lady Rowena had put her finger on it when she had said he didn't know Elise as well as he'd thought. Plainly he didn't know her at all. This—being mobbed by admirers—must have happened many times before.

Elise was moving towards the corridor, her smile dazzling enough to light the whole of Champagne. She was accepting many tokens—flowers, ribbons, trinkets. One of Count Henry's pages rushed to carry them. The crowd surged around her and Gawain found himself staring at a dozen men's backs. He glimpsed one man thrusting a ring on to her finger. The man must be high in her favour for she touched his arm and bent close. Briefly her face filled with sympathy. What she said to the man, Gawain would never know, but the man trailed after her when she went into the corridor. A cherry-coloured ribbon was wound round the sleeve of his tunic.

Sir Olier! Setting the silver-gilt goblet on to the board with a thud, Gawain swore under his breath and shoved back his chair. 'Excuse me a moment, my lady, I would like to congratulate Blanchefleur le Fay personally on her performance. I won't be long.'

Anger burned in Gawain's breast. Anger blinded him. Anger was all there was. Gawain prided himself on his control, but he hardly saw anything as he stumbled after Sir Olier. He got to the corridor in time to see the page and Sir Olier enter a side chamber. Gawain followed.

The chamber was small. Overcrowded. Elise was directing the page to put her offerings on a chest. Her hand, Gawain noticed, was trembling—she was elated after her performance. Still on edge. Likely it would take a while for her to return to earth. Baderon was sitting on a stool turning a peg on his lute and Sir Olier—bruises and all—was smiling adoringly at Elise.

Gawain clenched his fists, caught the page's eye and jerked his head in the direction of the door. 'You,' he said, 'out.'

The page shot him a look and obeyed.

Gawain walked up to Sir Olier. 'You have finished your conversation with Blanchefleur, I believe.'

'But, my lord—'

Gawain looked at him and Sir Olier recoiled. Gawain grappled for calm. 'You may speak to her later.'

Elise shifted. Gawain almost bit his tongue when she touched Sir Olier's arm—the arm that bore her cherry-coloured ribbon.

'Sir Olier, I look forward to speaking to you later,' she said.

Sir Olier gave a brusque harrumph and when the door had closed behind him Elise sighed. 'Gawain, what on earth—'

Gawain turned to Baderon and gave another curt jerk of his head. 'You too, Baderon. Out.'

Baderon's jaw dropped. *'Mon seigneur?'*

'You heard. No one is to enter this chamber until I give my leave. Understood?'

Clutching his lute and a coil of lute strings, Baderon rose uncertainly. 'Elise? You will be all right?'

'It's fine, Baderon. I shall call you in a moment.' Her voice went hard. 'I am sure that whatever Lord Gawain has to say won't take long.'

Won't take long? Gawain clenched his fists. Dimly, he heard the latch click and then all he could hear was the blood roaring in his ears. And all he could see was Elise. Blanchefleur in that shimmering gown. It was the gown. The wretched thing was bewitched. He stepped closer. 'Who are you?'

'My lord?' Dark eyes studied him as she tucked a tendril of hair out of sight beneath her veil.

'Who are you? I thought I knew you, but I don't. Who are you?'

Elise looked doubtfully at Gawain. A *frisson* of alarm ran through her. Since meeting him she had been in his company several times, but this was the first time she had felt uneasy. Telling herself not to be ridiculous, she fluffed out her golden skirts and adjusted her veil. Clearly, she had not yet shaken off the wild excitement of the performance and was being oversensitive. 'Whatever's the matter? I didn't think to speak to you tonight.'

'I didn't come for conversation.'

'Why are you here?'

'God knows.'

His tone was so curt Elise's nails bit into her palms. Drunk with success a moment ago, she sobered quickly. There was anger here, much anger. Flexing her fingers, she wiped them on her skirts. 'Does Lady Rowena know you are here?'

'This has nothing to do with Lady Rowena.'

His tone had Elise swallowing. Her mouth was dry as dust. What was he doing? What did he want?

They stared at each other for what seemed like hours, but in reality it couldn't have been long. Gawain was so tall, she had to tip her head back to look at him. His fair hair gleamed in the candlelight. A muscle moved in his jaw. Lord, he was grinding his teeth. A tight smile appeared as he looked her up and down. He'd come to the banquet in formal attire—a red surcoat emblazoned with his golden griffin. The anger was coming off in waves. The kind and chivalrous knight was gone—she was looking at an angry stranger.

He was betrothed to Lady Rowena. What reason did he have to be angry with her?

'Lord Gawain.' Hoping formality would give him a chance to cool down, she held out her hand.

Powerful fingers closed on hers. He cleared his

throat and kissed the back of her hand. It was a courtly gesture. Elise's heart stuttered. He'd kissed her in just that way last year, after the All Hallows Tournament. He'd kept those dark eyes on hers then too, exactly as he was doing now. Not quite a stranger. But almost. She thought—hoped—he was calming down.

'Blanchefleur le Fay,' he murmured.

'It is good to see you, my lord.'

He pulled her to him and the golden gown rustled as their bodies met. 'Is it? You misled me.'

She bit her lip and tried not to enjoy the feel of him next to her. 'You are referring to my singing. Yes, I regret that I never told you everything. There never seemed to be the right moment.' There was no chain mail beneath his red surcoat—she could feel the heat from his body. His strength. Another *frisson* went through her. There was a crease between his eyebrows. He was not yet himself, some tension remained.

That fair head bent, his mouth hovered an inch above hers, an odd smile played about the edges. 'Was it all a lie?'

'My lord?'

'You didn't want me in your life. You didn't trust me.' She made a sharp movement, but he swept on. 'I was simply a means to an end. If you had trusted me you would have told me about Blanchefleur Le Fay. You simply said you were a singer. Blanchefleur is clearly far more than any singer. Her success is integral to what you are and yet you never breathed a word. You bedded me purely to gain entry to Ravenshold.'

Elise shook her head. 'Gawain, the attraction I felt for you was true.'

'Was it?'

He gripped her shoulder firmly with one hand, touched her cheek with the other, and the crease in his brow deepened. His expression was that of a man who had received a blow from an unexpected quarter. It twisted Elise's heart to think she had put it there.

Strong fingers ran up her neck and her stomach ached. *I remember that feeling.* It had only ever happened with him. Telling herself that she had no business reacting in such a way to his touch, Elise held herself still.

He was eyeing Blanchefleur's gilt circlet with obvious dislike. He lifted it from her head and threw it carelessly on to the side table. He found the ties of her veil, tugged at them and tossed it aside. When his hand went to the silver bow at her bodice, her heart jumped. She put her hand on his. 'What are you doing?'

'Looking for Elise Chantier.' He shook her off and studied the way the ribbon was laced.

'My lord?'

'You misled me, Blanchefleur. You said you were not well-known. No matter, I am here to see Elise.'

His grip on her shoulder eased. He bent over the silver ribbon and pulled on the bow.

He is undressing me! Lady Rowena is waiting for him in the great hall with half the nobility of France and he tries to undress me!

She put her hand on his. 'Gawain, stop this.'

The fair head shook. In the shadowed chamber, his brown eyes were black. Unreadable. He didn't look angry any more, that small smile played about his lips, but...

'Gawain?'

'I must speak to Elise.' He tugged at the lacings and before she had time to blink he'd unlaced it enough to peel the gown from one shoulder.

She swallowed as she saw the way his gaze flickered down, lingering on the curve of her shoulder, moving to the shadow between her breasts. 'You can speak to Elise without undressing me.'

He ignored her. With a sigh, his arm tightened on her waist as he aligned their bodies even more closely. Bending his head, he kissed her bared shoulder. Sensation rang along every nerve. Elise held in a moan. This was wrong. Gawain was betrothed.

'Gawain, you mustn't.'

He wasn't listening. Dark eyes looked into hers long enough for her to catch a glimpse of the grey flecks in them and then he dipped his head again and nuzzled her neck, nipping lightly just below her ear.

Her thoughts scattered. She'd never been able to resist him when he did that. She closed her eyes and steeled herself to ignore the tingling that rushed through her. It wasn't easy. She loved that tingling. And surely, just for a few moments, she could allow herself this pleasure.

'This is wrong.' She shoved at his chest. She could smell wine on his breath. 'Gawain, you have forgotten yourself. We are in Count Henry's palace and you are shortly to be married.'

He smiled. 'Yes, I am. There is a difficulty though. She's not the right woman.'

Her eyes went wide. 'Gawain, you are not being serious. You have to marry Lady Rowena.'

'Do I?' He shrugged. 'Maybe.'

She shook her head at him. 'How much wine have you had?'

'Not much. It tasted vile.'

Saints, in this strange mood there was no understanding him. But thankfully, the anger seemed to have dissipated. Then he leaned forward and his mouth touched hers, and it was All Hallows all over again.

All Hallows.

The world fell away. Elise was no longer conscious of standing in a small chamber off Count Henry's great hall. There was only Gawain's arms wound tight about her and his lips teasing hers apart. His body felt as strong and warm as it had done on All Hallows Eve. A haven in a dark and desperate world.

Sounds faded. Somewhere far away, Baderon was probably standing guard outside in the passage. People would be talking in the great hall. Laughing. Elise couldn't hear them. As Gawain lifted his mouth from hers and stared deep into her eyes, she could hear her flurried breathing; she could hear Gawain's indrawn breath; and his muttered, 'Last year you left without saying goodbye.'

'I couldn't.' She hadn't been able to say it, not to him.

His scent filled her nostrils—the tang of musk and bay, strong and masculine. He pushed at the neck of her gown, drawing it down, pulling it away from skin that warmed at his lightest glance.

Blanchefleur le Fay was lost. Gone. It was Elise who gripped Gawain by the shoulders; Elise who slid her hands into his sun-streaked hair and brought his lips to hers. It was just Elise and Gawain. And, just as it had been after the All Hallows Tournament, there was no need for words. Except…

'Gawain, think.' She heard herself sob. 'You are betrothed.'

Slowly, inexorably, Gawain peeled the golden fabric from Elise's other shoulder.

'You chose your stage name wisely. Even as Elise you have me bewitched.' He picked up her hand and scowled at the ring. 'What is Sir Olier to you?'

Elise blinked. Frowned. 'He is one of Blanchefleur's admirers. Gawain, what did you do to his face?'

Gawain shrugged. 'Nothing. He got in the way.'

Elise tried to pull back, but his grip tightened.

'He follows you about like a lost puppy. Has he asked you to be his mistress?'

'No.' Her chin lifted. 'He's asked to marry me.'

'*Mon Dieu*, he's offered marriage?'

She stiffened. 'Am I not worthy of marriage?'

'Hell burn it, Elise, I didn't mean that.' He searched her eyes. 'Have you accepted him?'

Elise's answer shouldn't matter.

Gawain knew that whatever lay between them should stay firmly in the past. None the less, he found himself holding his breath for her answer. Last year, Elise had used him—she'd wanted to be certain to gain entry to Ravenshold. Back then one glance at her brown eyes, one glimpse of that bewildering combination of strength and vulnerability, and he'd been lost. It had happened again tonight. What was it about this girl? She robbed him of his will. She disordered his mind.

When Gawain had stormed in to the chamber he'd been braced for the effect she might have on him. She lured him as no other and he'd been determined to resist. He needed to tell her about the manor. He would feel easier with her knowing about his gift before he left for Sainte-Colombe. He wanted her to know she had some security. But the moment he'd looked at her, his good intentions had flown to the four winds.

'Have you accepted him?' Her lips tightened and Gawain's gut cramped. Frustration? Resentment? He had no idea. 'You have to refuse him.'

She drew her head back. 'I beg your pardon?'

'Elise, you have to refuse him. He's not right for you.'

A surge of possessiveness shot through him. It was so powerful Gawain felt like hitting something. Not Elise, of course, he would never hurt Elise. Even though she had him utterly confused. He stared down at her, a doll of a woman who was and who was not the woman he had met last winter.

She was all prettied up in that golden gown, a gown that was, if he were not mistaken, pure silk. She'd painted her face. It was subtle and effective. The slim charcoal line outlining her eyes made them look enormous. She'd rouged her lips and possibly her cheeks. The cosmetics gave her added allure. They gave her power. Don't touch, they said. Did she use them to keep her admirers at bay?

Gawain clenched his jaw. He had never liked following orders. He tightened his grip on her and rubbed the pad of his thumb over her bottom lip. He wanted to see the girl he'd met all those months ago. He wanted Elise. The urge was as irresistible as the urge that had brought him to first comfort and then bed her after the All Hallows Tourney.

It was disturbing to discover that the urge was as overpowering as it had been all those months ago. She couldn't marry Sir Olier. It would be a travesty. But he knew he had no right to order Elise's life. And he could see she knew it too. Her eyes were narrowed as they watched him. Her lips were pressed tightly together.

'What have you done to your mouth?' He felt his brow crease as he stared at the trace of pink staining his thumb. 'And your cheeks? Your eyebrows?'

'It… Blanchefleur wears cosmetics to enhance her looks.'

'Enhance?' He snorted. 'Close up, you look like a whore.'

He waited, half-expecting a sharp answer. Would almost welcome one, for it would be an excuse to let fly and tell her exactly how disappointed he'd been when she'd fled Ravenshold so abruptly at the turn of the year. She tried to edge back, but he kept his hold firm.

'Blanchefleur le Fay is not a whore.' She spoke with remarkable calm.

Carefully, Gawain ran his thumb over her cheek, noting the way she seemed to lean into his caress. 'You enjoy my touch,' he said, moving his hand to cup one bare and tempting shoulder. She didn't deny it. The flush on her cheeks deepened as she watched the movement of his hand. It was a natural flush, not brought about by paint, and he responded to it instantly. Deep within, he felt the insistent beat of desire.

Huge brown eyes studied him. 'Gawain.' Swallowing, she adjusted the neck of her gown.

He shook his head and tugged it insistently in the opposite direction, succeeding in getting the golden bodice almost completely off one breast. He tugged again and more breast—creamier and fuller than he remembered—came into view. Desire swirled through him. She was even more of a woman than she had been on All Hallows Eve.

Scowling, she pushed at his hand.

'Elise, don't. I want to see you.'

'Gawain, you can't!' Her eyes were wide. Shocked.

'Blame the burgundy. I am not myself.' He twitched at the silken bodice, baring another inch of gorgeous, womanly breast. 'Lord, Elise, I know I should not, but I want you still.' He felt his mouth twist and heard himself say what he had sworn he would keep to himself. 'I've never stopped wanting you.'

She tossed her head and her hair, bound into a single glossy rope, bounced.

He frowned. 'Undo it.'

'What?'

'Your hair.' He kissed her shoulder and heard a subtle hitch in her breath. It told him he had Elise in his arms and not Blanchefleur le Fay. 'That first night, Elise wore it loose. Undo it.'

'I will not.'

'Then I will.' Keeping one arm planted round her waist, he drew her hair over her shoulder. Silvery ribbon was woven into the plait and finding the end, he untied it. She didn't struggle. Those dark eyes watched him, rather sadly, he thought. His heart squeezed as the heady scent of ambergris surrounded him.

'Gawain.' Small fingers curled into his scarlet tunic as he unravelled her hair.

'Beautiful,' he murmured, stroking a shining brown wave, arranging it over her breast. Bending, he blew on it and watched her nipple tighten. He heard another slight hitch in her breath.

'Gawain, you must stop this. What if someone comes in?'

'Baderon will keep them out.'

'Gawain, don't. You will regret this.'

'You missed me,' he said, cupping her breast through her hair.

She shook her head.

'Yes, you did. When you went back to your friends and your singing, you missed me. Blanchefleur le Fay might not miss me but you, Elise, you missed me.'

She sighed and stared at his throat. 'Yes, I missed you.'

Heart lifting for the first time since he walked into this chamber, Gawain lowered his head and his mouth caught hers. He couldn't stop himself.

She slid her fingers into his hair and he heard himself groan. He kissed her gently, carefully, so as to absorb the sensation—to fully savour it. The deep throbbing was becoming more insistent. He pressed himself against her and with a moan she responded in kind—pushing ever so slightly against him. Silk rustled. Easing back, he stroked at the bodice and sighed with pleasure as it fell to her waist. She was lovely. Lovely. Around her neck a pendant shaped like a daisy hung on a silken cord. A delicate jewel, it was made from gold with white enamel petals. He'd seen it before, on All Hallows Eve.

'A white flower. Blanchefleur,' he murmured, meeting her gaze. 'I didn't realise its significance before. Why didn't you tell me?'

'It...it didn't seem relevant.'

Gawain's mind was fogged with desire, but the hurt cut to his core. 'Not relevant? This touches at the heart of what you are. Of course it was relevant.'

'I am sorry, my lord. I didn't think you'd be interested in the life of a singer.' She smiled and ran her hand down his shoulder. 'You were so much the knight.'

Her eyes were dark. His knees weakened and so, it seemed, did hers. There was another swift, almost greedy exchange of kisses and a tangling of tongues, and when Gawain came back to himself he was sitting on a stool with Elise on his lap. With the golden silk down to her waist, her breasts were bared for his—and her—delight. There was quiet in the chamber as the exchange of kisses slowed. A candle sputtered as he shifted to dot a row of kisses over one breast and up the next. He reached a nipple, but she caught his head and held him away.

'No. Gawain, please.' The white flower gleamed in the lamplight as she started to hitch up her bodice.

Gawain let her. There was such joy in having her in his arms, he could no longer think. Besides, there was more of her to explore. More to rediscover. While she wrestled her bodice back into place, he caught at her skirts and pulled. Her legs were bare. For the first time in weeks, he found himself blessing the heat.

'Too hot for stockings,' he murmured, stroking along her leg.

'Mmm.'

Lost in a sensual haze, Gawain stroked on. Her expression was pained, but she sighed and shut her eyes and did not stop him. He stroked again, nuzzling her neck. He was easing her legs apart, hoping that Baderon would have the sense not to disturb them, when a brisk rap on the door had her jumping from his lap.

'One moment,' she called, yanking at her gown.

By the time Gawain had reached the door, she was just about decent. Her bodice was straight, and she'd managed to twist her hair into some semblance of a braid. Cheeks bright as a poppy, she looked confused. Lost. Briefly, Gawain closed his eyes. He knew exactly how she felt. His guts were in a complete tangle.

'I don't understand you,' she said, waving in the direction of the hall. 'This shouldn't be happening. Tonight is your betrothal feast.'

'I don't understand myself,' Gawain muttered.

The latch rattled and Raphael put his head round the door.

Raphael nodded briefly at Elise. 'Gawain, I am

sorry to interrupt your conversation with Blanche-fleur, but I thought you ought to know that Lady Rowena is on the point of coming to find you.'

Raphael vanished into the corridor and Gawain made to follow him. At the threshold he turned and caught Elise's hand. 'Farewell. I leave to meet Count Faramus of Sainte-Colombe in the morning.'

'You go to discuss marriage settlements.'

Gawain grimaced, he couldn't discuss that with Elise. But there was one more thing he had to say to her.

Chapter Ten

'Elise, before I leave there's something you must know. I am making arrangements for the deed of Le Manoir des Rosières to be signed over to you—life tenures for you and Pearl.'

Her mouth dropped open. 'I...I beg your pardon?'

'One never knows what lies around the corner,' he said softly, 'and I will sleep easier knowing you and Pearl will always have a home. There are legalities though, documents to be signed. Since the manor is in Champagne, Count Henry will have to agree. Sergeant Gaston will bring you word when everything's in order. If I haven't returned by then, he will see you moved into the manor.'

Pale as a ghost, she stared at him. 'You...you are giving me a manor?'

'You and Pearl, yes. Do with it as you wish. Your friends may go with you. There's some income from the vineyards and peasants' holdings. The steward will explain all in due course. For today I just want you to know. You may plan to move to the manor very shortly.'

She rubbed at her temple. 'What does Lady Rowena think about this?'

'Lady Rowena does not know.' Bowing over her hand, Gawain kissed it and followed Raphael into the passageway.

In the torchlight, Baderon's face was sheepish. 'I am sorry, my lord, I tried to stop him. Sir Raphael was most insistent.'

'Don't worry,' Gawain said. He was still reeling at the effect Elise had on him. One look, one touch, and he'd not known himself. 'It was probably just as well. I had overstayed my welcome.'

At the entrance to the great hall, Raphael stayed him with a gesture and lowered his voice. 'I'll be brief. I've news concerning André de Poitiers.'

'Go on.'

'A man answering his description was seen leaving Troyes on the Provins road.'

A door slammed and a torch flared at the other end of the passageway—Baderon had gone back into the chamber.

'Gabrielle told you this?' Gawain asked. Raphael

nodded. His manner was far too serious for Gawain's liking. 'Raphael? What's wrong?'

'Nothing's wrong save that I need more men.'

'You think Gabrielle's source is reliable?'

'Yes, yes.'

Gawain clapped Raphael on the shoulder. 'Well, as I am sure you will have worked out, I am bound for Sainte-Colombe tomorrow and it's only a stone's throw from Provins. You want me to nose around when I'm there?'

Raphael's face cleared. 'If you wouldn't mind.'

'Consider it done.'

'Thank you, my friend.'

Baderon came back into the chamber as Elise was gathering up Blanchefleur's gifts. She wrapped them in her shawl—the night was so warm, she didn't need to wear it. She was aware of Baderon talking, something about being pleased at how well their performance had gone. Understanding that this was his way of easing his tension and that no response was required, she let him run on. It was just as well that Baderon wasn't expecting a response, because one thing filled her mind.

Gawain had given her a manor. She couldn't take it in. A manor!

'It can't be true,' she murmured.

Baderon was standing by the door, ready to leave. 'What can't?'

'Lord Gawain has, apparently, given me a manor.'

Baderon's mouth fell open. 'What?'

'He's given me Le Manoir des Rosières.' She picked up her bundle and together they went into the corridor and out into the night. 'It's incredible.'

Baderon took her arm and looped it companionably with his. 'He wants you as his mistress.'

She shook her head. Her heart felt heavy. 'Does he? It could be his way of saying goodbye.'

Flaring torches were set at intervals along the courtyard walls. They glowed like coals through the dark.

Baderon patted her arm. 'He wants you as his mistress. There's no other explanation, *chérie*.' He eyed her bundle. 'You are used to receiving gifts, but let me assure you that counts don't give singers manors simply because they hear them in good voice.'

Elise struggled to find a suitable response. She wasn't certain whether Baderon knew that Pearl was Gawain's daughter. If he did, he would surely understand that the main reason Gawain was giving her the manor was to ensure that Pearl's future was secure. She bit her lip as she recalled the heat in Gawain's eyes as he had pulled her on to his lap—as he had peeled her gown from her shoulders. She didn't like to think that Baderon could be right about Gawain wanting her as his mistress. She'd always thought that Gawain was too honourable a man to consider such a thing on the eve of his wedding. However, she had to admit that his behaviour tonight had been less than exemplary. And the gift of the manor was ambiguous.

On the one hand Gawain might simply want to ensure that Pearl would always have a roof over her head. On the other—might she have misjudged him? Might he be planning to claim her as his mistress too? If so, he was in for a shock. It was one thing to conduct a liaison with an unmarried man, but one who was married? She couldn't do it.

'Baderon, Lord Gawain is going to marry Lady Rowena.'

'He won't be the first man to break his marriage vows.'

'Lord Gawain is an honourable man. Every time I have met him he has behaved with complete honour.'

Baderon's head was silhouetted against the light shining through the windows of the house behind him. His soft laugh reached her through the dark. 'Apart from kissing you at his betrothal feast, you mean.' He paused and a moth flitted silently past. 'How honourable is that?'

Elise had no response, so they walked on in silence and the thoughts whirled through her brain, melting into one another in complete confusion.

She—a mere nobody—was being given a manor. It was easy to summon an image of Gawain looking down at his daughter, gently stroking her cheek. The gift of the manor wasn't merely to ease his conscience. Gawain had a strong protective streak. He wanted Pearl to be safe. She sighed. How wonderful it would be if he wanted her to be safe too. She wanted him to love her. She wanted it so much her chest hurt.

And yet…

Frowning, she glanced at her shawl—it was bulging with gifts. Small gifts. Tokens. Trinkets that were easy to accept. Sadly, Gawain's gift—a manor!—simply served to prove how little he understood her.

'I am not sure I want a manor,' she said, slowly. It was too much. It would tie her down. What would she do with a manor? If Gawain truly understood her, he would know that she loved her life on the road. She wasn't one to be tied down.

Baderon looked askance at her. 'Excuse me?'

'Baderon, like you my life is spent travelling. I have freedom and I follow no one's rules but my own.'

'Our life is harsh. Elise, with a manor you'd never have to worry where the next penny was coming from. You would have a home.'

A bat streaked out of the dark and vanished again. 'Pearl is my home. My singing is my home. How would I sing if I was tied to a manor?'

Baderon grunted. 'You don't have to spend the whole year there. Sing in the summer and return to the manor in the winter. Singing is a cold bedfellow on an icy January night. It would be better for Pearl too.'

Elise walked silently, thinking. What would it be like to live in a manor given to her by the man she loved? Le Manoir des Rosières had been Gawain's family home. Would she see him at every turn? She wasn't sure she could bear it.

'Baderon?'

'Hmm?'

'What use is love?'

Baderon stopped walking. 'You ask me that? You?' His tone was incredulous. 'I should have thought that you of all people would have the answer to that.'

'I don't understand.'

'Lord, Elise, you make your living from love. You sing about it from dawn to dusk. And you ask me what use it is?'

She gripped his arm. 'Tell me, Baderon. What is love for?'

The pain in her chest was heavy, like lead. She wanted Gawain to love her even though he was marrying someone else. She wanted him to understand her. It wasn't right but that was the truth of it. Why did she feel this way? She could never accept him as her lover, but she couldn't deny that she wanted the gift of the manor to be because he cared. She wanted his understanding. Love—if that indeed was what she felt for Gawain—hurt.

Baderon covered her hand with his. 'Love is a great mystery, *chérie*, and that is its wonder. It's useful.'

'Useful?'

'Singing about love puts bread and meat in the stomachs of the likes of you and I.'

'Love hurts,' she muttered. 'It really hurts.'

Through the dark, she saw him nod. 'Assuredly it hurts, but the pain is irrelevant. You, *chérie*, are a *chanteuse*. And in my opinion one of the greatest alive today.'

Elise blushed. Baderon, the famous Baderon, thought she was a great singer?

'I am sorry you are in pain, of course,' he continued softly. 'But the pain merely deepens your singing. It adds colour and vibrancy to your voice. That day you came to find me, I noticed at once how your voice had matured. Your tone has a deep plangency—there were hints of it before, but now...' his voice trailed off '...it is moving beyond words. You have a great talent.' He touched her bundle of gifts. 'It is no coincidence that you have received so many tokens today. I am not the only one to have noticed. Your experience informs your singing.'

She peered at him through the dark. She couldn't see him well enough to read his expression. 'You've known all along?'

'About you and Lord Gawain? I wasn't certain it was him. Something had changed you. Your singing has always been good but recently—Elise, you would be welcome at any court in the land. You've had a baby. It wasn't a great leap from there to work out that the baby's father might be responsible for the richness of your voice. It was easy to conclude that the man must have been Lord Gawain. He's been taking a particular interest since you arrived in Troyes. I take it Vivienne and André know that he's the father?'

Elise nodded. 'I am not sure how many others know.'

They walked on. The moon was rising over the roofs. 'When I told Gawain about Pearl, I wanted to ask him how he would feel when others learned she was his. I knew it was a matter of time before word got about. However, once I learned of his betrothal there never seemed to be the right moment.'

'I am sure you will be able to discuss these matters with him in due course. He wants you as his mistress.'

Sighing, Elise shook her head and her hastily braided hair started to unravel. 'That would be wrong, Baderon.' They had reached the house in La Rue du Cloître. She put warmth in her voice. 'Goodnight. My thanks for accompanying me tonight. I am in no doubt that it was your playing rather than my singing that was at the root of our success.'

He shook his head. 'Believe that if you wish, but I know the truth. Lord Gawain has put fire in your veins.' Lightly, he touched her chin. 'Don't be downcast. He'll be back.'

* * *

Elise had crept into bed. She'd been bursting to discuss the gift of the manor with Vivienne, but Vivienne was worn out with tending to the babies at all hours and it would have been cruel to wake her.

She managed to contain herself until the next morning when Vivienne had settled on the cushioned bench downstairs and was feeding the babies. Dust motes danced in the light filtering through the shutters. Elise could hear the low rumble of voices—Sergeant Gaston and his men were talking outside.

Vivienne followed Elise's gaze and raised an eyebrow. 'Those men are nothing if not diligent,' she said. 'Do they never tire?'

Elise came to the bench. 'You may have to get used to them.'

'Oh?' A bowl of apricots stood on the table. Elise took one and offered it to Vivienne. Vivienne shook her head. 'I'll have it later.'

'Vivienne, I have news.'

Vivienne went white. 'You've heard something. André's not—'

'No. *No.* Vivienne, this isn't about André.' Cursing herself for her clumsiness, Elise rushed to apologise. 'I'm sorry, I didn't meant to worry you.'

'Elise, you would tell me if you had heard something?'

'Of course. I've heard nothing. I keep asking about the town and I'll try again later. Someone must have seen him. He can't simply have vanished.'

Vivienne let out a great sigh. 'Thank goodness. I feared for a moment that… Never mind.' She brushed the hair from Bruno's brow. 'What were you trying to say?'

'Something extraordinary has happened. Lord Gawain has gifted me his manor. I'm not sure what to do.'

Vivienne looked blankly at her. 'His manor?'

'He has a manor outside Troyes.'

'Le Manoir des Rosières, yes, I remember hearing about it.' Vivienne's brow wrinkled. 'He's given it to you?'

'Apparently.'

Vivienne's eyes filled, she looked as though she was on the verge of bursting into tears. Then she blinked and bent her head swiftly over Bruno and Elise was left wondering if she had imagined the tears. Elise turned the apricot in her fingers. 'He wants to ensure Pearl is not brought up as a vagabond.'

Vivienne looked up, smiling. 'If Lord Gawain

means it, I am happy for you. It does sound as though he wants to ensure you are both safe.' She hesitated. 'Are you sure you can trust him not to change his mind?'

'I trust him.' Elise stared at the apricot, running her thumb over its downy surface. 'Last night when he told me, I did find it hard to believe. After all, noblemen don't go about handing out manors to their cast-off mistresses.'

Vivienne's eyes were sharp. 'He didn't cast you off. As I recall, you left him.'

'Our arrangement was of a temporary nature.' Elise smiled sadly. 'We hadn't signed a contract.'

'It must have meant much to him,' Vivienne said slowly. She touched Pearl's cheek and watched as the baby's hand opened and closed on her breast. 'And I'm sure he wants to see Pearl safe.' She looked up. 'You understand what this means?'

'Vivienne, I am not sure I can accept his gift.'

Vivienne's jaw dropped. 'You'd turn down a manor? Are you mad?'

Elise bit her lip. Lord, this was becoming more tangled by the moment. If she accepted Gawain's manor, she would be able to house Vivienne's little family in the hard times. If she rejected it… Heavens, in thinking about rejecting Gawain's gift, she was only thinking of herself. She was being selfish.

She stiffened her spine. 'Vivienne, I need your opinion. If I accept the manor, it means that you and I will no longer have to fret about where we will spend our days if takings fall away. Gaw... Lord Gawain has said that you and André may take up residence there too.'

Vivienne's eyes widened. 'That is generous of him. Elise, you should accept it.'

'You sound very certain.'

'I am. You cannot turn this down. Think of Pearl, if nothing else.'

Elise let out a sigh. Vivienne was right. She had to think of Pearl. Anything might happen and it would be good to know that Pearl would always have somewhere to live. 'You're right, of course. I have to think of Pearl.'

'Thank goodness.' Smiling, Vivienne shook her head at her. 'You had me worried for a moment. Will you go and see it soon?'

'I imagine so.' Elise stared pointedly at the bars on the windows. 'There'll be more space at the manor. And land. Lord Gawain says the revenues are to be mine. Vivienne, don't you see what this means? We no longer have to worry.'

'Elise, it's your manor.'

Elise felt her face fall. 'You won't come with me? Do say you will. I shall need both you and André.' She spread her hands. 'What experience do I have of running a manor?'

'Elise, running a manor is not something I am familiar with either.'

'I'd rather learn how to do it with friends at my elbow. I shall need help, and I'd like people I trust around me.' Elise jerked her head in the direction of the street. 'And helpful though Sergeant Gaston is, I don't really know him. Besides, Pearl won't be weaned for some time—Pearl needs you too.'

'There are other wet-nurses,' Vivienne said slowly.

'Please say you'll come.' And, as if Pearl sensed what the two women were talking about, she chose that moment to finish feeding and gave Vivienne such a beatific smile that Elise had to laugh. 'See? Pearl agrees with me.'

Vivienne's lips curved. 'Elise, she has wind. I am not sure it's a real smile.'

'It's a real smile. Pearl wants you to come with us. Please say you will.'

'I shall think about it.'

'Thank you.'

A trill of laughter outside caught Elise's attention and she peeped thorough a gap in the shutter. Gabrielle, the girl from the Black Boar, was flirting with one of the men-at-arms. Her laugh was light and her expression carefree. Gabrielle glanced at the house and Elise's heart jolted. Did she have news of André? Gabrielle's face was bright with laughter. She didn't look as though she was bearing bad tidings. None the less, Elise didn't want to hear what she had to say with Vivienne as witness. If it was bad news, Elise wanted time to work out how best to break it to Vivienne.

Rising, Elise took up her shawl and wound it about her before picking Pearl up and securing her next to her heart.

'I am going to stock up on flour,' she murmured. 'Until we move to the manor we shall still be doing our own cooking.'

Vivienne blinked. 'We'll have a cook at the manor? Lord.' She paused. 'Not that I've agreed to come with you, you understand. I'm going to wait until André returns. We shall decide together.'

'Of course.' Elise put her head to one side. 'We'll have a steward and men-at-arms. We might even have a maid.'

Vivienne's eyes were as round as pennies. 'A maid?'

'I thought that might tempt you,' Elise said with a grin. 'Think about it. I won't be long.'

Chapter Eleven

In the street, Elise gestured for Gabrielle. With a toss of her head and a farewell smile at Gawain's men, Gabrielle followed her to the crossroads. From inside the shawl, Pearl gurgled. A small arm appeared around the edge of the fringing.

Gabrielle leaned closer to touch her. 'She's beautiful,' she said softly, and some of the gaiety left her expression.

'I think so,' Elise murmured. 'Though I'm bound to be biased.'

Gabrielle sighed and stepped back. 'Which way?'

The bishop's palace lay on their right hand; the bridge over the canal on their left. Elise nodded towards the bridge. 'I'm headed for the market. I'll walk with you to the tavern.' She met Gabrielle's eyes. 'Thank you for your discretion back at the house. I don't want to worry Vivienne unnecessarily and I can see you've heard something.'

Gabrielle picked up her skirts to avoid a bundle of hay that must have fallen off one of the merchant's carts. 'It's not much, but I thought you'd want to know. Yesterday morning some castle guards came to the tavern. They were talking about you.' She smiled. 'Well, not you exactly. They were talking about Blanchefleur le Fay. They knew she was going to sing at the palace. One of them was determined to hear you. He was most concerned about how you would sing without your lute-player.'

'I hadn't realised that you knew I was Blanchefleur.'

Gabrielle's smile was mischievous. 'I didn't at first, but it's hard to keep secrets in Troyes. Anyhow, your admirer in the guard had been on patrol on the city walls and he'd seen André take the road to Provins. He thought it curious that André had his lute with him—it made him suspect that André was intending to be away for some time.'

'André was heading for Provins?' Elise thought quickly. Provins was another of Count Henry's market towns. As well-known as Troyes, it lay halfway between Paris and Troyes. André had never mentioned knowing anyone in Provins, but if he had become involved with rogues and counterfeiters elsewhere in Champagne he would have good reason not to mention it. Lord, what was he embroiled in? Her stomach sank. Was he in over his head?

In the shawl, Pearl whimpered. Elise was holding her too tightly. Relaxing her grip, Elise kissed Pearl's forehead and concentrated on what Gabrielle was saying.

'Your admirer hadn't heard about Baderon agreeing to play for you—he was most anxious on your behalf. He's been watching out for André's return.'

Elise took Gabrielle's arm. 'Do you know when André left exactly?'

'The guard didn't say, but I got the impression it was fairly recently—within the past couple of days.'

They crossed the bridge over the canal and took the main thoroughfare. Shadows were shortening and the streets were already filling with townsfolk.

Gabrielle glanced at the sky. There wasn't a cloud in sight. She sighed. 'It will be hot again today.'

'I fear so.'

Gabrielle touched Elise's hand. 'I'm sorry I don't have more to tell you.'

'You've been a great help, thank you. At least we know that André was alive a few days ago.'

'What will you do? Will you go to Provins?'

Overhead, a swift screeched, darting back and forth over the tall, wooden houses. Eyes on the swift as it wove patterns in the sky, Elise hesitated. 'I don't know.' Her thoughts churned. She might well have to go to Provins, but she was reluctant to admit as much to Gabrielle. True, the girl had been helpful, but Elise hardly knew her. Could she be relied upon to be discreet?

'Provins is on the Paris road,' Gabrielle added. 'It is quite a way. Do you ride?'

'A little.'

'You could walk it over the course of a few days but your feet are likely to be blistered at the end of it. And what with this heat—'

'It would be unbearable.'

'Exactly.' Gabrielle slanted her a look. 'It's a pity Lord Gawain is occupied with Lady Rowena, otherwise you might have joined his party. I heard he was heading for Provins.'

Elise looked coolly at her. 'He was headed for Sainte-Colombe.'

Gabrielle grinned. 'Which lies cheek by jowl with Provins.'

Elise held down a sigh. Did the world know about her and Gawain? 'I am not certain I need to go. Likely André will return in a day or so.'

'Very likely.' Gabrielle squinted towards the sun. 'Heavens, it's late. Agnes needs help in the kitchen.' She pointed down a shadowy alley. 'I'm going that way. It's quicker. Fare you well.'

'Farewell, Gabrielle. Many thanks.'

'You are most welcome.' Gabrielle took a few steps down the alley, skirted round a heap of yellowing cabbages and looked back. 'Elise, one thing further—if you find yourself in Provins and can't find your friend, you might make enquiries about the caves.'

'Caves?'

Gabrielle's smile was crooked. Her voice was low, rushed. 'Ask about the caves. Farewell.' She hurried into the shadows and Elise was left staring after her, a statue in the stream of people flowing past the alley.

Caves? What caves? It was clear Gabrielle knew more than she was prepared to say. Elise stared blindly at a sagging door frame and grimaced. The stink of rotting cabbage in this street was unbearable.

Hand covering her nose, she turned thoughtfully

towards the market. Provins. Saints, with Gawain pursuing his courtship of Lady Rowena nearby, it was the last place she wanted to go. Of course, André might not have gone to Provins. He might have stopped off en route. Except it sounded extremely likely that Provins would have been his destination. A town that was similar to Troyes would be exactly the sort of place that low-life fraudsters might choose for their headquarters. There would be plenty of hiding places. Caves?

André's welfare was what counted. Like it or not, she must go to Provins. And she must go soon. Before the Guardian Knights learned that André had been seen on the Provins road. André needed her and, compared to his welfare, worrying about avoiding Gawain was a trivial matter. It wouldn't stop her from going. In any case, it should be easy to avoid the Count of Meaux. He would be moving in very different circles. He would be staying with Count Faramus in Sainte-Colombe. If Elise went to Provins, she was unlikely to see him. André was in deep trouble. She was sure of it. And before she set off, she would find out about the caves.

Baderon! Elise's spirits lifted. Baderon knew

Champagne like the back of his hand. He would surely tell her about the Provins caves.

Vivienne flung the wooden spoon aside and slammed down the lid of the cooking pot. 'I'm coming with you!'

Elise flinched. 'Careful, love, I only just bought that pot.'

'Jésu, as if I cared! André is in peril. I know it. We both know it. I'm coming with you.'

Elise shook her head. It was evening already and the babies were resting in their cradles upstairs. For the past hour she and Vivienne had been arguing in circles, with Vivienne insisting she too must go to Provins, and with Elise trying to convince her otherwise.

'Vivienne, please be calm.' Elise gestured at the ceiling. 'If you come, we'll have to bring the babies. They will slow us down. Why, they might even be put at risk. You have to stay here. Sergeant Gaston will look out for you. He will ensure you have everything you need.'

'I need André.' Vivienne bunched her fists. 'I don't need Sergeant Gaston, and I certainly don't need you ordering me about.' Her voice broke and she covered her eyes with her hand. 'I just need André.'

'I will do my utmost to find him. Lord, we don't even know for certain he will be in Provins. All I was told was that he was seen taking the Provins road.' Moving to the fire, Elise put her arm about Vivienne's shoulders and hugged her. 'I will do my best to find him.'

Shakily, Vivienne returned the hug. 'I know you will. I'm sorry to snap at you, but I miss him so. When he's not with me I feel as though I've been torn in two.'

Elise nodded. She understood how that felt. The thought of Gawain riding off to Sainte-Colombe with Lady Rowena had her in shreds.

Vivienne blinked at her, eyes watery. 'However, I don't want you rushing headlong into danger either. You can't go alone.'

'I had worked that out for myself,' Elise said drily.

'What will you do?'

'Baderon knows every highway and byway in Champagne. I've asked him to come with me.'

Vivienne brightened. 'That's a good idea. Do you think he'll agree?'

'He jumped at the idea. Provins is just as important as Troyes. There will be plenty of opportunities for him to play at the castle.'

'You could sing too! Follow up the success of

last night's performance at the palace. You'll have all of Champagne at your feet.' Vivienne gave her a wobbly smile and Elise knew she would have her way. Vivienne and the babies would be staying in Troyes, safe under the watchful eyes of Sergeant Gaston.

Gawain had to admit he was given a warm welcome at Jutigny Castle, the Sainte-Colombe holding. As his cavalcade trotted into the bailey under a crimson evening sky, Count Faramus appeared at the head of a long flight of stone steps. Gawain and Lady Rowena were swept into the great hall.

Count Faramus beamed with bonhomie as he gave his daughter a brief hug before focusing his attention on Gawain. 'Wine, my lord? Ale? Whatever you wish is my command.'

'My thanks.' Gawain accepted a cup of wine. His surcoat was more grey than red—he was covered with the dust of the road. He was hot and sticky and his neck itched. 'I confess I would kill for a bath.'

'Of course. I've never known heat like this.'

Count Faramus—a round, bewhiskered man in his early fifties—was less imposing than Gawain had imagined. So this was the ally his uncle had taken such pains to cultivate? He looked like a benevolent uncle rather than the great warrior Gawain had heard so much about. Gawain tried to look interested and listened with half an ear as Lord Faramus outlined the entertainments planned for the coming weeks. It was hard to concentrate and ever harder to keep smiling. He was becoming increasingly concerned about his forthcoming marriage.

A door opened at the end of the great hall and a stately lady swept in. This must be the Countess of Sainte-Colombe. The countess held out her arms and Gawain watched with astonishment as Lady Rowena's face transfigured. All smiles, she flew into her mother's embrace. It was galling to see Lady Rowena look so happy. Not that Gawain didn't wish for her happiness, but the most he had been able to wring from his betrothed had been a polite smile. Arms wrapped round each other, the women left the hall, heading doubtless for the ladies' solar.

Gawain held down a sigh as his betrothed whisked out of sight. He had taken his time over the journey from Troyes. They had passed a night at an inn. He had hoped that Lady Rowena would become less skittish in his presence and that, if he gave her the chance to be alone with him, she would see that he wasn't an ogre. Naturally they hadn't actually been alone. An escort of twenty men and a couple of maids had seen to that. But you'd think she might have reconciled herself with the idea of marrying him. He'd been polite. He'd been attentive. To no avail, she'd sat there clutching her cross and chewing her lips, plainly so terrified that at times she'd been barely able to speak. Did she fear all men, or was it just him?

'You don't like tourneys?' Count Faramus had seen his frown and thought Gawain was questioning his plans for the coming days. 'I had heard of your prowess on the Field of the Birds and I assumed—'

'No, no.' Gawain forced a smile. 'A tourney would be most invigorating. Thank you, my lord.'

'It's a pity we can't go hawking, but the birds are in moult.' Count Faramus gestured at one of the men standing a few yards away. 'And now, my lord, permit me to introduce my steward, Sir Macaire. He will show you to your quarters. We dine in an hour. Macaire, see to it a bath is brought for Lord Gawain.'

Sir Macaire bowed. 'Yes, my lord.'

Gawain's chamber was at the top of the north tower. The bed was large and the oak canopy was draped with purple silk. Purple. The image of a purple pavilion with silver stars leaped into his brain and his head began to throb.

Aubin and a manservant staggered in with one of his travelling chests. 'Shall I put this by the wall, my lord?'

'Please.' Gawain's mind seemed sluggish. He wondered if he had a touch of heatstroke. Rubbing the bridge of his nose, he went to the window. A double lancet, it looked out over the Sainte-Colombe acres—a patchwork of field strips, vineyards and forest. Provins lay just over two miles away.

There was a heat haze. The Sainte-Colombe acres seemed to waver as he looked at them. They looked well cared for. Orderly. In due course, if his marriage went ahead, this land would one day be under his stewardship. Gawain leaned his forearm against the stone window embrasure. The ditches were clear; hedges had been trimmed; people were walking up and down between the lines of vines, harvesting the grapes in the last of the light, putting them in baskets. It was an idyllic sight.

Gawain had never felt more miserable in his life.

Marriage with a woman who started at his every touch—no, it was worse than that, she started every time he breathed—Lord, what a nightmare.

Behind him, Aubin and the manservant were ordering his belongings. He heard a bath being heaved in and the sound of pouring water.

Is it worth it? The question appeared out of no-where and another swiftly followed.

How on earth was he going to go about bedding Lady Rowena? The purple pavilion lingered in his mind's eye and he gritted his teeth. He'd never been one to look for love, but he'd hoped for a little passion in his life. Lady Rowena—merciful heaven, this felt so wrong.

Sighing, he moved away from the lancets. The bath was ready and waiting. His headache would surely leave him once he had bathed.

Riding pillion behind Baderon was more challenging than Elise had imagined. Progress was slow. And hot. Clouds of dust hung over the highway. Baderon's horse, Magpie, was pestered with flies. Elise was no great horsewoman and after the first couple of hours her bottom felt bruised. Her arms ached from hanging on to Baderon. Sticky with sweat, she'd had more than enough. Still, she was pleased to have escaped the watchful eyes of Sergeant Gaston. When Baderon had appeared with his lute, saying that Countess Isobel d'Aveyron had summoned them to a private performance at Ravenshold, the sergeant hadn't objected. Of course, there was no private performance. Elise and Baderon were riding to Provins.

'How far are we going today?' Elise asked, brushing a damp strand of hair from her brow.

'We should manage about fifteen miles, but if Magpie tires, we'll stop sooner. She's not used to the extra weight and I don't want to lame her.'

'Of course not. Baderon, you're a saint to come with me.'

'It's no hardship. There will be just as much work for me in Provins as there was in Troyes.' Baderon paused and Magpie clopped stoically through the flies and the dust. 'In any case, Lord Gawain asked me to watch out for you. He wouldn't think much of me if I let you travel alone.'

Elise curled her fingers round Baderon's belt. It had been kind of Gawain to have taken such an interest in her welfare—he was very protective—but it wouldn't last. How could it? He had many responsibilities and giving her the manor was his way of ridding himself of an unwanted and embarrassing burden. She was getting the manor because of Pearl. Her throat ached. Dragging her mind away from Gawain—it hurt to think of him—she changed the subject.

'Baderon, have you played often in Troyes?'

'Many times, at the castle and the palace.'

'And how long have you known Lord Gawain?' Elise bit her lip, but the question had escaped before she could stop it. So much for her changing the subject! Every thought she had seemed to wind back to Gawain.

'Not long.'

'Oh? I assumed you had known him for some time.'

Baderon shook his head. 'Until recently I knew him only by repute.' He laughed. 'Lord Gawain hasn't shown much interest in the world of the troubadour before now.'

Swallowing hard, Elise gazed past Baderon's shoulder at a line of poplars on the horizon.

'Courtly love,' Baderon continued, 'and all that entails never interested him until this summer. You must mean much to him.'

Involuntarily, forgetting Baderon could not see her, Elise gave a swift head shake. 'That's not true. He's helping me because—'

Baderon snorted. 'Holy Mother, Elise, the man's given you a manor! He must think well of you.'

Elise took a deep breath. If only that were true. The fact that Gawain had given her the manor proved how little he understood her. How could he think well of her if he didn't understand her?

However, she didn't want to argue—not when Baderon was going out of his way to help her. 'Where will we stop tonight?'

'I'm hoping we'll reach the Haywain. We can pass the night there. The innkeeper will be able to tell us if he's seen André.'

'Have I seen another lute-player?' A wide grin spread across the innkeeper's face. 'As a matter of fact, we were lucky enough to have a visit from one of your calling a few nights back. It was a lively night.' He looked expectantly at Baderon. 'Are you of a mind to entertain us too, *monsieur*?'

Elise felt herself relax as relief flooded through her. They were on the right track! 'Excuse me, landlord,' she asked, 'did you get the lute-player's name?'

The landlord scratched his nose. 'Anton, I think it was. No, wait a moment, it was André, yes, André.' His brow puckered. 'He hailed from somewhere in the south.'

'Poitiers?'

'That's the place.'

'*Monsieur*, André is a dear friend and it's vital I find him. I don't suppose he mentioned where in Provins he was headed?'

The landlord smiled. 'As a matter of fact, he

did. He was trying to find a friend of his, name of Jerome. I know Jerome of old. He's the son of a wine merchant—the same wine merchant who supplies most of the inns along the Provins road.'

Elise exchanged glances with Baderon. 'Where might I find this Jerome?'

'In Provins lower town. The family have lodgings over the Sun Inn—it's next to the church of Saint Ayoul. Ask there and you'll soon find your friend.'

Elise released her breath in a sigh of relief. 'Thank you, landlord, that is most helpful.'

The landlord turned his attention back to Baderon. 'Will you play for us, *monsieur*?'

Baderon's eyes danced. 'For the right inducements, I might. You'll throw in our board and lodging?'

'Naturally.'

Baderon looked expectantly at Elise. 'Elise, what about you? Will you sing?'

Elise was hot and tired, but discovering the name of the man that André was looking for was invigorating. *Jerome. The son of a wine merchant who lives over the Sun Inn.* She pulled her travel-stained gown away from her body with a grimace. 'Aye, provided I can refresh myself first.'

She smiled at the landlord. 'Please tell me you have a bathhouse.'

'We do indeed.' The landlord swept them a bow worthy of royalty. '*Madame, monsieur*, you are most welcome.'

The next day, Elise and Baderon continued on the main highway. They stopped at the Four Princes on the second night and again they sang for their supper. And again they learned that André had trod the same path and that when he had left the Four Princes, he had taken the road to Provins.

The day after that, the wooden fortifications of Provins hove into sight. A brace of towers flanked the main gates to the lower town. The grass on the margins of the approach road was brown, desiccated by weeks of scorching sun. Butterflies hovered hopefully over wilting wildflowers— poppies, clover, cornflowers. Baderon and Elise clopped through the gate, nodding at a guard whose face was as brown as a nut.

'We'll go straight to the Sun Inn,' Elise said.

'Very well.' Baderon twisted round in the saddle to look at her. 'Are you of a mind to sing again?'

Elise grimaced, rubbing her thigh with the heel of her hand. 'Not tonight.'

'You've enough money? I can help you if—'

'Thank you, but I have money.' Elise had the fee from the Harvest Banquet. She also had some bezants her father had given her before he died. They were pure gold and she'd tucked them into the bottom of her purse. She had been saving them for Pearl, but she'd happily part with them if they helped bring André back in one piece.

Elise took note of the lie of the land as they rode into the lower town. The streets were very like those in Troyes, narrow and lined with wooden houses. House martins' nests clung beneath the eaves; smoke curled through roofs and louvres; geese honked; cartwheels rumbled. Some of the streets ran sharply uphill. Higher up, she could see stone fortifications, the top of a tower. She looked at Baderon. 'I assume that's the castle?'

Baderon nodded.

Elise wasn't sure how open she could be with Baderon. He knew she was looking for André, but so far she hadn't breathed a word about counterfeiters. She would have liked to tell him everything, but she had a strong suspicion that if she mentioned the fakers, he would refuse to go on helping her. Still, she had a name—Jerome—and Gabrielle had mentioned the caves. Apparently, everyone knew about the Provins caves, she could surely ask him about them.

'And the caves? Do you know where they are?'

'They're everywhere in the town. A network of tunnels runs under the streets.'

Gripping Baderon's waist, Elise found herself staring at the dusty ground. 'They're beneath the streets?' She had assumed the caves would be some way from the actual town, but beneath the streets?

'For the most part the townsfolk rent them out to foreign merchants. They use them for surplus stock and as lockups for their goods between trade fairs.'

Elise's heart sank. 'How many caves are there?'

'I've never seen them myself, but I was told it's an underground maze. There's an entire network cut into the chalk. Why the interest?'

'I...I am not sure exactly. A friend suggested I find out about the caves. But I am afraid of asking about them too closely in case...' Her voice trailed off. If André was mixed up with fraudsters and they were using these caves as their headquarters, she didn't want her questions to put him in danger. 'Baderon, we need to be discreet.'

Baderon grunted. 'The landlord at the Sun Inn

will surely know about the caves. And so will this Jerome if his father is a wine merchant.'

The Sun Inn lay in the shadow of St Ayoul. Leaving Magpie in the stable, they went inside.

The inn was busy and the landlord so surrounded by customers it was impossible to claim his attention for long. Once they'd managed to secure a place for the night, Elise went straight to the heart of the matter.

'Landlord, we are looking for a friend. André de Poitiers. Have you seen him?'

'Never heard of him.'

'Then what of Jerome? I believe his father is a wine merchant with lodgings here.'

'Jerome? Haven't seen him lately, but I will ask about for you.'

'Thank you, *monsieur*.'

Elise and Baderon elbowed their way to a table, and after a short wait a serving boy brought them a jug of wine. The wine jug was half-empty by the time the boy returned with a platter of chicken and onions.

'You want to speak to Jerome, *ma demoiselle*?' the boy asked. 'He is not here at present, but if you are prepared to offer something in the way of a *pourboire*, I am sure something might be arranged.' His fingers wiggled under Elise's nose, and she slipped him a coin. The boy's teeth flashed white in the lamplight and the coin vanished. 'He'll meet you by the market cross in the lower market. At noon. The market cross at noon. Come alone, *ma demoiselle.*'

Baderon made a sharp movement as though to catch the boy's arm, but he twisted like an eel and vanished in the direction of the cookhouse. 'I don't like it,' Baderon muttered, swearing softly. 'Why the devil can't he meet both of us? I'm coming with you.'

Elise hesitated. If only Gabrielle had been able to tell her more. She didn't know why, but her instincts were telling her that the mystery of André's disappearance would be solved if only she could speak to Jerome. 'Baderon, I have to talk to this man. I have to. André must have been coming here, yet the landlord hasn't seen him. Doesn't that strike you as odd?' She felt a prickling sensation, shivery fingers trailing down her back despite the heat. She took Baderon by the hand. 'I have to go. And if Jerome wants me to go alone, that's what I shall do. You would do the same if André was your friend, I'm sure.'

Baderon sighed into his wine. 'Very well. Take

heed though. I shall be watching you—following you every step of the way. Agreed?'

She bit her lip. 'You'll be discreet? You won't let him see you?'

'Elise, I have some intelligence. Naturally I'll be discreet.'

At noon, Provins lower town was so busy that the market square didn't seem big enough. The townsfolk pushed and shoved, flowing past the market cross like a stream running round an island. The sun beat down on everyone's heads, as relentless and blinding as it had been these many days. The tang of overheated bodies hung in the air. Ducks quacked. Goats bleated. The cheese on one of the stalls, though shaded by a thick awning, looked sweaty. It was surely on the point of melting.

Elise eyed the sun. The bells of Saint Ayoul had chimed the hour some time since. Jerome was late. Irritably, she plucked at the neck of her gown. There was no shade by the market cross. She was melting along with the cheeses. Baderon was lounging against a house a few yards away, in the shade, lucky thing. Elise hadn't looked at him once since she'd come to stand by the cross, nor would she, but she was aware of him and grateful for his watching presence.

'*Ma demoiselle?*'

A young man broke free of the heaving crowd and nodded at her. 'You are the young lady who wishes to speak to Jerome?'

'Yes, I—'

Hand on his heart, the young man executed a bow worthy of the Paris court. Oddly, his smile had cold fingers skittering down the back of Elise's neck.

'Permit me to introduce myself,' he said, smoothly. 'My name is Jerome. My father and I have been importing wine from Burgundy for many years. Count Henry is one of our most valued customers.'

Count Henry had vineyards of his own, but Elise knew it was likely he bought other wines, so she simply nodded. She shivered. This young man—Jerome—seemed perfectly civilised. He was unusually personable with his neatly cut tawny hair and amber eyes, but she didn't warm to him.

'You are searching for your friend André, I believe? This way, *ma demoiselle.*'

Jerome set off, diving in and out of the townsfolk as they cleared the market square. Elise followed as he ducked into one alley and then another. Lord, Provins was a maze. Thank God for Baderon, she thought. If not for him, she doubted that she'd have the courage to follow Jerome. The street began sloping upwards, which likely meant they were headed for the upper town. When the stone ramparts of Count Henry's castle came into view above them, Elise knew she had guessed aright. The street narrowed as the way got steeper. Jerome paused and looked back at her.

'Walking is hot work this summer,' he said, smiling.

Elise's skin crawled. Every instinct was telling her that the less time she spent with Jerome the better, but she couldn't walk away. 'Indeed.' Elise swallowed and managed to smile back. She thought about André.

A lichen-encrusted wall rose up on her left, curving along with the rising street. Widely spaced steps took them higher. They were yet some way from the top when Jerome halted at a door in the wall. It had thick iron hinges.

'The entrance to our vaults, *ma demoiselle*.'

A clump of ivy, crisp and brown through lack of rain, trailed along the cracks at their feet. Jerome produced two large keys. The lock grated and the door swung inwards. Elise's pulse began to thud. Several steps ran down into a gloomy cavern.

'*Ma demoiselle*, the family cellar.'

Elise felt her throat work. It came to her that if she went into the cave with Jerome, she might never come out again. On impulse she ran her hand round the back of her neck, lifting her hair as if to cool herself. She cast a swift look down towards the lower town. The street was empty.

Where was Baderon? Holy Virgin, had he lost her? With the press of people in the market square and the crooked route they had taken, it was entirely possible. In a flash of inspiration, she hooked her fingers around the cord of her enamel pendant.

'Saints, but it's hot.' She forced another smile.

The young man's eyes gleamed as he looked at her and she was put in mind of a cat toying with its prey. 'It's cool in the caves, *ma demoiselle*. You will find it a welcome change, I am sure.'

Elise took a deep breath. 'Lead on, sir.'

She saw him glance down the street—it remained deserted—and jerked hard on the cord of her pendant. It came away easily. Dropping it at the foot of the wall, she shifted her foot and nudged it into the sunlight. God willing, Baderon was on her tail. He would see it.

'After you, *ma demoiselle*.'

Elise started down the steps. A shaft of light lit

up a vast empty space that was edged with grey shadows. Round stone pillars held up the ceiling. As Elise's eyes adjusted to the semi-darkness, she saw faint glimmers of light filtering in through vents in the top of the walls. If someone had told her she was descending into the hall of a dwarf king, she wouldn't have been surprised. Her heart thumped. Her breath quickened. Though large, it felt very enclosed. Her skin seemed to shrink.

A hiss and a flicker of light made her turn. Jerome had a torch. She watched him push the door shut and heard the crack of a bolt being shot home.

They were shut in! Every muscle in Elise's body seemed to freeze. She found herself humming the Magnificat. 'My soul doth magnify the Lord...' The nuns had chanted it daily in the convent and though Elise wasn't made for convent life, though she found the life there restricting, she had found solace in the chanting. *I am here for André,* she reminded herself. *I am here for André.*

Jerome came down the steps. 'This way, *ma demoiselle.*'

He disappeared into an archway hewn from the bowels of the earth, leaving Elise with no choice but to follow him. She didn't want to be left in the empty hall alone. She chanted softly under her breath. 'Glory be to the Father...' It took her mind from her fear.

They entered a tunnel where the wavering torch-light gleamed on ochre-coloured walls that were flecked with white. Chalk, she supposed. The walls were rough to the touch and the air frigid. Goosebumps ran up her arms. She could smell mushrooms. The silence was unearthly.

Beyond the wavering light, the corridor ran deep into the earth. The walls glistened. And there—yes, tiny mushrooms were indeed thriving in the crevices. Tipping back her head, Elise could see an iron grille. They must be walking beneath one of the streets. Dried grasses blocked the opening. She fancied she heard the screech of a jay.

There was movement behind her. Something hit the back of her head and everything went black.

Gawain was roused before dawn by Aubin. That was not unusual. What was unusual was the anxiety in his squire's voice. 'Lord Gawain, you have a visitor.'

Gawain opened weary eyes and blinked at the candle wobbling in Aubin's grasp. '*Mon Dieu*, Aubin, go away. Daybreak's at least an hour away. It's far too early for visitors.'

Aubin set the candle on the coffer by the bed

and Gawain rolled over, turning his back on him. He was aware that his uncalled-for visitor had had the temerity to step into the bedchamber, but it really was too early.

'You'll want to see me,' a familiar voice said.

Gawain rolled over again. 'Baderon? What the devil are you doing here?'

'It's Elise, my lord. I thought you'd want to know. She's missing.'

Gawain felt himself go still. 'Missing? Elise's isn't missing. I know exactly where she is. In Troyes.'

'No, my lord, she is not.'

Slowly, Gawain sat up. It crossed his mind that this might be some ghastly joke, but Baderon's expression was earnest. 'You're serious.' He was aware of Aubin opening trunks; laying his tunic and hose at the foot of the bed; lifting his sword and belt down from the hook on the wall. A cold dread settled over him.

Baderon's expression was grim. 'Lord Gawain, Elise left Troyes shortly after you did. She went to Provins in search of André de Poitiers. He was seen heading that way.'

Gawain swung out of bed and padded to the ewer to splash water on his face. 'You let her come?' He reached for a drying cloth.

'There was no stopping her. She was convinced that she could find him and bring him back to Troyes. His woman—Vivienne—is frantic.' Baderon swallowed. 'Since Elise was set on coming, I thought it best to escort her. If I hadn't done so, she would have set out on her own.'

Head thumping—he must have drunk too much wine last eve—Gawain looked at him.

'My lord, there was no stopping her.'

'I understand.' Gawain tossed the cloth at Aubin and turned for his clothes. 'While I dress, you had best tell me everything. Everything.'

The men were none too pleased to be roused from their sleep, but they'd been well trained. Gawain's troop was trotting through the wooden gateway and into the lower town as the first rays of sunlight began creeping across the ground.

Gawain didn't know Provins as well as he knew Troyes, so he'd commandeered the Count of Sainte-Colombe's captain to act as his guide. The man had been born in the town and claimed to know the location of every last entrance to the caves that Baderon had spoken of. The cellars would be locked, of course, but the captain swore he knew where to find the key holders.

'Where do we start?' Gawain asked as they trotted smartly along sun-baked streets. It took effort to keep his voice calm. He felt as though his world had disintegrated. Elise was in danger and he only had himself to blame. He'd promised Raphael he would make enquiries about André in Provins, only he'd been so taken up with his wretched betrothal that he had yet to do so. 'Regret is pointless,' he muttered.

'My lord?'

Sainte-Colombe's captain was looking anxiously at him. Gawain clenched his jaw. He didn't feel calm, but he must present a calm face to the men. He was afraid, very afraid, for Elise. His fear must not show—a commander who couldn't control his own fear wasn't fit to command men.

'The caves,' Gawain said. 'Tell me about them.'

'The town sits on a bed of chalk—it has been mined for years. My lord, there are tunnels down there, side passages. Winter or summer the temperature never changes.'

'That's why it's good for storage.'

'Yes, my lord. Merchants rent cellars from the townsfolk. It's always cool in the caves. Ideal for storing wine, for example. The space is highly prized because merchants don't necessarily shift all their stock at the fairs. If they store it in the caves, they know it will be safe between fairs.'

She will be cold.

Gawain looked thoughtfully at the captain. 'It sounds as though the caves would make a good prison.'

The captain nodded. 'They have been used for that purpose too.'

Gawain gripped his reins. *A prison?* He shot Baderon a look. Dragging off his helmet, he hooked it over the pommel of his saddle and shoved his hand through his hair. Wild thoughts careered through his mind. For Elise not to have returned last eve she must be under constraint. And that was looking at matters in an optimistic light. At worst she might be… His mind refused to complete the thought. However, if her search for André had led her to the counterfeiters, they might want her silenced.

Mon Dieu, that must not happen. It would not happen. He would find Elise and she would be well. Pearl needed her. Lord, he needed her. Elise had to be alive.

He heard the captain talking about leaving their horses under guard beneath a plane tree. The words washed over him and he forced himself to focus on the task in hand. He would find Elise. The knots in his stomach eased, some tension remained to be sure, but he would feel better when he had found her. *She will be safe.*

'How many entrances do you know of, Captain?'

'At least half a dozen. There may be more.'

'And you know the key holders, you say?'

'Yes, my lord.'

'Very well.' Dismounting, Gawain surrendered The Beast's reins to one of the men. 'Where do we start?'

Chapter Twelve

The door to the first cellar was set into a wall halfway up a sloping street.

Gawain tapped his foot impatiently while Sainte-Colombe's captain went through the ritual of rousing the key holder and gaining entrance. As the door creaked open, Gawain pushed through it and went down into the dark. It was much smaller than he had expected, a cramped cave rather than a cellar. His head almost brushed the ceiling. There were a few barrels, a broken hoist. Nothing of interest. There were no doors or passages leading elsewhere, just a cold, cramped cave.

'Is that it?' he asked, frowning. 'I thought the caves were larger than this. Don't they connect?'

'Some do, some don't.' The captain spread his hands. 'I'm sorry, my lord. This is one of the smaller cellars.'

Grunting, Gawain went back into the warmth of the street.

Four cellars later, the captain pointed across the street to another door. 'That one's said to be larger, my lord.'

Gawain strode across. On the ground something flashed in the morning sun. He picked it up and his heart stopped. A tiny enamel pendant with a broken cord lay in the palm of his hand. Mouth dry, he stared at the exquisite enamelling, at the white daisy with its golden centre. His fingers closed over it and he examined the door. It was oak, studded and strengthened with iron. He cleared his throat. 'This one, captain. We look in here.'

The captain nodded. 'Very well, my lord, I'll send for the key.'

Gripped by a sense of urgency, Gawain thrust Elise's necklace into his pouch. 'No time for the niceties.' Elise was in there. He knew it. A look at the hinges told him that the door opened inwards. He signalled at one of the men. 'Sergeant, do the honours, will you?'

The sergeant and a couple of troopers put their shoulders to the door.

Moments later, they stepped down into what appeared to be an underground hall. The ceiling was vaulted. Two rows of pillars marched deep under the town. A shadowy archway led further into the dark. The air was cool and smelt vaguely of earth.

Snatching a torch from a soldier, Gawain made straight for the archway. Here, the walls were more crudely formed and he found himself staring down a tunnel roughly hewn out of the rock. The surface of the walls was gritty and uneven. Clusters of tiny mushrooms were flowering in cracks. The men crowded after him, their footsteps loud in the subterranean quiet.

A trooper coughed. '*Mon Dieu*, what devil's lair is this?' He hastily sketched the sign of the cross on his breast.

Ahead, the passage divided. Gawain lifted his hand. 'Quiet.' He picked out two men. 'You two follow myself and the captain. The rest of you wait here until you are called. In silence.'

The captain fell in behind him and they progressed to the point where the tunnel divided. Gawain examined the floor. He was hoping to find footprints or telltale scuff marks. There was nothing. And he had yet to see any goods.

'This place doesn't look as though it's been used in years,' he said.

'There may be locked vaults ahead of us, my

lord. Anything of value would be stored in the vaults.'

'You take the right-hand tunnel, Captain. I'll take the left. Take this man with you.' He then pointed at the other trooper. 'You come with me.'

'Very good, *mon seigneur*.'

Gawain's torch made the walls glisten. He had only proceeded a few yards when he came across a door with a barred opening near the top. Even before he tried the latch, he knew it would be locked. He held the torch up to the grille.

'Elise? Elise?' The silence was that of the tomb. Gawain grimaced and pushed the thought away. God save him, let it not be the silence of the tomb. At the back of the vault, there was a neat stack of wine barrels. 'Elise?'

Nothing stirred. There was no scuttling that might indicate rats or mice. Just frigid air and the smell of damp earth and mushrooms.

Ahead was another door. A little way on there was another—indeed, a whole line of doors seemed to run on into infinity.

'Elise? Elise?'

The sputter of the torch was loud in the quiet. Gawain cursed under his breath. He knew she was down here somewhere, but where?

And then he heard something. A sighing of breath. A whisper? No, a sob.

'Who's there? Help! Please help.'

Small fingers curved round the bars of one of the grilles. Heart in his mouth, Gawain angled the light towards the door. A pale face peered out at him. Eyes huge, black against the white of her face. Elise!

He exchanged glances with the guard and they dropped their torches into a bracket by the door.

'Stand back, sweetheart.'

Elise's fingers withdrew. He and the guard put their shoulders to the door. With a crack, the door burst open. Gawain snatched up the torch. She was crouched on the floor, huddled protectively over the body of a young man. The light flickered over a face that was tight with worry.

'Gawain!' He saw her swallow. 'Thank heaven. I think André's been here for some time. He won't wake up.'

Thrusting the torch at the guard, Gawain fell to his knees and reached for her. He'd never seen her look like this. He took her hands. Lord, they were cold. 'You're like ice.' He touched her forehead. '*Mon Dieu*, Elise, you're half-frozen.'

Hand to her throat, Elise swallowed. 'Mostly,

I'm thirsty.' She grimaced. 'I'm so thirsty I had to stop singing.'

Gawain could feel the anger rising. They'd been locked in here without water? As he suspected, the counterfeiters were afraid that they were about to be betrayed. Elise and André had been left to die.

Pretending calm, Gawain lifted her into his arms. 'Let's get you to where there's warmth and water.'

'But, Gawain,' she spoke hoarsely, 'André—'

'I've men outside. They'll fetch a litter.' He shouldered his way out into the passageway and raised his voice. 'Captain!'

A distant shout reached them.

'To me! On the double!' He looked down at Elise and gentled his tone. 'I'm taking you to Provins Castle.'

Nodding, she slipped her arm about his neck and laid her head on his chest.

Gawain couldn't help himself. He nuzzled her cheek. He hadn't recognised how panicked he was until she put up her hand and stroked gently down his nose. It was a gesture he recalled from last year, and immediately it calmed him. Last year she had looked at him in just the way she was looking at him now. As though she...

He dipped his head, conscious of the guard's interested gaze yet unable to resist, and his mouth found hers. Her lips were cold and they softened to his touch. He kept it brief. 'Thank God you're safe.' If he had lost her… It didn't bear thinking about. His eyebrows drew together as another thought occurred to him. 'Elise, you are a mother. You shouldn't have put yourself at risk. You knew I was nearby. Why didn't you apply to me for help? And I left my men at your command in Troyes. Why did you come to Provins without them?'

She pulled her head back. 'I wasn't alone. Baderon—'

'A lute-player? What protection could he have given you? Dear God, Elise, didn't you think of the danger? What if we hadn't found you?' She made as if to interrupt, but Gawain swept on. 'You've seen André's condition. How long do you suppose he's been here without food? Without water?'

Sainte-Colombe's captain ran up. 'My lord?'

'There's an injured man back there in one of the vaults. Use a horse blanket as a litter and bring him out with all speed.'

'Yes, my lord.'

Elise looked at the captain. 'His name is André. If he wakes, please give him something to drink.'

Gawain tightened his hold on Elise. 'Captain, we're going to the castle. Bring the man there.' He strode on until they reached the large chamber that resembled a hall. Stalking past his men with her fast in his arms, he climbed the steps.

Sainte-Colombe's captain followed, Gawain heard him issuing instructions about bringing André out of the cellar. He gripped Elise. He wanted nothing more than to bury his head in her neck and inhale her scent. *Control, man, control...*

'I was near mad with worry,' he muttered. He hadn't meant to confess it aloud. Her fingers clenched and unclenched on his tunic.

'I am sorry, Gaw—my lord.' Her voice was small. 'I never meant to go in alone, but I lost sight of Baderon and...Gawain, I had to find him.'

Gawain glowered down at her. 'That is no excuse.'

She let out a breath. 'When I saw him it was clear he'd been down there some time.'

Gawain carried her across the street. A dazzle of sunlight made her blink like an owl and a shudder went through her. 'They didn't mean for us to leave.'

Gawain felt his throat tighten. He jerked his

head at the man standing guard over the horses. 'My horse, if you please.'

He shifted her in his arms. She looked dainty and fragile. Beautiful. And so worried. It came to him that he would move heaven and earth to lift her worries from her. He found a smile. 'You're happy to ride before me?'

She smiled and leaned her head against his chest.

There was no chance for private speech until they were inside Provins Castle. Gawain commandeered a guest chamber on the second floor, just off the solar. Placing Elise carefully on the bed, he stood back and looked her over with a critical eye.

'You're pale as a ghost.'

A maidservant bustled in with a tray and set it on a side table. 'Here's the small beer you asked for, *mon seigneur.*'

'My thanks.'

'Shall I fetch food, my lord?'

'Elise?'

'I'm ravenous. May I have some bread, please? With honey.'

Of course, how could Gawain have forgotten Elise's sweet tooth? One night at Ravenshold, they'd demolished an entire almond cake between them. He looked at the maidservant. 'Do you have any almond cake?'

The maidservant smiled. 'I think I might find some, my lord.' Dipping into a curtsy, she left the chamber.

Gawain had barely opened his mouth to ask Elise if she remembered that almond cake when another woman appeared with a towel and a water jug.

'My lord, if you wouldn't mind.' The woman bobbed him a curtsy as the first one had done. 'I would see to the lady. Perhaps you should withdraw.'

Gawain did mind, but, recollecting that he was a betrothed man, he nodded. 'I'll be on the landing.' He met Elise's eyes. 'I'll be back when you are more comfortable.'

Despite the thick walls the August heat had penetrated the heart of the castle and Gawain was itching to be out of his gambeson. No sooner was he in the stairwell, than he eased it off. While he waited, he fixed his gaze on a slice of blue sky visible through the window slit. He could hear murmuring in the bedchamber, although he couldn't make out the words. The sound was oddly calming, which he supposed was a good thing because inside he felt anything but calm.

Why hadn't Elise appealed to him for help? She should have known she was courting trouble when she went into the cellar. Had she even thought about what would happen to Pearl if she had never returned? Why didn't she trust him?

Delving into his purse, he pulled out the daisy and studied the enamelling. It was smooth and perfect—top-quality Limoges probably. Who had given it to her? His guts felt cold. Was her heart taken? Had it been taken last year when they had become lovers? Gawain could see her standing in Count Henry's palace after her performance, besieged by admirers. Doubtless Blanchefleur le Fay had hordes of men willing to fight for the privilege of paying her homage.

Gawain thought about Sir Olier—of the eagerness with which he had solicited her favour for the tourney; of the way he had rushed to her side in the palace great hall. Sir Olier had been desperate to be the first to congratulate her after her singing. Elise's response had been cool. Polite. Distant. If there was a man with a place in her heart it wasn't him.

She keeps men at a distance. Why?

Gawain glanced at the bedchamber door. He

hadn't thought to check, but when he'd found her in the cave he didn't recollect seeing Sir Olier's ring on her finger. Yet clearly she'd been wearing this necklace. It had to be of great significance.

Last winter, the warmth that had flared between them had felt so real. He ran his thumb over the tiny white petals. Blanchefleur. She'd been wearing this then, but he hadn't appreciated what it meant. She hadn't breathed a word about her success as a singer. She'd kept that from him. He understood her reasons now. She'd been reserved because her purpose in Ravenshold had been to learn how her sister had met her death. She hadn't wanted complications, and even if she had told him about the reality of her life as a *chanteuse*, he wouldn't have appreciated the extent of her fame.

Gawain's life was military. He knew about garrisons and armouries; he knew how to man a castle and manage an estate; he knew the qualities to look for in a warhorse. Until he had heard Elise sing at the palace, he had thought her world— that of the troubadour—to be trivial, mere flummery. It hadn't seemed relevant. Witnessing the way she had transported everyone at the banquet had given him new insight.

The maidservant opened the bedchamber door.

'You may go in now, my lord, though if you ask me you shouldn't stay long.'

Gawain's lips twitched. The woman was very forward with her opinions. It was possible she disapproved of him bringing Elise to Provins Castle. But what else could he have done? He could hardly have taken her back with him to Sainte-Colombe! He merely smiled. 'Thank you. I won't be long.'

'She needs rest, my lord. That knock to her head—'

Gawain gripped the woman's arm. 'She's hurt?' Lord, he'd known she was thirsty and hungry, but they'd hit her? He felt sick at the thought.

'Not badly, my lord, but she has a lump on her head the size of an egg.'

Pressing silver into the maidservant's hand, Gawain went straight to the bedside. Elise was lying back against the pillows. 'You were hit?'

'Gawain, it's nothing.'

'Let me see.' Perching on the edge of the mattress, he drew her to a sitting position.

Her hair had been wound into a loose knot at her neck. Gently, he undid it, parting the strands to get a closer look. There was a reddened area and, yes, a definite lump. Thankfully, the skin didn't appear to have been broken. He sucked in a breath. 'That must hurt.'

The scent of her hair—familiar, womanly, with that tang of ambergris—evoked memories of large dark eyes smiling into his, of warm kisses and soft skin. Of…

'It's nothing, Gawain. I… Oh!' She caught hold of his shoulder and he found himself fixated by her mouth. Those lips…he could remember exactly how soft they had felt. How warm…

However, she wasn't looking for a kiss. She'd seen the cord of her pendant wrapped around his fist.

'You found it!' Her face lit up. 'I am so glad. I would hate to lose it.'

Easing back, Gawain held out his wrist so she could take it from him.

'I dropped it hoping that Baderon might see it,' she said.

'I saw it glinting in the sun. The cord is broken. Allow me to retie it.'

Fixing the pendant round her neck, he found himself closing his eyes as once again that tantalising scent—*Elise*—wound through his senses.

She squeezed his hand and a small thrill shot through him. 'Thank you, Gawain. This has great value to me.'

'A gift from a lover?' He kept his voice light.

'Gawain, contrary to what you seem to believe I don't have legions of lovers. You are the only man—'

His eyebrows shot up. 'I surely wasn't your first?'

'No, no. There has been another lover.'

'But there were no babies with him.' Oddly, that pleased him.

'The herbs worked well with him, which is why I assumed that there would be no issue after we… after we…' Blushing, she trailed off. 'Gawain, I want you to know that I enjoyed our time together. You have given me so much. Pearl is the greatest gift.'

He gave her a stern look. 'Pearl might have lost her mother today.'

She touched his sleeve. 'Thankfully she didn't. Gawain, I should like to see André.'

She made as if to get up, but Gawain caught her hand and gently, firmly, pushed her back against the pillows. He laced his fingers with hers and found himself staring at her hand. It was so small. And she was not wearing any rings. He bit back a smile.

'André is being taken care of. You may see

him later. You must rest first.' His eyes held hers. 'You're not wearing Sir Olier's ring.'

'No.'

'Don't you like him?' Gawain had no right to ask, but the question was out before he could stop it.

In the back of Gawain's mind a reckless plan was forming. If he saw it to fruition it would mean going back on his word. It would mean him turning his back on one duty to honour another. He would have to run the gauntlet of his aunt's disfavour; the King would have every right to question his honour; and Lady Rowena—Gawain wasn't sure how she would react. Before he took the first step, he needed to know Elise's mind.

She gave him one of her quiet smiles. 'Sir Olier has always been most generous, but it might mislead him if I were to wear his ring.'

'He has offered you marriage.' The idea of Elise marrying Sir Olier was so repellent it didn't bear thinking about, but Gawain had to know what she thought. Watching her like a hawk, he added, 'Many people would consider it a good match.'

'It would be if Sir Olier was…' She paused, as though choosing her words carefully. 'I cannot marry him.'

Gawain felt a smile begin to break and fought

to keep his expression neutral. 'He would provide you with security.'

She stared, looking at him as though he had started to speak in tongues. 'Me? Marry Sir Olier? Gawain, how can you—a count—suggest such a thing? The disparity between Sir Olier and myself is far too great. He is a knight whilst I am the illegitimate daughter of a troubadour.'

Gawain waved his hand, dispensing with her parentage and illegitimacy. 'Sir Olier doesn't see any obstacles.'

Breaking eye contact, she looked towards the window. 'I thought at first Sir Olier was not serious in his suit.' She drew in a breath and her breasts lifted. Gawain tried not to notice. 'Though of late he has renewed his suit so often and with such vigour that I am coming to believe he sees no barrier between us.'

'The man wants you. You are a very beautiful woman.'

She gave another sigh. 'Vivienne said he meant it. I didn't believe her.'

'Believe it. He wants to marry you. Elise, if he sees no barrier and you want him, there is no barrier.'

She blinked. 'That is truly your belief?'

He squeezed her hand. 'Can you doubt it?'

Her eyes were shadowed as she gazed thought-fully at him, and he wondered what she was see-ing. A man who loved her and would do what he could to win her? Or a man who belonged in her past? He burned to know.

'Elise, it would make me happy if you under-stood that I have your interests at heart.'

She simply looked at him. Gawain's heart sank. If only he could open his heart to her. He ached to tell her what was in his mind—he wanted her and Pearl in his life for all time. He wanted their relationship to be legitimate. He didn't want a shady affair. Yes, he had duties to his liege and his aunt. He also had duties to Elise and his daughter. And, provided Elise was willing, he would rank his duty to Elise and Pearl over his other duties. Unfortunately, until he was free he couldn't dis-cuss this openly with her.

'Do you want Sir Olier?' He couldn't breathe as he waited for her reply.

She tipped her head to one side and the petals of the enamel flower at her throat glinted as she moved. 'Why do you ask?'

Gawain felt his skin scorch. He hated that he wasn't free to give her a full answer. He decided to take a different approach. Briefly, he touched her pendant. 'Who gave you this?'

'No lover, I assure you. It was a gift from my father to my mother. When she married she gave it to me. She didn't want to cause trouble with Sir Corentin.'

'Sir Corentin was her husband?

A nod.

'When did your mother marry? Was this after your father's death?'

'No, no.' She gave a look he could only describe as wary. 'Mother left Father long before that.'

He waited.

'Ronan Chantier wasn't an easy man to live with.'

She bent her head, ostensibly to adjust the pendant. She was avoiding his eyes. Her cheeks were pink. With embarrassment? Shame? Gawain opened his mouth to tell her that she need never feel shame with him when her head came up.

She fiddled with the daisy. 'Father gave Mother this in the early days, when they were courting.' She shrugged. 'After that he thought only of his next performance. Mother told me once that she had never truly had his heart, that no one could truly touch him and that he wasn't fit to be a father. That was why she left him. She found a knight and married him.'

'And now? Is your mother still living?'

'I am not certain. When she married, Mother made it clear that Morwenna and I were not to contact her.'

Gawain felt his jaw drop. 'You never saw your mother after her marriage?'

She was staring at the wall, turning the daisy round and round between finger and thumb. Her head shook and a tress of hair fell across her breast. 'Shortly before Mother's marriage we were taken to the convent. That was when she gave me this pendant. She said Sir Corentin might be upset to see a reminder of her former life.'

He squeezed her hand. He didn't know what to say. Here was yet another side of her that she'd kept from him. Sad to say, the more time he spent with her, the more he was coming to see that that past winter when her beauty had ensnared him, he'd scarcely known her. 'You are a brave woman,' he murmured. Elise had had a terrible start in life and yet she was managing to make a success of it.

'Brave? Me? You must have been at the wine, my lord. Sometimes I dream my courage fails just before a performance. If I couldn't sing, I don't know what would happen to us. I fear many things. In the main I worry about Pearl.' She gave a strained laugh. 'You have helped me enormously, my lord. Your gift of the manor is more security than I ever hoped to achieve. I can't thank you enough.'

Gawain's fingers curled round hers. 'I would give you more than that, if I could.'

She tilted her head and a tress of dark hair fell over her breast. 'I don't understand. Speak plainly, Gawain. You are about to be married—are you asking me to be your mistress?'

Dark eyes watched him and not for the first time, Gawain wished he could read the thoughts behind them. If only he could ask for her hand. However, until he had freed himself from his commitments, that wasn't possible. He must content himself with giving her hints and hope that she would understand what he was trying to say. As a man of honour he could do no more. 'I would offer you the world. *Mon Dieu*, Elise, last year I was free. If you hadn't walked away without a backward look, I would never have opened marriage negotiations with Count Faramus. These things are not easy to unravel.'

Reaching up, he ran his fingertips down that shining strand of hair. His touch was light, familiar—it was the touch of a lover. He shouldn't touch her in this way until their path was clear. The trouble was he couldn't help it.

Her breathing faltered and the enamel daisy

trembled on her breast. The scent of ambergris was muddling his mind. His gaze settled on her mouth. 'So pretty,' he murmured. How was it that the longer he spent in her company the harder it was to remember that he must do the right thing? 'If…' He swallowed. *Mon Dieu*, she had moistened her lips and he was transfixed. 'Elise, if I were free, what would you do?'

Carefully, she placed the palm of her hand against his cheek. 'Lord Gawain, do you truly not know?'

He was baffled by her use of his title when they were sitting together so intimately. Was it her way of holding him at bay? A small finger ran down his nose, and he looked blankly at her. She used his title, yet a heartbeat later she was touching him as though they were lovers again. What did she want of him? A pulse of desire, deep in his veins, urged him on. He shifted and pulled her fully into his arms. 'Elise.' He nuzzled her neck, closing his eyes as he inhaled her. Elise. 'Beloved.'

Her hand slid round his neck and into his hair, sifting it so his scalp warmed. Whatever else he did, he must not kiss her. If he kissed her, he'd be lost. However, he hadn't bargained for those delicate fingers to tighten in his hair so as to align his mouth with hers.

'One kiss, Gawain,' she murmured. 'Just one.'

Their lips met, tentatively. Somehow he kept it innocent. He was hoping that if he didn't act as though they had been lovers, if he didn't act as though there was nothing that he would rather do than join with her, his body would forget it. She gave a slight murmur of frustration and then she was leaning closer, pressing her breasts fully against his chest. 'Properly, Gawain.'

Gawain groaned. She hadn't used his title. Just his name. He caught her fully in his arms and deepened the kiss. Briefly, he drew back. 'Lord, Elise, this feels so good.'

His body wasn't doing what it was supposed to be doing and Elise wasn't helping. His hand slid to cover a breast through the fabric of her gown. She moaned and pressed her body to his. She was kissing his collarbone. She dragged his tunic and chainse clear of his belt. Delicate fingertips trailed fire along his back.

'Elise.' His voice was hoarse. He was actually panting, hot and aching with need and frustration. He had yearned for her for too long. His tunic and chainse were dragged off him, by him or by her he could not say. His mind was a mind divided. He had to have her. He couldn't have her. He wasn't sure what to do about Lady Rowena, never mind the assurances he had given to Count Faramus and the King. And add to that the fact that Elise had given birth recently—Gawain wasn't certain how soon a woman might be approached after childbirth.

With a shaky laugh she fell back against the pillows. He followed, groaning. This was torment. This was delight. He must be careful. Much as he wanted her, he would simply caress her. Her hands were busy smoothing the skin of his back and chest, making him throb and ache. He pressed against her thigh and she stroked his cheek. The slight smile as she touched his nose almost undid him.

'I adore your nose.'

She plunged her fingers deep into his hair. The flower at her breast trembled.

They kissed and her moan was an echo of his. Holding her head, he looked into her eyes as she shifted beneath him. Her breasts were straining against the fabric of her gown. They were distracting. Tempting. Her bodice was laced from neck to waist and fastened with a bow. Gawain worked at the lacings to undo her gown and inch by inch, more glorious womanly curves were revealed. His mouth went dry. She arched up, nibbling his ear. Her breath was warm and flurried as he succeeded in teasing the fabric apart and covered a breast with his palm. Her breath caught in a sound that was halfway to a sob. He caressed first one breast, then the other. This was torment and he wanted more. The voice in the back of his mind, the voice that urged caution, was becoming very faint.

'So womanly,' he murmured, cupping a breast. Her eyes shone into his. 'So beautiful.'

Somehow, the coverlet was gone. She lay half under him. Their legs were entwined and she was rubbing her foot up and down his calf. Her hands were gripping his buttocks, holding him to her, scattering what was left of his wits to the four winds. He was nothing but want.

Drawing up her gown, he sighed his pleasure against her neck. His fingertips skimmed over the warm skin of her thigh. Up to her waist. He burned with need.

She stopped caressing his buttocks. She was wrestling with his hose, stroking him through the fabric. He sucked in a breath.

'Have a care, beloved.'

Soft brown eyes smiled into his.

'Gawain,' she said, huskily. And again, 'Gawain.'

He pressed his lips to her cheek, her temple, her brow—dotting her face with kisses. He was moving down towards her breasts when a change of atmosphere gave him pause. Her body was no longer soft and pliant beneath him, but stiff and unyielding.

Elise tugged on a lock of sun-streaked hair. 'Gawain?'

'Beloved?'

'This is wrong.'

Gawain stared blankly at her. Dazed with want, his mind refused to accept what she was saying.

'We shouldn't be doing this. Gawain, I am sorry. I don't know what came over me.' Easing out from under him, she sat up and bent her head over the lacing of her gown.

Gawain grimaced. He was throbbing with need and rather surprised at the speed with which he had lost himself. 'You are right, of course. My apologies.' Hauling himself off the bed, he padded uncomfortably over to the ale jug. He heard the creaking on the landing at the same time as Elise.

Wide brown eyes met his. 'Gawain, the door! Someone's outside.'

The latch clicked and Lady Rowena de Sainte-Colombe walked in.

Chapter Thirteen

Elise blinked. She wanted to die. Lady Rowena!

Gawain's fiancée froze on the threshold with her jaw open. Slowly she closed her mouth and stepped into the bedchamber. Elise heard herself groan.

Lady Rowena ignored her. She looked at her betrothed, a gold cross glinting at her neck. 'Good morning, my lord,' she said, calmly. 'I heard that your friends had suffered with an accident and wondered if I might be of assistance.'

Hot-faced, Elise tied the bow on her lacing. She had never felt so small. What could she say? *I am sorry, my lady, this isn't what it seems.*

Except it was. It was exactly as it seemed. Elise hadn't been able to keep her hands off Gawain last winter. She had returned to Troyes to find him betrothed to the woman standing near the door with that cool expression on her face and nothing had changed. She still couldn't keep her hands off him. Heavens, what had she done?

It struck her that Lady Rowena might appear calm, but she was rather too pointedly avoiding looking at Gawain's naked chest. It was such a beautiful chest. Wasn't she the least bit curious to see his body?

Guilt went through her like a lance. *What have I done?*

Elise swung off the bed, conscious that Lady Rowena's eyes hadn't flickered in her direction. It was almost as though she couldn't see her. Lady Rowena didn't want to see her. She was pretending Elise was not there.

Thank goodness she and Gawain had come to their senses. Otherwise Lady Rowena would be staring at them *in flagrante*. Briefly, Elise closed her eyes. *Gawain must want to kill me.* She bit her lip. This was her fault. She'd asked him to kiss her. He would surely hate her.

Gawain set down his ale and reached for his chainse. Elise found herself cursing the feelings he engendered in her. She of all people should know better. She did know better, but once again she had allowed herself to be carried away. Only this time it was worse, because last year he had not been betrothed. He shot her a dark look and went to take Lady Rowena's hand.

Elise struggled to recall what it was that he had said that had prompted her to fall into his arms so easily. *'I would give you the world if I could.'* She looked at his broad back, aching to wind her arms about him, and wondered. Had that been a lie? It could hardly be otherwise, particularly since he hadn't actually said his marriage with Lady Rowena wasn't going ahead. No, he hadn't said that.

She massaged her temple. Her head was throbbing and it wasn't simply due to the knock on her head. *'These things aren't easy to unravel.'* He'd said that too.

He'd been warning her. And she, blinded by love and want, hadn't understood what he'd been saying. Gawain and Elise had no future. Yes, he'd given her a manor, but that was the end of it.

When Gawain's blond head bent over Lady Rowena's hand, Elise's heart felt as though it would break. Glancing over his shoulder, he inclined his head at her.

'*Madame*, if you will excuse us, I have matters to discuss with Lady Rowena. May I suggest that you rest awhile longer before going to find André?'

Throat tight, Elise nodded.

The latch lifted, the door sighed and she was alone.

Elise sank back on to the bed. She felt as insignificant as an ant. She'd read too much into his words—it had been wishful thinking on her part. Why would Gawain want to marry her? She had nothing to offer a man like Gawain except her body. Well, he'd given her a manor. That, at least, she could be thankful for. She and Pearl would never starve.

She fingered the enamel daisy, twisting it round on the cord, and sighed. Lady Rowena's cool reaction to walking in on them was puzzling. If Elise had been in her shoes she would have flung the ale in Gawain's face. What was wrong with the woman? Was she blind? Or did she simply not care? Did she have no pride?

Elise's head was really throbbing. Wincing, she explored the lump on her skull and wondered how long her headache would last. She had no right to be upset about Lady Rowena. She set her teeth and scowled at the door. *I should know better.* Next time, she would. There would be no more kisses. Not one.

* * *

At the foot of the spiral stairs, Gawain offered Lady Rowena his arm. He fully expected her to reject it, but after the briefest of hesitations, long white fingers were laid on his arm.

'My lady, I should like to talk privately with you. May I suggest the chapel?'

She nodded and her veil shifted. 'Of course, my lord.'

They passed along a stone passageway with Gawain bracing himself for a difficult conversation. Save for the rustle of Lady Rowena's skirts and the pad of their feet, there was little sound in this part of the castle. In the distance he could hear the chatter of servants; the laughter of the men-at-arms; the banging of a hammer.

The chapel must have been designed purely for the use of Count Henry and his immediate family. It was small and built to the old Roman design with chunky pillars and stone seats set into the walls. The sanctuary light flickered behind the altar, a *prie-dieu* stood before it.

Lady Rowena genuflected before the altar and crossed herself. Gawain escorted her to a cushioned seat.

'My lady, I am sorry that you should have witnessed that. It was not well done of me.'

Lady Rowena gave him a candid look. 'You hoped to keep your liaison a secret?'

He grimaced. 'It is not a liaison.'

Her eyebrows shot up. 'It certainly looked that way.'

'Elise and I have…history. It was never my intention to shame you in such a way and I can only apologise.'

Her sigh was loud in the quiet. 'You love her?'

Gawain felt himself go still. 'That is between Elise and myself.' *Yes, I love her.*

Lady Rowena gave him a quiet smile. 'In Troyes I couldn't help but notice that Blanchefleur le Fay has many admirers.'

'That is true.'

'But you hold a special place in her heart?'

'I thought so, once.'

'How long have you known her?'

'My lady, you should know that when your father and I opened negotiations for our betrothal, I thought Elise had gone from my life. It stunned me to see her in Troyes again.' The image of Pearl leaped into his mind, but Gawain held his tongue. He wasn't going to discuss Pearl with Lady Rowena. It simply wasn't fitting.

Lady Rowena folded her hands neatly in her lap. 'Lord Gawain, I am not naïve. Marriages among the nobility are made for dynastic reasons—to strengthen ties such as the one that exists between my family and yours.' A hint of a smile lifted the edges of her mouth. 'I understand that noblemen—and sometimes noblewomen—take lovers. I make no judgements. I think you should know that I can accept anything as long as I know exactly where I stand.' Her eyes met his directly. 'I want the truth. I should like to know whether you plan to continue with this liaison.'

Gawain stood up abruptly and found himself staring at the cross on the altar. 'That would be wrong. It would be a sin.'

'Knowing it was a sin would not stop many men.'

'It would be wrong,' he repeated, turning back to face her. 'My lady, I am not sure I understand you correctly.' He smiled, watching for her reaction. 'I too like to be sure of my ground. Tell me, are you saying that if we were married you would condone my having a liaison with Elise Chantier?'

Her head dipped. 'It is not ideal, Lord Gawain.' She shrugged. 'I am a realist. If you are prepared to deal kindly with me, I am prepared to turn a blind eye on your liaison with Elise Chantier.'

Gawain felt a frown form. 'I need heirs. Legitimate heirs.' Again Pearl leaped into his mind and his gut clenched. Lord, he really was in the briars. Cutting himself free wasn't going to be easy.

'I shall give you heirs, my lord. As long as you treat me with every courtesy, I see no reason why we should not have a happy marriage.'

'Happy?' Gawain stared at his betrothed and shook his head.

Briefly, her cool blue gaze was uncertain. 'Why not? I like you, Lord Gawain, and I have to tell you that is beyond my expectations.'

Her attention fastened on the sanctuary light, and in a flash of insight Gawain knew that Lady Rowena's calmness was assumed. There was more that she was not saying.

She drew in a breath. 'You don't love me and I think we both know I don't love you. Love, or the lack of it, need not signify. Liking should be sufficient. We have both been brought up to do our duty. I can assure you I shall never take a lover. You will never have to worry about me trying to foist a cuckoo child on you.'

Puzzled, Gawain came back to the wall seat and sat next to her. 'You are an extraordinary woman. How can you know that you'll never want a lover? You might fall in love.'

Slowly, she shook her head, and her gaze went

past him and fixed on the cross on the altar. 'That will not happen.'

'How can you know?'

Her veil shifted. 'I know.'

Gawain looked narrowly at her. 'I was told you are seventeen years of age, yet today you strike me as having lived a deal longer than that. There is...' He struggled to give voice to the awareness that was forming in his mind. 'There is an authority about you that is remarkable in one so young.'

She let out a shaky laugh. 'Thank you. I think.'

'And now to the meat of the matter. Lady Rowena, I have a suggestion to put to you.' He rubbed his brow. After hearing Lady Rowena's views on marriage, Gawain was convinced he was doing the right thing. Having found Elise again he wasn't about to lose her a second time. A passionless duty marriage wasn't for him. 'When I entered this chapel I feared that you might not like my suggestion. I am no longer sure what you will think, although I am beginning to suspect that it might bring you happiness.'

Lady Rowena arched an eyebrow at him. 'You intrigue me, my lord. Pray continue.'

'I agreed to our betrothal in the best interests of Meaux and Sainte-Colombe. My lady, I have to tell you that I have changed my mind.'

'You wish to be break with our betrothal?'

'Yes, I do.' Gawain found himself clenching his fist while he waited for her response. 'Well? What do you say?'

After André returned to consciousness, he recovered quickly. By suppertime, Elise was relieved to find that he was well enough to accompany her to the great hall.

Count Henry's servants and retainers had taken the lower tables. The boards were spread with cream cloths and someone had thought to place jugs of flowers at intervals along them. Roses and lilies. It was an unexpectedly homely touch in a castle this size. Candle flames fluttered in stands and on wall sconces. There were flowers on the top table too. There weren't as many people jammed on to the benches up there, just a handful of noblemen: Count Henry's steward; his senior knights and their ladies. An array of arms hung on the walls—shields, lances, swords. Knights' banners were displayed in stands at either end of the hall.

Elise picked one of the quieter tables and went to sit at the end of a bench. For herself, she didn't expect any fanfare. Tonight she wasn't Blanchefleur le Fay, she was simply Elise Chantier, a guest of

Count Henry. She looked André over. He looked remarkably well considering his recent ordeal. 'How long did they keep you in the cellar?'

André shrugged and leaned forward to skewer a chicken leg. 'Lord, I have no idea. Two days? Three? It might have been longer. I lost all sense of time.' He dropped the chicken on to their trencher and as he did so, his sleeve fell back. There were rope burns on his wrist.

Elise smothered a gasp and lightly touched his wrist. 'Did they beat you? They didn't touch your hands, did they?'

His mouth turned down. 'They didn't touch my hands, but they took great pleasure in smashing my lute.'

'Oh, André, the devils.'

He shot her a rueful look. 'Elise, it was my fault. I shouldn't have had dealings with them in the first place.'

'Well said, lad.' The voice came from behind them. *Gawain.*

Elise turned and frowned at him. 'Gawain, his lute! How is he to play without one?'

There was a small space left next to Elise. It was surely only large enough for a child. None the less, Gawain gestured at it. 'May I?'

Elise scooted along the bench to make room and

then Gawain's thigh was warm against hers. Remembering what they had been doing in the bedchamber, she felt her cheeks flush. 'Should you be here, next to me?' she asked quietly. What would Lady Rowena think? To her horror, Gawain's hand ran down her thigh in a surreptitious caress and a bolt of longing shot through her. She shook her head at him, wondering how it was that she could like the man, for like him she undoubtedly did. 'I shouldn't like you. You are a complete brute.' The words she could never say shrieked through her mind. *I love you, Gawain. Why it is I couldn't say, but I love you.*

Gawain's eyes danced and for a horrible moment she thought he could actually read her mind. Another illicit caress stroked fire down her leg. 'I can't stay long,' he said. 'I'm returning to Sainte-Colombe with Lady Rowena this evening and I wanted to speak to you before I left. Do you have everything you need for tonight? André?'

'Yes, thank you, my lord.'

Gawain looked her way. 'Elise?'

'I have more than I need, Lord Gawain.' *Except you.* Tears burned at the back of her eyes. He was a brute. She loved him.

'Good. I've arranged to escort you both back to Troyes when I have finished my business with

Count Faramus. I hope we shall be able to leave some time tomorrow.'

Elise blinked. 'You are to be our escort, my lord?'

He gave her an odd look. 'Who else? Unfortunately, I shall have to leave again almost immediately and the house in La Rue du Cloître won't be available for much longer. I think it best if you remove to the manor as soon as possible.' A dark eyebrow lifted. 'Are you in agreement?'

Elise made an exasperated sound. She simply didn't understand him. 'As you wish, my lord.' Elise wasn't sure she would stay long at the manor—life there would be very different to life on the road—but whilst the babies were young she couldn't deny it would be useful.

Gawain turned back to André. 'Since I can't stay long in Troyes, I hope I may rely on you to see that Elise and Pearl settle in at the manor.'

Elise had already told André about her manor, so he took this request in his stride. 'Yes, *mon seigneur.*'

'My thanks,' Gawain spoke softly. 'I don't like to think of Elise being without her friends. It would relieve my mind if you and your lady took up residence with her.'

'Thank you, Lord Gawain, you are more than generous.'

Gawain shook his head at André, eyes serious. 'I am not so generous that I do not expect something in return.'

André looked warily at him. 'My lord?'

'I overheard you talking just now. Do I take it you have seen the error of your ways?'

André frowned at the platter of chicken in the centre of the table and cleared his throat. 'You're going to report me to Sir Raphael.'

Gawain made a dismissive gesture. 'Not necessarily. Are you ready to make amends?'

'Mon seigneur?'

'I want you to go to Sir Raphael yourself. Make a clean breast of things. Tell him all you know about the counterfeiters.'

'My lord!' Elise gripped Gawain's sleeve before she remembered herself and quickly loosed it again. 'You can't ask him to do that—the Guardians will arrest him. He'll be locked away. He might be hanged!'

Dark eyes met hers. 'Elise, Count Henry and Captain Raphael are reasonable men. They will take André's youth into account. If he gives them a full explanation, they will soon see he got in over his head. All he has to do is be open with them. I'm certain he'll be granted a pardon.'

André reached for his wine and gulped it down. 'My lord, I…I am not sure where to begin.'

'You might begin by telling the captain what the sword was doing in your possession in the first place,' Gawain said, in a low voice.

'I was keeping it for Jerome.'

Elise touched André's arm. 'What about the players? You mentioned a troupe of players.'

'The players,' André muttered, avoiding her gaze. 'The sword was made in Toulouse, the players brought it from the south and I was to hand it to Jerome when he came to Troyes. He was booked to bring a consignment of wine to Count Henry's court.'

'The players and Jerome are part of a network?' Gawain asked.

'Aye.' André's face was full of anguish. 'My lord, I was only meant to be passing the sword on to Jerome. I couldn't see much wrong in that.'

Gawain gave a swift head shake. 'You were to be paid for this service?'

'Yes, my lord.'

'They were using you as a middleman. You must have known it was wrong.'

'I am truly sorry. *Mon siegneur*, I had no idea how…how ruthless they are. Jerome in particular.'

'He's the gang leader?'

'I believe so. When I came to Provins and told him I'd lost the sword, he was like a madman. Said I'd destroyed years of work and he would have his revenge.' André drew a shaky breath and he glanced at Elise. 'It doesn't surprise me that he struck Elise when she came in search of me. That man will do anything to protect his interests.'

Gawain glanced briefly at Elise. 'Never fear, I protect my interests too. You have my word you will both be quite safe. André, I will speak for you. Most men have done things in their youth that they regret. I am sure you will find yourself forgiven. Make a clean breast of it and you can live your life with your head held high. If not, you'll be jumping at shadows for the rest of your life. I imagine that might make life as a troubadour something of a challenge. You may be interested to learn that after we brought you out, the Provins Guard scoured the cellars for evidence. They've found nothing. Any evidence has been removed.' He looked meaningfully at André. 'The Guardians need your testimony.'

Gawain eased himself off the bench and squeezed André's shoulder. 'Think about it. Think about that woman of yours. That son. I am sure you will come to the right decision.' Dark, glittering eyes smiled briefly at Elise. He bowed his head and golden firelight gleamed in his hair. '*Madame*, I bid you *au revoir*. Until tomorrow.'

Shortly after breakfast, Elise and André took up a position by the mounting block near the stables to wait for Gawain. They weren't there long, for Gawain proved as good as his word and the bailey was soon ringing with the sound of trotting hoofs as his troop poured into the yard. One of his men had a couple of spare horses on leading reins.

Gawain dismounted and gestured for the trooper to bring the two horses across. One was a pretty grey mare, the other a larger-boned chestnut gelding.

Gawain saw Elise looking them over and checked. 'Lord, Elise, I never thought to ask—can you ride?'

Elise smiled sadly. Gawain's hesitancy was a humbling reminder of the difference in their status. Gawain wouldn't dream of asking Lady Rowena if she could ride. A lady would have been in the saddle practically from birth. Whereas she, the illegitimate daughter of a troubadour and his *belle-amie*…

'I am no great horsewoman, but, yes, I can ride. Actually it will be a relief to have my own mount. I practically roasted on the way here.'

'Oh?'

'I sat behind Baderon.'

'I assumed you would have hired a horse.'

Elise simply smiled and shook her head.

'You have the money now,' Gawain muttered. 'You will have the revenues from the manor.'

'I…I hadn't thought of that.'

'Elise, you can stop worrying about money.' His mouth relaxed into a smile. 'It will take some getting used to, I imagine.'

He turned to André. 'I take it you can ride?'

'Yes, *mon seigneur.*'

Elise and André had little in the way of baggage. Gawain made a point of checking their girths and saddles personally and they were soon riding through the gates of Provins. Rather to her surprise, Elise found herself at the head of their party, alongside Gawain.

'My lord, should I be riding at your side?'

A muscle pulsed in his jaw. 'It is my wish that you ride with me.'

Elise drew her brows together. She wasn't sure about the wisdom of riding next to him so openly. Was it seemly? Was it right? A number of other questions rolled about at the back of her mind. Had Gawain concluded his negotiations with Lord Faramus? She pushed that one to the side—she might long to know how matters stood with Lady Rowena after that disastrous episode yesterday, but Gawain's relationship with his betrothed was not her business. Still, if he wanted it she would ride at his side today. This might be one of her last chances of talking to him and she must make the most of it.

She found a question that seemed safe enough. 'I take it Count Faramus loaned you this horse?'

Gawain nodded, and then Elise realised her question hadn't been safe at all—it led to a whole raft of other questions. Did Count Faramus know that Gawain wanted the horses for his…what was she to him? His discarded mistress? The mother of his firstborn child? A woman with whom he hoped to renew an illicit love affair?

I will not become his mistress. I will not. The good sisters at the convent had failed to turn Elise into a nun, but they had instilled in her a horror of the idea of stealing another woman's husband. Her relationship with Gawain must change. It should change now. Eyes prickling, she made a show of adjusting the fall of her skirts to hide her legs. She shouldn't really be talking to him.

'There's no sign of the heat relenting,' Gawain said.

'No.' Elise went on twitching her skirts, conscious of his gaze on her. When she looked up, she kept her gaze firmly on a dust cloud that was being kicked up by a train of mules ahead.

'You ride well,' he said.

'Father taught me. It was after I left the convent. He said riding was a necessary accomplishment if we were to spend so much time on the road.'

'You keep no horses though. They are too costly, I suppose.'

She nodded. 'We have a mule and a cart. Vivienne dislikes riding. And now we have the babies a cart is essential. Occasionally André and I hire horses.'

'You'll find horses at the manor. As I recall, there's a mare there that would suit you very well.'

She felt her eyes go round. 'You are giving us horses too?'

'I am giving *you* horses.' He shrugged. 'You will need them when you ride out with Sir Bertran to inspect your land.'

Slowly, Elise shook her head. She had a manor with revenues. She was rich. She had horses. A home. 'My lord—'

'Gawain,' he muttered. 'It would please me if you would call me by my Christian name.'

'Very well. Gawain.' She fiddled with the reins and tried to ignore a rush of longing that had her eyes misting with tears.

She heard him sigh. 'Elise? What is it?'

She stared at her reins. She wanted to ask him if Lady Rowena minded that he was personally escorting her to Troyes, but she couldn't ask that. She wanted to tell him that she loved him, but she couldn't do that either. Blinking hard, she glanced across and her eyes seemed to drink him in. His tall, broad-shouldered body was completely at home on the back of his destrier. He turned slightly towards her. His manner appeared warm, affectionate even. The summer sun had brightened his hair to the colour of ripe wheat and his eyes shone down at her, dark and mysterious and as fascinating as ever. Today his eyes were unfathomable and somehow at variance with his smile, which had an openness about it that was achingly dear. Her gaze settled on the long fingers loosely holding the reins. Yesterday those fingers had sent fire streaking through her.

She inhaled slowly and couldn't help but notice how the movement of her chest drew his gaze to her breasts. Gawain, Count of Meaux, was not hers. He never would be. And if she were to judge by the expression on his face—there was no denying the flash of hunger in his eyes—it was up to her to maintain a seemly distance between them. No less a person than the King was promoting his marriage. For Gawain's sake, she must never place herself in a position where he would be tempted to take advantage of her. There must be no repeats of that shameful incident of yesterday.

She wound the reins round her forefinger, unwound them and started all over again—winding, unwinding, winding. 'My l—Gawain.' With a swift glance behind her, she lowered her voice. 'I should like to ask you about André. I am worried about what will happen when he goes to Sir Raphael.'

'I have told you that I will speak up on his behalf.'

'Thank you. I only pray that you are right when you say he will be judged with compassion.'

Leather creaked and Gawain's hand closed on hers. 'Do not fear for him. Count Henry and Captain Raphael are bound to see, as I see, that there is no evil in the lad.' Broad shoulders lifted. 'He is young. He made an error of judgement.'

Gawain's words echoed through her mind, and Elise stared thoughtfully at the hand on hers. 'You said something similar yesterday.'

He looked blankly at her. 'Did I?'

'In the hall at suppertime, you said most men had done things in their youth that they came to regret.'

Again, he shrugged. 'What of it?'

'Were you thinking of yourself when you said that? Is there something in your past you regret?'

His hand withdrew and he shifted in the saddle. 'I have many regrets.'

His smile was crooked. It made Elise wonder if Gawain numbered her among his regrets. She didn't want him to regret his liaison with her. True, it had brought her pain when they had separated, but it had also brought her Pearl. Their time together had brought great joy, and—albeit briefly—she had experienced the sense that she and Gawain were bound together, that they were family. It was rare for Elise to feel that. The closest she'd ever come to feeling anything like it had been with her sister, Morwenna.

Her mother and father hadn't had room in their lives for their daughters. She and Morwenna had been carted off to the convent as soon as they had become *de trop*. After leaving the convent and finding her father again, Elise had been desperate to stay with him. She had wanted a home for her and Morwenna. She had fought to win her father's love—why, she'd learned to sing in hope of winning his affection. Ronan had been pleased with her as a *chanteuse*, but Elise had never felt there was a real bond between her and her father. Certainly nothing like the bond she'd felt with Gawain. That had been breathtaking. Instant.

'How about you?' he was asking. 'What's your biggest regret?'

'Leaving Ravenshold—and you—at the turn of the year.'

A muscle twitched in Gawain's cheek. 'Truly?'

'Truly.' Elise let out an airy laugh, guiltily aware that she should not have admitted as much. He wouldn't want to know. She rushed on. 'Now it's your turn. Your remark about youthful regrets has aroused my curiosity. What did you do in your youth that you regret?'

Somewhere a church bell was ringing. The rooks were cawing in a nearby stand of trees, just as they'd been cawing in the woods around Ravenshold when they had become lovers. Gawain looked steadily ahead. Elise was beginning to fear that he thought her question impertinent when he let out a large sigh.

'I have many regrets,' he said softly. 'And if you want one that has shaped my life, I have to mention my cousin, Lunette de Meaux.'

'Your uncle's daughter.'

'Aye. As a boy I never expected to inherit my uncle's county. My father was his younger brother. Father did have the manor near Troyes and I thought myself lucky—in time it would be mine. Many second sons inherit nothing. However, my father and uncle were close, and when it became clear that my uncle would have no male heir, they applied for a dispensation so that Lunette and I could be married.' Dark eyes looked across at her. 'It was their way of keeping my uncle's land in the family.'

Elise nodded. Such arrangements were common. 'What happened?'

'I loved Lunette as a sister. We were both young and I trusted that in time I would love her as my wife.' His mouth was unhappy.

'Gawain.' Reaching across, Elise lightly touched his sleeve. 'Tell me. You married her?'

He gave a curt head shake. 'There was an accident shortly before the wedding. Lunette died.'

His expression was bleak. 'It was my fault—a sin of omission, if you like. I killed my cousin.'

Elise caught her breath. How could that be? Gawain was the soul of honour. 'Gawain, that can't be true, Lunette's death cannot have been your fault.'

'Believe it.' His voice was bitter, his eyes bleak. 'My uncle certainly did. We were riding. Lunette's saddle had a faulty girth. I should have checked it before we set out. We were racing along the riverbank and her horse stumbled. The girth snapped.'

'She was thrown?'

'Aye. She was killed instantly.'

'Gawain, I am so sorry.'

He heaved in a breath. 'It's ancient history. Suffice to say that Lunette's death caused a rift in the family. It never healed. My father took my part—'

'I should think that he did!'

'Well, that's as may be, but my uncle refused to accept any apology. And it was my fault—I should have checked that girth.'

'How old were you when this happened? How old was Lunette?'

'We were fourteen.'

'At that age your cousin should have known to check her own saddle. You were not to blame,' Elise said firmly. She recalled how carefully

Gawain had checked her saddle and harness earlier in the bailey of Provins Castle. Gawain was careful in all things, responsible in all things. Lunette's death had made him the man he was. Sensing that it might not be the moment to point this out to him, she said nothing.

'A sin of omission is still a sin,' he was saying, grimly. 'And it galls me to know how my uncle will be turning in his grave to see me inheriting his county.' A muscle ticked in his jaw. 'It galls me very much. That is why I considered that marrying Lady Rowena was perhaps the best course. At least in that one thing I could please him.'

Gawain had used the word 'considered'. Elise's stomach swooped. It was as though he was speaking in the past tense. Had he changed his mind about marrying Lady Rowena? She found herself staring at her horse's mane. 'Oh?'

'My uncle favoured the marriage,' he said, bluntly. 'Lord Faramus was his friend and ally.'

She cleared her throat. 'I understand the King is promoting the match.'

Gawain grunted and frowned.

Elise fiddled with her reins. Behind them, André was talking to one of Gawain's men. She could hear his every word, which likely meant that the entire troop could hear what she was saying to their lord. It really wasn't the place for intimate conversation, particularly when it was veering on to shaky ground.

Had Gawain changed his mind about marrying Lady Rowena? It was possible, but it would be beyond impertinent for her to ask him. And she must be realistic. Even if he had changed his mind about Lady Rowena, Elise Chantier would never be his match. The Count of Meaux would never marry a *chanteuse*. Just because he had given her his father's manor did not mean he would consider marrying someone of such low birth. He'd been driven by duty when he'd given her the manor. He took his responsibilities as a father seriously and he wanted to provide for his daughter. It meant no more than that.

She mustn't delude herself. As yesterday had so embarrassingly proved, passion was alive between them, but passion alone was not enough. Gawain might have feelings for her, indeed after yesterday both she and Lady Rowena knew beyond doubt that he did, but they were carnal feelings. Carnal feelings and marriage did not necessarily go together. Did Gawain love her at a deeper level? Could he love her? She couldn't ask that either.

Lunette's death had made Gawain conscious of his responsibilities, but that was not all. It had taught him to guard his feelings. Elise had known him as a friend and a lover, but this was the first time he had mentioned Lunette and the pain and guilt her death had brought him. He kept his emotions to himself.

When Elise had learned that Gawain had inherited a county, she had thought only of his good fortune. Sir Gawain Steward had become the Count of Meaux! But it wasn't that simple. Gawain viewed his inheritance with mixed feelings. Guilt over Lunette's death and the ensuing family rift weighed heavily on his conscience. Overscrupulous to a fault, Gawain was shouldering the blame for the mistakes of others. Lunette forgot to check her girth and in time his uncle should have accepted this.

'Your uncle was wrong to blame you for your cousin's death,' she said softly. 'I can see how distraught he must have been after the accident, but I believe that over time he must have come to forgive you.'

Gawain looked sharply at her. 'How so? After the funeral he and my father never spoke again. I was never summoned to Meaux.'

'Your uncle forgave you. Surely he was involved in negotiating your betrothal with Lady Rowena?'

'So I've been told, but I didn't learn about the

negotiations until after his death. Why did he never contact me himself?'

'Your uncle was clearly a proud and determined man, otherwise the rift between him and your father would soon have been bridged. Such a man might find it hard to approach you. Is there someone at Meaux you could speak to? Someone who would know your uncle's mind before he died? It might set your mind at rest.'

Gawain's expression was thoughtful. 'I could speak to my aunt—my uncle's widow, Lady Una. She's entered a convent in Paris. I adored her as a child.' He grimaced. 'I must confess I cannot imagine her taking the veil. She was the liveliest of women. Anyone less suited to convent life would be hard to find. I shall visit her and see how she is faring.'

Elise smiled. 'I am sure Lady Una would like that.'

Chapter Fourteen

The walls of Troyes had just come into view and instead of heading directly for the Preize Gate, Gawain kept The Beast on the road that led to his manor. He should have anticipated what would happen.

Elise gestured towards the gate, a furrow in her brow. 'Gawain? What about Pearl and Vivienne? They are coming with us?'

'I shall send for them shortly,' Gawain spoke curtly.

The worries of the past few days were flooding into his mind. He hadn't realised how unsettled he would feel until he'd seen the town walls. Elise's safety was his main concern. Jerome appeared to have fled Provins, but he might have come to Troyes. Until Gawain had seen the city on the horizon, he'd assumed it would be easy leaving Elise in the care of Sergeant Gaston whilst he went to

Paris. Unfortunately, he couldn't stop thinking what might go wrong. What would Jerome do if he was in Troyes and he saw Elise? From what André had said, it was clear Jerome saw her as a troublemaker. Jerome wanted her silenced and he was ruthless enough to try anything.

And it wasn't simply Elise's safety that was at issue here. What about Pearl? Icy fingers ran down his spine. The word 'kidnap' leapt into his brain. If the fraudsters found out that Pearl was his daughter they might…

'Captain?'

'Mon seigneur?'

'Take four horse soldiers and go straight to La Rue du Cloître. You'll find Sergeant Gaston on guard outside one of the houses. Enquire after Vivienne—she's a nursing mother presently lodging in the house. Escort her and the babies—there are two of them—to the manor.'

'At once, my lord.'

The captain wheeled his horse about and Gawain turned to Elise. 'Satisfied?'

A line deepened on her brow. 'I thought we were going to meet them at the house and go to the manor together.'

'You thought wrong.' Gawain didn't want to worry her, but it might be best if she was brought to see some of the dangers. Elise was staring mutinously after the captain. A blind man could see that she was within a hair's breadth of spurring after him. She took no heed of herself—she must be made to see her worth. Gawain reached for her reins. 'I wouldn't if I were you.'

She looked at him, all innocence. 'My lord?'

Gawain brought her mare close to The Beast and his knee bumped hers. He glanced pointedly at his hand on her reins. 'Think. What would it look like if we rode into town with an entire troop at our heels? It would draw all eyes. The men would have to wait outside with the horses whilst André was reunited with Vivienne, you would start fussing over Pearl—it would likely take hours.'

Some of the anger left her face. 'It would be a circus.'

'Precisely. All Troyes would know that you had returned. Elise, I am concerned for your safety and the sooner you are behind the manor walls, the better I will feel.' She opened her mouth and Gawain swept on regardless. 'It's not only your safety that concerns me, André too might be at risk. My aim is to get both of you to the manor, where you will be safe.' Releasing her reins, he ran his finger down her cheek. 'La Manoir des Rosières has curtain walls and a dry ditch. It's easier to guard than the house in La Rue du Cloître.'

Her face clouded. 'You're locking us up? I thought the manor was mine, yet you speak of your men guarding it? Gawain, why leave your men behind if the manor is truly mine?'

'The manor *is* yours. My men aren't guarding you—I'll be leaving them with you to help you settle in.'

She searched his face. 'There's something else, isn't there? What are you not saying?'

Mind in turmoil, Gawain kicked The Beast into a walk and they continued down the road in the direction of the manor. André and what was left of his troop snaked along behind them. What else could he say? He didn't want her seriously alarmed.

Briefly, it occurred to Gawain to mention his petition to the King—it might act as a means of distracting her from his concerns over her well-being. Swiftly, he dismissed the idea. In all honour, there was nothing he could say until after he had spoken to the King. After that—well, the outcome was as yet unknown. What he did know was that he had to be sure Elise and Pearl were protected. He wanted that as he had wanted nothing else in his life.

Sad to say, there were no guarantees. Elise was a free woman. While he was in Paris, she might decide she missed being Blanchefleur le Fay. She might decide to pack up the purple pavilion and take to the road. Summer was the best season for singing and it was in her blood. She might even— his hand curled into a fist—accept Sir Olier's offer of marriage.

His stomach felt hollow. He could return to the manor only to find that Elise and Pearl had vanished from his life. How could he protect them then? He loved them. He would do all in his power to protect them. Years ago, he had failed to protect Lunette—he would not fail now.

What had she just said? *You are locking me up.* The words had a peculiar resonance. *You are locking me up.* He hid a smile. In a thousand lifetimes, such a thought would never have crossed his mind. However, since it had…

'Gawain, what are you not telling me?'

Mind working, he struggled to keep his expression bland. Elise was nothing if not tenacious and if she agreed to marry him, she would lead him a merry dance. She would soon learn that he was equally tenacious. She had walked away from him once and that wasn't going to happen again. He would protect her. The question was, how best to ensure that she stayed safely at the manor until he returned?

You are locking me up.

Gawain's thoughts took an unexpected turn and he found himself thinking about King Henry of England. The world knew that King Henry and his Queen had a turbulent relationship. They quarrelled often. Queen Eleanor was rebellious and disloyal. Recently, she had sided with her sons against her husband. The word 'treason' had been bandied about. Of course, Gawain wouldn't dream of comparing his relationship with Elise to that of King Henry and Queen Eleanor's. For a start, he and Elise weren't married. Yet. And whilst he and Elise didn't always see eye to eye, Elise didn't have a disloyal bone in her body. However, the King's method of restraining his queen had caught everyone's interest. King Henry had captured his queen and imprisoned her. For almost a year no one had known where she was.

Heart thumping, Gawain glanced at Elise. His troubles were entirely different to those of King Henry's, yet the King's method of resolving his problems was strangely compelling.

Gawain wouldn't imprison Elise. Not exactly. He would simply ensure that she was safe. There would be no wandering off with Pearl whilst he was in Paris.

Unfortunately, keeping her safe was likely to require drastic measures. No matter. He had the men and the means. She would be furious with him, but far more important, she and Pearl would be safe.

Elise pushed her veil over her shoulder. Her dark eyes were watchful.

'You'll love the manor,' he said cheerfully. 'I'll show you around before I leave. You can choose a bedchamber for yourself and decide which one will suit Vivienne and André.'

She arched an eyebrow at him. 'I can choose a bedchamber? Gawain, at this moment I couldn't care less about bedchambers. You're hiding something and I want to know what it is.'

'I'm not hiding a thing.'

This was a barefaced lie. Gawain didn't like lying. However, in this case, he had no choice. He wasn't going to confess that he had decided to use King Henry's method of restraining his queen on Elise. Jerome was at large.

Sergeant Gaston would be given orders to permit Elise the run of the manor. She would be allowed to ride out around the estate, provided she took a decent escort with her for her protection.

She would *not* be allowed to go into Troyes; nor would she be allowed to take to the road again. She had to learn to look after herself. As Blanche-fleur le Fay she received accolade after accolade—she must learn Elise Chantier was equally precious. Elise's past—her mother's rejection of her and her father's lack of warmth—must haunt her still.

'Elise, I am curious about the convent. Was the regime harsh?'

She gave him a puzzled look. 'It was no worse than life in any other convent, I imagine.'

'Were the nuns cruel?'

'They were kind enough given that Morwenna and I must have been a grave disappointment to them. We showed no sign of having a calling.' She grimaced. 'I spent much of my time trying to get out of the continual penances.'

'Penances?'

'Every day we were expected to spend hours on our knees praying for forgiveness for our parents' sins.'

'Every day?' It sounded grim beyond belief. Gawain struggled to imagine what it must have been like for a sensitive young girl like Elise to have been thrust into such an environment.

'Apparently daily contemplation of one's sins is

good for the soul. As is fasting. I expect that saved money.' When Gawain looked blankly at her, at a loss for words, she added quietly, 'Our illegitimacy was a source of great shame.'

A pang of guilt shot through him. Pearl. He had given her an illegitimate child. He hadn't meant to, hadn't known, but he must have made her burden seem almost intolerable. He didn't know what to say. 'Lord, Elise, I am sorry.'

'Gawain?'

'You and I. Pearl. I am sorry. I had no idea. You must loathe me.'

Her smile was warm. 'Not at all. I broke free of guilt when I left the convent. I no longer allow it to affect me.'

Gawain wasn't sure he believed her. She might think she was free of guilt, but the daily round of penances must have clouded her view of herself. It was a miracle the nuns hadn't warped her good nature. He gripped her hand. 'Your parents' sins are not yours. Their shame is not yours.'

'So I believe. Sadly, that was not the view of the sisters.' She shrugged. 'Every day we had to list our parents' sins and pray for redemption. I did learn something useful at the convent though. I learned to sew.'

'You sew?' Sewing was a lady's occupation. It

occurred to Gawain that Elise took pride in her appearance. He'd never given it much thought, but she dressed like a lady. Admittedly, the everyday attire she wore as Elise Chantier was very different from the costumes she wore as Blanchefleur le Fay. Elise dressed with simple elegance; Blanchefleur was all show. Today Elise's gown, a pale leaf green, matched her veil. The neckline was bordered with cream embroidery in a wispy Celtic pattern; the hem of the veil bore a similar design. Both were beautifully worked.

'Embroidering altar cloths was a good way of escaping the endless ritual.' Her eyes shone, her lips curved. 'Who did you think made my clothes?'

'I...I hadn't really thought about it. I assumed Vivienne made them.'

'I enjoy sewing. It's restful.'

'It's good to think that your time at the convent was not all bad. Did your father visit you?'

Some of the light went out of her eyes and she looked swiftly away. 'He...he was too busy.'

Gawain's heart sank. After such treatment it was hard to credit how warm-hearted she was. How loyal to her friends. André and Vivienne were lucky to have her.

'You are a jewel, Elise,' he muttered. 'A jewel.'

Startled eyes met his. 'Are you feeling quite well, my lord? The heat must have got to you.'

He scowled. 'Don't do that.'

'What?'

'I paid you a compliment and you rejected it.' He was taken with the urge to drag her from her horse and kiss her senseless. He glanced swiftly at the troop behind them, caught a man's gaze and thought better of it. 'Lord, Elise, if Blanchefleur can accept compliments, why can't you?'

'I don't think I follow you, my lord.'

Gawain sighed. She was back to addressing him as 'my lord'. Holding him at arm's length again. Well, for the moment he would let her have her way. When he got back from Paris, however...

Elise saw Le Manoir des Rosières long before they reached it. The keep loomed up from behind a curtain wall, stark grey against the endless blue of the sky. At the top of the tower, a guard's spear sparked in the sun. Further down the tower Elise caught another flash of light—Lord, the window slits were glazed! Would she really be living behind glass, like a princess? Lichen-encrusted walls encircled the manor in long sweeping curves and as they drew nearer, she saw a dry moat very similar to the one around Troyes. There was a wooden drawbridge, an open portcullis and an archway that opened out into the manor yard.

Conscious of Gawain studying her, Elise guarded her expression. Her heartbeat wasn't so easy to control—it was thudding like a drum. Dear Heaven, this manor was hers.

'Welcome to Le Manoir des Rosières,' Gawain said, as they rattled across the drawbridge.

The place wasn't all military. A couple of trees cast shade on one side of the tower—an apple tree, a bay. There were flowers too. A woman in a grey gown was watering a pink rose bush. Nearby, a froth of white roses formed an archway, a shady bower over a bench.

'Le Manoir des Rosières,' Elise murmured. 'They must water the roses daily in this heat.'

'They do indeed.' Dark eyes met hers. 'My mother planted them.'

Elise nodded and tipped her head back to examine the tower. She had no words. It was one thing to be told by Gawain that he was giving her a manor. But to actually ride into the forecourt and see the place for herself—she could barely speak. It was beautiful. A fortified manor that looked pretty and welcoming. She might not want to live here permanently—how could she abandon singing?—but it was wonderful to know that she had this to come back to. There would be no more cold winters. No more counting every penny.

She looked at the roses and cleared her throat. 'Gawain, thank you.'

'It is my pleasure,' he said, smiling warmly at her. 'Would you care to refresh yourself before I show you your new domain?'

'Thank you, I would.'

Elise stood in the manor hall, staring with her mouth agape at a huge hanging on the south wall. Facing the dais, Gawain's golden griffin stalked across a blood-red canvas. It was magnificent and terrible. Half eagle, half lion, the griffin's beak was curved like a scimitar. Its claws gleamed with gold thread and the lion's tail seemed to twitch as she looked at it. Walking up to it, Elise ran her fingers over the cloth.

'Your mother's handiwork?'

'My aunt, Lady Una, worked it. It used to hang at Meaux.'

Elise touched his hand. 'You see? Lady Una does love you.'

'Not necessarily. That is the device of the Count of Meaux. She sent it along with news of my uncle's death.'

She smiled at him, shaking her head. 'Gawain,

this will have taken years to work. Each stitch is imbued with love and dedication. Your aunt wouldn't have given it to you if she didn't love you.'

'It's simply my coat of arms.'

'It's far more than that. Your aunt loves you, Gawain, as I am sure you will discover when you visit her at the convent.' She stepped back a pace, focusing on the griffin. 'Look at those feathers! And the fur of the lion's hindquarters, his tasselled tail. It really is marvellous work.'

Gawain's mood seemed to change as he took Elise on a tour of the rest of the keep. Her hand was taken in a tight grasp, and he strode off at such a pace it was hard to keep up with him. Elise found herself towed up the spiral stairs and they stepped into a large room lit by five lancets. Stone seats had been built into the window embrasure—they were heaped with cushions. There was a wide fireplace and, on a side table, an ivory-and-ebony chess set.

'The solar,' he said, in a curt voice. His mouth was tight. He looked almost upset.

Giving him a thoughtful glance, Elise found tongue for the most basic of questions. 'Does the solar take up the whole floor?'

'Aye, the family bedchambers are higher up. This way.'

His mouth was a tight line and his manner had become brusque to the point of rudeness. Elise preceded him up another turn of the stairs. What had caused his change of temper? On the landing outside one of the bedchambers, she hung back. Remembering the roses curling round the garden trellis—Le Manoir des Rosières had been his family home—she thought she understood it. Gawain was regretting his generosity.

'Gawain, what's wrong?'

His eyes were unreadable. 'Nothing. Come, this way.'

Elise couldn't shake the idea that he was having second thoughts about giving her the manor. 'You're in a very great hurry.'

'My apologies. I shall be setting out for Paris at first light, which means I must speak to Sir Raphael tonight. And I have messages to deliver to Count Henry.'

Elise's fingers curled into her palms. 'I hadn't realised you would be leaving so soon,' she murmured. He was very eager to get away. When would she see him again? It would be good to know. Her chest ached. 'Won't you stay until Pearl arrives? Don't you want to see her?'

His expression softened. 'If Pearl arrives before I leave, I shall be pleased. If not, I have to get back to Troyes with all speed.'

'You might pass them on the road.'

'True.'

Elise found herself staring at the pulse on Gawain's neck. 'You're going to tell Sir Raphael about André and the counterfeiters.'

'He has to be told what happened in Provins.' He tilted her chin up and forced her to meet his gaze. 'Elise, I have promised to speak up for André and I will honour that promise. The rest is up to him. He will have to convince Sir Raphael that he is fully reformed.'

'I understand.'

'When I return to Troyes I shall visit you. I can see Pearl properly then.'

Elise had the distinct impression that Gawain's mind was elsewhere. Certainly he had much to think about—his betrothal, visiting his aunt... She searched his face. 'I thought you'd be dashing off to Sainte-Colombe after your audience with the King.'

'That rather depends on the outcome.'

'Oh?'

Lips curving into a slight smile, he shook his head at her. 'If possible, I will come to see you.'

Heart lifting, she returned his smile. 'You want to check up on me. Make sure I haven't caroused the nights away and drunk your cellars dry.'

'They are your cellars now. I will return because I need to know that you have everything you need. And that you are happy here.'

He pushed opened a door and ushered her into a large bedchamber. Aubin was before them, he had a heavy wooden trunk by the handle and was dragging it to the door.

Gawain made a sound of exasperation. 'Use your head, Aubin. That's far too heavy for you to take down on your own. Get someone to help you.'

'Yes, *mon seigneur.*'

Aubin vanished down the stairwell and Elise met Gawain's eyes. 'This was your bedchamber?'

'It is yours, if you choose,' Gawain said. 'You may prefer another bedchamber. However, this fireplace is the largest. In winter the extra warmth is most welcome.'

The rest of the tour proceeded in like manner, with Gawain moving at breakneck speed. Elise was whisked in and out of three small bedchambers. She was given scant seconds to glance at a larger one that put her in mind of the novices' dormitory in the convent. Gawain muttered something about this being the bedchamber the womenfolk used. There were more bedchambers higher up and, at the very top, a guardhouse.

Almost before she knew it, Elise was standing outside at the foot of the steps to the hall, waiting to bid Gawain farewell. He had told her so much about the manor her head felt as though it was going to burst. How long would it take for her to feel at ease here? The purple pavilion had been home for so long. Still, if she didn't take to manor life, the pavilion would be waiting for her.

Gawain was standing outside the stables, fair hair catching the sun as he issued last-minute instructions to Sir Bertran, the manor steward. Elise had learned that Sir Bertran's wife, Lady Avelina, was the woman who had been watering his mother's roses. Lady Avelina had been acting as chatelaine and Gawain had instructed her to help Elise settle in. Folding her hands together, Elise drew in a lungful of air. Sir Bertran and Lady Avelina looked pleasant enough. Elise thought she would learn to like them. Even so, it would take time for her to feel confident as lady of the manor.

Peering through the gateway, she looked down the road to Troyes. She was hoping to see André returning with Vivienne and the babies. However, save for a priest on a mule, the road was empty. Tears pricked at the back of her eyes. Despite Gawain's reassurances that he would return after his audience with the King, she doubted he was being realistic. He had so many responsibilities. It could be weeks, even months, before he returned. She would have liked him to see Pearl before he left.

Aubin led The Beast out of the stables and looped the reins round a ring in the wall. Then he went back into the stable.

Sir Bertran's voice, though low, drifted across the yard. He appeared to be questioning something Gawain had said, '…not under any circumstances?'

Elise pricked up her ears.

'None,' Gawain said, firmly.

Elise hid a smile. Gawain had told her this manor was entirely hers, but the habit of issuing orders was clearly hard to break. He remained very much in command. No matter. Until she found her feet, that was probably just as well. Running a manor was not something she had been bred to. She had much to learn. Hopefully Sir Bertran and Lady Avelina would guide her. Sir Bertran struck her as being a reasonable and straightforward man. Gawain had chosen him as his steward, and since

Gawain had himself been steward at Ravenshold, he would know what qualities to look for. She trusted his judgement.

'Furthermore, when André...' Gawain turned his head and his voice faded before strengthening again '...Troyes, make sure he has an escort. Sergeant Gaston and half a dozen troopers are to accompany him. Understood?'

Sir Bertran nodded. 'Understood.'

Gawain strode back to Elise. Taking her hand, he pressed warm lips to the back of her fingers and released her. '*Au revoir*, Elise.'

Conscious of Sir Bertran hovering nearby, Elise replied formally, '*Adieu*, my lord.'

A pleat formed in Gawain's brow. '*Adieu*? I much prefer the sound of *au revoir*.' He was looking at her mouth and she felt her colour rise. 'I shall be returning, you know.'

Cheeks aflame—Gawain really ought not to look at her in such a way in public—Elise dropped into a curtsy. Out of the corner of her eye she saw Aubin had brought out his horse and was already mounted. 'Farewell, my lord.'

A long finger traced a line down her cheek. Spurs chinked as he turned and went for his horse.

Elise stood very still as the Count of Meaux and his squire clattered over the drawbridge and on to the road. A wide dust cloud trailed in their wake, rolling over the fields like a mist. When would they return? She had no idea.

Taking a deep breath, she smiled brightly at Sir Bertran. 'You have much to teach me, sir, I am sure.'

Sir Bertran smiled. 'You won't be bored, *madame*.'

It wasn't long before Elise's friends arrived. She was in the hall with Sir Bertran as he outlined his plans for her induction into her role as lady of the manor when the rumble of cartwheels had her lifting her hand.

'One moment, sir,' she said, going to the door.

Vivienne and the babies were ensconced in the cart and hedged about by outriders. André pelted across the forecourt and Vivienne fell into his arms.

Elise's vision misted. Blinking hard, she hurried over to the cart and reached for Pearl. Elise nuzzled Pearl's cheek. Pearl cooed. Elise kissed Pearl's nose. Pearl gurgled and waved her arms about, catching hold of a strand of Elise's hair. She seemed to be trying to tug it out from under her veil.

'No, you don't.' Elise twitched her hair free and

kissed Pearl again. 'I missed you, my love,' she said, fiercely. Cuddling Pearl, she walked about the forecourt to allow Vivienne and André to exchange their news. They looked very intent. Doubtless André was talking about what had happened in the caves.

Elise wandered tactfully away, taking Pearl to the bench beneath the white roses so that Vivienne and André might speak privately. The sun moved slowly across the sky and at length she returned to her friends. They were still wrapped round each other.

Vivienne smiled at her, eyes sparkling.

'Did you see Lord Gawain on the road?' Elise asked.

'Briefly. He didn't stop to talk.' Vivienne shifted away from André to take stock of the manor. Her jaw dropped. 'Saints, Elise, we can live here?'

'If you wish.'

In the hall it was immediately clear that Vivienne was thrilled to be brought to the manor. Bruno clutched to her breast, she rushed round touching everything—the polished trestle on the dais; the crimson wall hanging; the embroidered bedcovers in the bedchambers.

'André and I won't be bedding down in the

hall—we are to have our own bedchamber?' she asked, in hushed tones.

'Certainly.'

Elise and Vivienne left André introducing the babies to Lady Avelina and went back upstairs to set up the babies' cradles. There was an alcove in one of the bedchambers that would make a perfect nursery.

As Elise watched Vivienne's excitement she felt a twinge of guilt. 'Vivienne?'

'Mmm?' Vivienne moved to the window slit and peered out at the fields.

'Would you prefer living here to life on the road?' Elise asked.

'Wouldn't you?'

'I…I am not sure.' Elise nudged the leg of a wooden stool with her toe. 'Until now I've never given it much thought. Singing is how I make my living and it never occurred to me that I had a choice.'

'You didn't before this.' Vivienne gestured about her. 'This changes everything.'

Elise sank on to the stool. 'I suppose it does.' She felt like pinching herself. 'I haven't had time to think.'

Vivienne squeezed her arm. 'It's not surprising.

In your heart, you didn't believe it would really happen. I can't say I'm surprised.'

Elise frowned. 'I don't follow you.'

'You're not used to dealing with someone like Lord Gawain—an honourable man who values you highly.'

Elise remembered the heat in Gawain's eyes as he had kissed her hand in the manor courtyard. 'He values me, all right,' she murmured. 'As a bedfellow.'

Vivienne made a tutting sound. 'Elise, at times you are quite ridiculous. Lord Gawain holds you in very high esteem. André has already told me what happened at Provins—how Lord Gawain dashed to your rescue the instant Baderon came to him for aid. It is so romantic, better than one of the ballads.'

'It is no such thing,' Elise spoke sharply. 'André won't have told you how Lady Rowena found Lord Gawain and me alone in a bedchamber. He had barely a stitch on. There was nothing romantic about that, I can assure you. It was mortifying.' *Particularly when Gawain dragged on his tunic and went off with Lady Rowena without as much as a backward glance.*

'Count Gawain wants you, of course.' Vivienne

shrugged. 'That is natural. The man is in love with you.'

Elise felt herself go still. Sounds seemed louder than they had a moment ago. She could hear the rumble of Sir Bertran's voice in the hall below. She could hear the crowing of a cockerel and the clang of the blacksmith's hammer. *The man is in love with you.* If only it were true.

'I blame your father,' Vivienne was saying. 'He treated you so poorly it has given you a dislike of men.'

'I don't dislike men!'

Vivienne narrowed her eyes at her. 'Don't you?'

'Of course not. You know I like André and Baderon and…and I like Lord Gawain too.'

'You *love* Lord Gawain, but you would die before you admit it. And you do seem to enjoy punishing men.'

'What?' Elise was aghast. 'That's not true!'

'Isn't it?' Vivienne's gaze was steady. 'We could start with your first lover, poor Robert.'

'*Poor* Robert? What about him?'

'You broke his heart.'

'I did nothing of the kind. Robert and I agreed we did not suit and we parted, and—'

'There's Sir Olier too,' Vivienne went on softly.

'You never let him close either. Even when you are Blanchefleur you keep men at arm's length. Face it, Elise, you don't trust men. That's why you never let them close.' She sighed. 'It's your father's fault.'

'Father loved my singing. It was Mother who put Morwenna and me in the convent.'

'Maybe, but you idolised your father and you hoped he would fetch you out again. But Ronan Chantier was busy with his own life and he didn't want the burden of looking after two young girls even if they were his daughters. So you sought him out and when you found him you used your voice to persuade him to let you stay.'

'Father loved me for my voice. He didn't love me,' Elise agreed, quietly. Sad to say, she knew it was the truth. Her father had only allowed her to continue living with him because as a singer she was the perfect partner for a troubadour.

Vivienne squeezed her shoulder. 'Gawain is not the same. He is a good man and he sees into your heart.'

Elise swallowed. 'He did tell me he searched for me after I left.'

'Lord Gawain loves you, Elise.'

'He's going to be married.'

'He loves you.'

'Even if he does, he would never say.'

Vivienne shook her head. 'What a pair you make.'

Elise forced a smile. 'I wonder what he thinks of Blanchefleur.'

'He doesn't give a fig for Blanchefleur, though I am sure he admires her singing.' Vivienne shook her head. 'It is your misfortune that you left him at the turn of the year. Had you remained it is my belief he would have married you.'

Elise's throat was too tight to speak.

'Elise, he's a good man. You've allowed him closer than the others because of Pearl. Don't mess this up, try to trust him. Lord Gawain values you. And don't look so worried, I'm sure he'll be back.'

Chapter Fifteen

Shortly after sunrise, Elise rode out with Sir Bertran and a couple of men to learn the boundaries of her land. First she inspected the village and met the village priest. In the fields, scythes flashed—villagers were cutting hay for the manor horses.

Next Sir Bertran rode with her to a vineyard where the vines were weighed down with grapes. Whilst he talked, Elise couldn't stop thinking about her conversation with Vivienne. She didn't keep men at arm's length! And she certainly didn't punish them. For a start, Vivienne had misunderstood what had happened between her and Robert. They just hadn't suited. And when Elise had left Gawain she'd done so not to punish him but because he belonged in another world to her. He…

'Madame?' Sir Bertran looked expectantly at her.

Lord, he'd been talking about the vines and was

waiting for her to respond. Elise plucked a question out of the air. 'We make our own wine, sir?'

'Yes, *madame*. Our wine is very palatable, although we can't compete with Count Henry in terms of quantity.'

They inspected some nearby woodland.

'There is excellent hunting here, *madame*,' Sir Bertran told her. 'Plenty of game. We have deer and even boar. We set up nets to trap birds, and later in the year there will be hawking elsewhere on the estate.'

Elise tried to force herself to concentrate, but her mind was only half on what Sir Bertran was telling her. She hadn't forgotten André's promise to Gawain. André must go into Troyes and speak with Sir Raphael. By suppertime tomorrow, if he showed no signs of honouring his promise, she would have to remind him.

Fortunately, a reminder wasn't necessary. After inspecting the manor fish pond, Elise and her escort turned homewards. At the crossroads, a faint haze over the Troyes road marked the passage of a party of riders leaving the manor. A red pennon streamed behind them.

Marking the gleam of a soldier's helmet, Elise focused on the horses. She looked at Sir Bertran. 'Sir, those riders—is André among them?'

Sir Bertran squinted at the riders. 'Aye. Sergeant Gaston will be taking him to the castle barracks. I believe a conference has been arranged with Count Henry and Sir Raphael.'

'Thank goodness,' she murmured.

'Madame?'

'Lord Gawain will be pleased.' She threw Sir Bertran a worried look. 'I hope the Guardian Knights deal kindly with André.'

'Lord Gawain, if you would wait here,' the nun said. 'I will send for Lady Una.'

'My thanks.'

The nun closed the door behind her. Gawain was standing in an airy, high-ceilinged chamber—St Mary's guest house. It was lit by old-fashioned Romanesque windows and though the furnishings were sparse, being simply a large wooden table and two benches, it resembled a small knight's hall. A green curtain divided the chamber in two. Gawain guessed the sleeping area must lie behind it.

He didn't have long to wait. He had barely had time to draw breath before the door opened and his aunt hurried in, skirts sweeping the floor.

'Gawain?' Lady Una held out her hands. A faint smile lifted the corners of her mouth.

346 Lord Gawain's Forbidden Mistress

As Gawain took her hands and kissed them, he was pleased to see that she was not wearing a novice's habit. His heart lifted. 'My lady, it is a pleasure to see you.'

'It is?'

'Can you doubt it? You always were my favourite aunt.'

Lady Una's eyes twinkled. 'As I recall, I am your only aunt.'

He grinned. 'That helps, certainly.' He held her at arm's length. 'You look well, my lady. Hardly a day older than when I last saw you.'

'You're too kind.' His aunt's smile faded. 'What brings you to St Mary's, my lord? Are matters awry at Meaux?'

'Far from it.' Releasing her hands, Gawain grimaced. 'However, I have made a decision and you must be the first to hear of it. My lady, I intend to seek an audience with King Louis.'

'Something is wrong. I knew the moment Sister Ella came to find me. What is it?'

'My lady, I came to inform you—with much regret—that I cannot marry Lady Rowena.'

Lady Una drew herself up. 'Gawain, I cannot have heard you correctly. What are you saying?'

'I cannot marry Lady Rowena.'

Several wrinkles appeared on his aunt's brow.

'But…but you must! The King has agreed.' She gripped Gawain's arm. 'Your uncle fought tirelessly for the match. Does that mean nothing to you?'

Gawain held her gaze. 'It means more than I can say to know that Count Etienne promoted the match on my behalf.'

'He loved you, Gawain.' Lady Una's eyes glittered with unshed tears. 'We both loved you. It was just…'

'I know.' Gawain laid his hand on hers and sighed. 'Lunette.'

'She was our life.' Lady Una stared at the floor, gave herself a slight shake and looked up. 'Etienne found it hard to accept that she was truly gone and that you were blameless.'

'It was an accident.'

She nodded. 'Of course it was. And once Etienne had accepted it, he did his best to find you the perfect bride—the King's goddaughter, no less. Will you throw that away?'

'*Madame*, I am afraid that I must. I cannot marry Lady Rowena.'

The wrinkles deepened. The smile was quite gone. 'Why not?'

'There is someone else. I love her.'

'Who is she?'

'Her name is Elise Chantier. She—'

'Chantier? You're in love with a singer?' Lady Una's voice was laced with contempt. 'Gawain, are you seriously telling me that you are spurning Lady Rowena de Sainte-Colombe for a singer?'

'Elise is more than any singer. She is my life. And if she will have me, I will marry her.'

'If? Of course she'll marry you—you are a count and she is a singer.' Lady Una stared at him. 'You really haven't asked her?'

'Not yet. I am not free. I thought to speak first to you and the King.'

'What of Rowena?'

'Rowena has no more wish to marry me than I her.'

Lady Una's mouth worked. 'Her father swore she was eager for the match.'

'That is not the case. My lady, we really are not suited. But that is not the issue. I love Elise.' He paused. 'I also love our daughter.'

His aunt put her hand to her throat. 'Daughter?'

'Her name is Pearl. You would love her, my lady. She is beautiful. Small and perfect.'

Lady Una's expression softened. 'A daughter,' she murmured, in a choked voice. 'Daughters are very precious.' Sniffing slightly, she turned away.

'My lady, I intend to acknowledge Pearl. I will

do my best for her. I know you will be disappointed in me, and I regret that. But I cannot ignore my duty as a father.'

His aunt wiped her eyes on her sleeve. 'No.' She sniffed. 'You love her. And you say you love this Elise Chantier too?'

'With all my heart. My lady, there are difficulties in Troyes, which means I must meet with the King as soon as possible. Do I have your blessing?'

A day had slipped by with no word from André. There had been no word on the second day either. Or the third. By sunset on the fourth day, Elise was sitting on the bench with Pearl beneath a froth of white roses. She was humming a lullaby, presenting a serene face to the world, trying to ignore the maelstrom of questions whirling through her mind.

What was happening in Troyes? Had Sir Raphael heeded Gawain's request to listen sympathetically to André? Why hadn't André sent a message back to the manor? He must know how worried Vivienne would be. Why the silence? Why?

Vivienne came round the corner of the keep with Bruno over her shoulder and Elise stopped humming. Vivienne's eyes were shadowed, her mouth tight.

Elise waited until Vivienne was sitting next to her. 'You've heard nothing?'

'Not a word.' Vivienne smothered a sob.

Elise kept her voice calm. 'Very well, we shall wait until morning, and if we've still not heard from André, I shall ride into Troyes.'

'You'll go to the garrison?'

'It's the best place to start. Sir Raphael is Captain of the Guardian Knights. He and his men are based there. If I can't find him, I shall insist on speaking to Count Henry.'

Vivienne stroked Bruno's head. Her eyes were bright with unshed tears. 'This waiting is torture.'

Elise squeezed her hand. 'I know. Vivienne, I am sorry.'

'It's not your fault. Elise, I should dearly like to come with you, but the babies make that difficult.'

Elise gave her a bright smile. 'Don't worry. I will make faster progress on my own.'

'Thank you,' Vivienne said, in a small voice. 'Thank you a thousand times.'

At breakfast next morning, Elise took a place on the dais next to Sir Bertran and Lady Avelina. 'Good morning, Sir Bertran. My lady.'

'Good morning, *madame*.'

Lady Avelina offered her the bread basket and Elise took a chunk of bread.

'My thanks. Has there been any news from Troyes?'

Sir Bertran's good-natured face crinkled in puzzlement. *'Madame?'*

'I was wondering if André had sent a message.'

'There has been no news.'

'In that case I must ask you to arrange an escort for me.'

'You have plans for this morning, *madame*?'

'Business in Troyes.' Breaking off some bread, Elise started to eat. After a moment or two she became conscious of a strained silence. Her skin prickled.

Lady Avelina was biting her lip. She avoided Elise's eyes. 'Ex…excuse me, *madame*.'

The bench rocked as Lady Avelina left the table. With a sinking feeling, Elise saw that Sir Bertran's face was no longer as relaxed as it had been when she had first come to table.

'Sir Bertran?'

'My apologies, *madame*, but it will not be possible for you to go into Troyes today.'

Elise dropped her bread on the table and her

chin came up. 'I do not think I understand you, sir. You are my steward, are you not?'

'Indeed, *madame*.'

'And you have yourself been riding out with me these past few days.'

'Indeed, *madame*.'

'But I cannot ride today?'

'You may ride, *madame*, provided you remain on the estate.' Sir Bertran cleared his throat. 'You may not ride as far as Troyes. You must stay within the manor boundaries.'

A knot formed in Elise's stomach, an unsettling mix of anger and fear. 'You forbid me? How can this be? I thought this manor was mine and that all the retainers, including yourself and the guards, must follow my orders. Surely I may do as I wish?'

'Yes, *madame*, of course you may.' Sir Bertran shifted. He looked as though he was sitting on a heap of thorns. 'In almost every respect. It is just that—'

'Lord Gawain ordered you to constrain me.'

Her steward spread his hands. '*Madame*, it is for your safety.'

Elise gritted her teeth as the image of Gawain and Sir Bertran muttering together in the stable yard sprang into her mind. So that was what they'd been talking about! Before he had left for Paris, Gawain had given Sir Bertran orders forbidding her to leave the manor.

'Did he give you orders to have me cloistered here permanently?'

'My lady?'

'Am I your prisoner, sir?'

Sir Bertran's jaw dropped. 'Prisoner? Lord, no. It is for your protection, *madame*.'

'Protection?' She spoke through clenched teeth. 'It sounds very much like imprisonment.' She lifted her eyebrow at him. 'You won't let me go to Troyes.'

'With regret, *madame*, I will not.'

'Not even if all the men make up my escort?'

'I am sorry, *madame*, not even then. You may go anywhere you like within the estate.'

'That's not good enough. I need to go to Troyes.'

He bowed his head. 'I am desolate, *madame*, but that is not possible.'

'What about tomorrow? Will you take me tomorrow?'

'*Madame*, I cannot.'

Her nails bit into her palms. 'Lord Gawain has ordered you to confine me.' She couldn't believe it and yet the anger surging through her told her she must believe it. Gawain had confined her.

She had had enough of confinement after being dumped in the convent with Morwenna and she had vowed it would never happen again. Gawain knew this, and yet here he was, imprisoning her. Le Manoir de Rosières was a very pretty prison and it had large boundaries, but as far as she was concerned it was a prison, none the less.

What would Sir Bertran do if she told him that she had decided to pack up the cart and leave for Poitiers? Except she couldn't do that. Not without André. Not without Vivienne.

Her thoughts jumped this way and that. Was Gawain keeping her here so he could force her into being his mistress? He must know that she loved him. They had fallen upon each other in the bedchamber at Provins Castle. They had barely managed to stop. The attraction between them was as strong as it had ever been.

How humiliating. Gawain had deduced she wouldn't be able to hold him at bay for ever. He had galloped off to Paris to conclude his marriage agreements with the King and when he got back he wanted to ensure that she was conveniently waiting for him here.

No. *No.* Her thoughts were running away with her. She knew better than that—Gawain would never force her. She took a steadying breath. Controlling her anger—she was beginning to see it was induced by panic at the thought of being confined—she narrowed her eyes at Sir Bertran. 'Lord Gawain gave you these orders for my safety?'

'Assuredly. Lord Gawain is concerned for your well-being. *Madame*, he was most discreet about what happened in Provins. None the less, he made it clear that whilst you were to be given free rein in the manor, you were not to ride into Troyes. It is dangerous.' Sir Bertran curled his lip. 'The place is full of riff-raff and until the Guardians have rooted them out, you are to remain here.'

'I see.' Elise searched her steward's face. It was a kind face. It was also a strong face. Sir Bertran would not be swayed. Gawain had given him orders and he would obey them. Slowly, Elise unclenched her fists. It seemed that her only course was to persuade Sir Bertran to help her. 'Your loyalty to Lord Gawain is admirable, sir.'

He grimaced. 'I hope you will come to see my loyalty is also to you, *madame*.'

'I hope so, Sir Bertran, because I do need your help.'

'You are concerned about André.'

'It's been days since his meeting with Sir Raphael. We should surely have heard from him by now. Vivienne is mad with worry and, frankly, so am I.'

'Sir Raphael is a good friend, *madame*. Would it ease your mind if I went to the garrison myself today?'

Elise felt herself relax. 'Thank you, sir, that would be most kind.' Elise wasn't used to relying on others. It felt more than a little unsettling. However, if she was truly to become lady of this manor, she ought to try and start.

Sir Bertran took his time in Troyes. The morning dragged by, slow as a snail. He didn't return.

Elise paced the hall. She walked up and down the manor garden, rocking Pearl in her arms. She took Pearl to the bench beneath the white roses. She jumped up again and paced some more—around the bay tree, up to the apple tree and back to the bench. And still there was no dust cloud on the road from Troyes, just a charcoal smudge on the horizon where clouds were building. Elise narrowed her eyes at them for a moment, slightly surprised at what she was seeing. Could it be smoke? No, the sky really was darkening with the first clouds she had seen for weeks. There was no sign of Sir Bertran or André.

Elise went into the stables with a vague idea of

escape forming in her mind. She was showing Pearl the horses when Vivienne poked her head round the door. Vivienne was biting her lip so hard, she must surely draw blood.

'What can have happened?' Vivienne asked. 'Where's André and why isn't Sir Bertran back?'

'I've heard nothing.' Elise walked down the stalls, studying the horses. She was judging which one would be the fastest and whether she could handle it. The chestnut gelding was a possibility; the black mare didn't have enough muscle; the grey was too heavy boned. She homed in on the chestnut gelding. Most promising. 'If we've heard nothing by suppertime, I swear I shall charge past the guards and gallop into Troyes myself.'

Vivienne looked at her, worry in her every line. 'They'll follow you.'

'So? I shall ride like the wind. By the time they catch me I shall be at the garrison.' Vivienne went on chewing her lip and Elise gave her a friendly nudge. 'Don't do that, love.'

Noon came and went. Elise's stomach churned. She went back to the bench with Vivienne. More clouds were piling up. After weeks of endless blue they looked black and threatening.

Elise fanned herself with the edge of her veil.

'Saints, you'd think Champagne must melt in this heat.'

Vivienne focused on the clouds. 'Do you think it will rain?'

'I hope so. The land is parched. And rain might cool things down a bit.' Elise eyed the steps leading to the top of the curtain wall. Truly, the combination of heat and tension was enough to drive one mad. 'I'm going on to the walkway. I need to sing.'

Vivienne nodded and held out her arm. 'I'll take Pearl. She'll want feeding soon, in any case.'

'Thank you.' Elise was glad she didn't have to explain. Vivienne understood how her worries fell away when she sang. The song was all.

Gawain and Aubin were cantering along the road to Troyes. Triumph was a heady feeling, and the pounding in Gawain's chest matched the beat of The Beast's hoofs. The King had agreed to his petition. Count Gawain de Meaux and Lady Rowena de Sainte-Colombe were no longer betrothed.

Gawain was free. *Completely* free. A generous donation to the King's favourite monastery had bought him the King's leave to propose to the lady of his choice.

The Beast pounded along. His coat was flecked with foam and the heat rising from his body warred with the heat of the sun. Along the edge of Gawain's vision, a dark bank of cloud was swallowing up the blue. He tore off his helmet and wiped grit from his face. He grinned at Aubin. 'There will be a storm later.'

Aubin grinned back. They dug in their heels and sped along the dusty highway. Tall purple thistles rocked at their passing. The dry grasses waved.

Initially, Gawain's audience with the King had been awkward, but by the end of it he'd been more than pleased. First, he'd handed the King a letter from Lady Rowena. Gawain had seen the letter. Indeed, Lady Rowena had asked him to aid her with its composition. Lady Rowena's letter opened with her saying that she would, of course, obey her liege lord the King in all things—she would marry Lord Gawain if he so insisted. However, she felt obliged to inform the King that she had a higher calling. She wanted to become a nun.

Lady Rowena's letter hadn't cajoled or pleaded. She had simply stated her case and had closed by saying that she remained in all things her god-father's obedient servant. She sent the King her good wishes and reassured him that she held him in her daily prayers. She awaited his decision, trusting that God would guide the King as He seemed to be guiding her.

And the King—himself the most pious of men—had agreed.

Gawain's heart was lighter than it had been in weeks. He would shortly be seeing Elise. He was determined to make her his countess. They would marry and Pearl would be legitimised. Doubts remained, to be sure. Did Elise love him? Would she accept him as her husband? He brushed his doubts aside. The King had agreed to his petition. Today, all things were possible.

Poppies flashed by in a blur of red. They had reached the outskirts of Troyes.

Aubin waved at the castle rearing up behind the city walls. 'Aren't we stopping at the garrison?'

'No time.'

They stormed past Troyes. When the manor appeared, Gawain slowed The Beast to a walk and wiped more grit from his face with his sleeve. He grimaced at Aubin. 'I stink of horse and sweat.'

'You'll be wanting a bath, my lord.'

'If you please.'

Aubin nodded and then frowned. 'Which bedchamber will you be using?'

'*Mon Dieu*, Aubin, I don't care. But I can't greet my lady like this.'

'No, my lord.'

In Paris, Gawain had bought Elise a gold chain for her enamel necklace. He'd wanted to buy more, but he thought she'd enjoy the pleasure of choosing something for herself, and he knew she valued that enamel pendant. It would be safer on a proper gold chain. He would hunt out another gift—a betrothal gift—later. He glanced at the lute strapped to his saddlebag. He'd bought it for André, to replace the one the counterfeiters had broken. He intended to give it to the lad when he knew he'd done the right thing by helping the Guardian Knights in their quest to find the counterfeiters.

Gawain ran his gaze over the manor battlements, habitually checking the guards were in place. He could see the occasional glint of metal as they patrolled up and down and felt himself relax. He saw a splash of blue. A woman was up on the walkway. Elise? He couldn't quite make out her features, but Elise had a gown in just that colour.

When he heard the singing he knew it was Elise. The song seemed to hang in the warm air. It was as though Elise were greeting him. Except she couldn't possibly be greeting him, because she was facing east, facing that ominous bank of cloud. Gawain could imagine the look on her face though. It would be as rapt as it had been that night in Count Henry's great hall. She was lost in her singing, blind to the world.

'What are they doing?' Aubin asked, pointing. Several villagers were gathered on the other side of the moat and were looking up at her.

'Elise has an audience.' Gawain shook his head and smiled. 'Not that she's noticed.'

The song—a ballad from the south—seemed to resonate deep inside. Gawain couldn't make out the words, but the yearning in Elise's voice made his heart ache. As they rode closer he recognised it.

It was a love song, a tragic love song about two lovers—a knight and a fairy who, despite their love, failed to bridge the divide between their two worlds. Gawain drew rein and allowed Elise's voice to reach deep inside him.

His eyes prickled. Merciful heaven, what a voice! It was clear as a bell. Even though Elise was singing outside rather than in a hall, every word and syllable remained strong. The notes vibrated with passion. She was singing about love— was she singing from experience?

Gawain knew there was no other man in her life. *Does she love me? She must love me to sing with such feeling.* It was a heartening thought. The notes floated out over the estate, pure and true, wavering slightly when she reached the point in the story when the knight—afraid of losing his love—had her confined in a tower. Gawain stiffened. He had forgotten the ending.

The tale flowed inexorably on to its tragic climax. When the fairy flew out of the tower and vanished for ever, leaving only a handprint behind her. Gawain swore under his breath. Elise hated being confined. She really hated it. Lord, he ought not to have left instructions for her to be hemmed in on the estate. Still, he was back now and as soon as he explained that he had only been thinking of her safety, she would surely understand.

Chapter Sixteen

Having finished her song, Elise went through the hall on her way to the nursery. She was halfway to the stairwell when she realised that Sir Bertran's squire was on her heels.

'Gilles, you wanted to speak to me? You have news from Sir Bertran?'

'Oui, madame.' A pleat formed in Gilles's brow. 'Sir Bertran regrets that he was unable to send word earlier, but a fight broke out in Strangers' City. Sir Bertran has joined forces with Sir Raphael and they are combing the camp for the troublemakers.'

'And André?'

Gilles shuffled his feet and refused to meet her eyes. 'Sir Bertran lost sight of him in the skirmish. We think he's with Sir Raphael.'

Elise caught her breath. 'You *think* André is with Sir Raphael—are you telling me you don't know for certain?'

Gilles spread his hands. 'I am sorry, *madame*.'

Anxiety balled in Elise's stomach. She glanced at the hall entrance, but all she could see was the tawny hair and amber eyes of the man—Jerome—who had locked her in the cellar with André. He had such cold eyes. Dead eyes. The eyes of a killer?

André must be found. She had to get to Troyes—fast.

'Gilles, this is not the message I was hoping for.' She paused. 'You understand you must say nothing of this to Vivienne?'

'As you wish, *madame*.'

'Thank you.'

Assuming a calm she did not feel, Elise retraced her steps and went out into the bailey. Regardless of Gawain's orders, she was going to Troyes. Casually, humming under her breath, she drifted languidly towards the stable door. Once inside, her eyes landed, not on the chestnut gelding, but on an ugly black-stockinged bay being rubbed down by one of the grooms. The Beast. Gawain was back. She must hurry.

'Lord Gawain has returned, I see,' she said lightly.

'Yes, *madame*.'

The gelding was stabled only a couple of stalls

away. Moving towards it, Elise smiled at the groom. 'What a beautiful animal. I've a mind to put him through his paces in the forecourt. Might I trouble you to reach down that saddle?'

Gawain was dragging on a clean tunic after his bath, rehearsing what he would say to Elise, when the door bounced open and Aubin hurtled in.

'My lord, Elise has gone!'

Gawain's throat went dry. 'Explain.'

'She's taken the chestnut gelding. Gilles tells me that her friend André went into Troyes as you had hoped, but he didn't come back. Sir Bertran went after him and—'

'Elise has gone in to Troyes?'

'Apparently.'

'Why the devil wasn't she stopped?'

'She told the men she was going to try out the horse in the bailey. And with you having returned, the guards weren't expecting her to gallop straight past them.'

Swearing, Gawain snatched up his sword. 'Saddle fresh horses.'

Elise tore towards the city, clinging like a burr to the gelding's back. Its hoofs drummed on the dry earth and she prayed she wouldn't fall. Elise had never liked galloping—it took too much effort just to stay on. And today she was more distracted than she had ever been. Gawain was back. He would be furious that she had gone into Troyes, but he'd left her with no choice. She had to find André. What would she say to Vivienne if anything had happened to him?

The atmosphere was heavy, tense with the threat of thunder. Instinct kept Elise in the saddle. As the fields rushed past, hot air filled her lungs. After about three miles the tents of Strangers' City came into sight, and she became aware of a horse pounding up behind her. Hauling on the reins, she slowed the gelding enough to shoot a glance over her shoulder. A few lengths behind her was the raw-boned grey from the manor stables. The horseman wasn't wearing a helmet. His fair hair was whipped by the breeze. *Gawain.* The distance between them was closing fast.

Steadying the chestnut, Elise sighed. She wasn't a fine enough horsewoman to attempt to outrun him. Catching her breath, she waited.

The grey came to a shuddering standstill. Dust whirled. Gawain's hand came out as though to snatch at her reins before drawing back and coming to rest on the pommel of his saddle. 'You won't run?' he asked, eyes wary.

'Is there any point?' Elise glared at him. 'It seems you are determined to curtail my freedom.' She couldn't help notice there were faint shadows beneath his eyes. A sheen of perspiration gleamed on his face, and his hair was disordered by his race from the manor. To her eyes he would always be the most handsome of men and it irked her that even in her anger, she couldn't tear her gaze from him. 'Gawain, you told Sir Bertran to cage me. How could you?'

He grimaced. 'I am sorry.' His chest heaved and he jerked his head towards the encampment. 'I thought only for your safety. Those men you are so intent on finding are dangerous.'

She narrowed her eyes. 'You thought only of my safety.'

The grey sidled closer. 'Can you doubt it? Elise, I thought you understood.' His lips twisted. 'The bond between us is so powerful, I was certain you understood. It was my mistake, and I am sorry. Until I heard you singing up on the wall I didn't understand how strongly you feared confinement.'

Elise felt her cheeks burn. They were surely as red as the poppies fringing the highway. 'You were there? I hadn't realised.'

'That cellar in Provins—you were very brave, you must have been terrified.'

Her throat tightened and her eyes prickled. 'I was.'

'I won't confine you again, I swear it.'

Gawain's eyes held hers, dark and sincere. He held out his hand. Slowly she reached out and their fingers locked. He hadn't taken time to put on his gloves. 'Thank you.'

His mouth went up at the corner. 'Lord, Elise, it is good to see you.' Leaning in, he pressed his mouth to hers. Elise swayed closer. His lips felt warm and welcome and she let them linger. *Home.* Slightly startled by the thought, she drew back and touched her mouth. She had never had a home, not really, but when Gawain kissed her she felt as though she was where she belonged. She smiled and squeezed his fingers and glanced towards the encampment.

'Gawain, André—'

Nodding, Gawain kneed the grey into a walk. He didn't let go of her hand and Elise couldn't bring herself to let go either, so they continued towards the encampment with linked hands. They passed a couple of barns on the town outskirts in a companionable silence. It felt good to be holding his hand. Too good. Elise forced herself to remember what they were doing. 'We must find André,' she murmured.

The meadow next to the walls of Troyes was lost beneath the tents and pavilions of Strangers' City. Everything looked muted. Canvas was faded by sun and a coating of dust; grass was bleached to the colour of straw, and in patches it had completely died away. On the path between the purple pavilion and the ale tent the ground was cracked and dry. A desert must look like this. Overhead, dark clouds loured.

'I went to the King,' he said.

'Your audience went well?'

'Elise, I am free.' He looked intently at her. 'Lady Rowena and I are not going to marry.'

Elise's heart gave a painful twist and she forgot about André.

'Lady Rowena and I agreed we are not suited,' Gawain added. 'The King has released me from my betrothal agreement.'

'So that was why you went to Paris.'

Gawain smiled and his fingers tightened before he let go of her hand. 'We will talk more later.'

Elise followed his gaze. A troop of mounted knights was milling about in front of the ale tent, the Champagne pennon hung from a lance. The Guardians were out in force and they'd clearly seen action. Several sullen-looking men were roped together like cattle bound for market. Prisoners. The knights watched their prisoners in a relaxed manner. One leaned casually on the pommel of his saddle. Weapons were sheathed. Helmets had been removed. The fight, if there had been one, was over. Or was it?

Elise's heart skittered. She couldn't see André. Sir Bertran was among the knights guarding the prisoners. He had seen Gawain and was breaking away from his fellows, urging his horse towards them. Where was André?

A bolt of lightning shot out of the clouds. Thunder cracked and large raindrops bounced on the ground, sending up tiny puffs of dust.

Sir Bertran reached them. He met her gaze. '*Madame*, your friend's testimony has proved most useful. As you see, the counterfeiters have been caught.'

Rigid with tension, she clutched the reins. 'Where is he? Where's André?'

Sir Bertran looked uneasily at her. 'That, *madame*, is the difficulty. He is missing.'

Elise looked at the prisoners. Heart thumping, she urged the gelding towards them, examining the men's faces one by one, looking for a mop of tawny hair and cold amber eyes. She was mindful of the big-boned grey at her shoulder and of Gawain's watchful gaze.

'Elise?'

Sick to her bones, she brushed raindrops from her face. 'Jerome—the man who locked us in the cave—he's not here.'

Lightning flashed. Thunder rolled overhead and in its wake, Elise could have sworn she heard someone shouting.

'Over here! Help! Over here!'

The thunder crashed again and Elise and Gawain exchanged glances.

'The tent,' Elise said, digging in her spurs. 'That came from our tent!'

They reached the pavilion and flung themselves from their horses. Sword out, Gawain caught Elise's wrist. 'Wait here.'

Heart in her mouth, Elise nodded. Gawain dived through the opening. Rain poured over her. Hands shaking, she edged closer. *Lord, let André be safe. Lord, protect Gawain.* She heard a thump and a strangled gasp. Fighting. Her heart pounded. Someone gaze a sharp cry.

Elise couldn't bear to stand by and do nothing. She cast about for a weapon and her gaze fell on the water cauldron. It was sitting in a heap of soggy black ash that had once been her cooking fire. She snatched it up.

'Elise, put that down,' Gawain said.

She whirled round. Gawain was standing by the tent flap with his sword at Jerome's throat. A cut on Jerome's cheek was seeping blood, and the rain was washing it into his tunic. André—he had a black eye—was using a guy rope to tie Jerome's wrists.

Dropping the water cauldron, Elise stumbled over. 'André, thank God!'

'Thank Lord Gawain,' André said.

Jerome gave her a look of loathing. 'You witch, I knew you'd make trouble.'

André jerked on Jerome's bonds. The rain sluiced down. There was movement on the track between the tents. The Guardian Knights had followed them. Gawain smiled at Elise and gestured Jerome towards them. She seemed to have lost her tongue.

Gawain is no longer betrothed to Lady Rowena.

She stood by the pavilion as Jerome was handed over to Count Henry's knights. It was a relief to see him safely under guard. She said nothing as he was led off to join the other prisoners. Nor did she say much to André when the knights had gone. She simply gave him a hug and sent him on his way to Vivienne.

And then there was only Elise and Gawain standing outside the purple pavilion with the rain pouring over them. Incongruously, Elise found herself watching bubbles form along the cracks in the earth. It was too warm to become chilled, but she was drenched. Her veil was clinging to her neck and shoulders. Grimacing, she eased it away.

'You're uncomfortable.'

She shrugged. 'I'm not going to complain about a little wetting, Lord knows we need the rain.'

'That's true.' Gawain gestured at the entrance to the tent. She thought she saw him hide a smile. 'It's time to take shelter.'

An odd shiver ran down Elise's spine as she went in. It felt as though she was stepping into someone else's life. Stripped of most of their belongings, the place felt bereft. Rain beat on the canvas and trickled through the slash at the back. André had made that tear when he had to cut his way in to avoid being seen. It felt as though a hundred years had passed since then. Two coffers had been left behind. One held an assortment of cooking pots, a jar of herbs, some wooden spoons. The other contained bundles of ageing linens— a moth-eaten blanket; scraps of silk intended for ribbons; a red cloak that had once belonged to her sister, Morwenna.

Gawain ducked through the opening. A couple of strides brought him to her and he pulled her close.

'I'm surprised these things haven't been stolen,' she murmured, gesturing at the cloak.

'I asked Sir Raphael to watch the tent.'

'Thank you.' She smiled into his eyes and watched them go black.

'My pleasure.' He swallowed and went on looking at her.

The rain had darkened his hair. His gaze was hungry. It made her hot and she couldn't look away. Not that she wanted to. Not that she needed to. She eased closer and relaxed against him. Gawain was no longer betrothed. His arms tightened about her. Overhead, thunder rolled and crashed.

Gawain gave a strained laugh. 'So.' He kissed her ear. 'Your André is safe.'

'Thank you, Gawain.' They were standing toe to toe and Elise couldn't stop smiling. It was heaven to feel his arms about her again. Heaven to be able to slide her hands up his chest and grip his wide shoulders. Her heart was all fluttery. She felt nervous. Excited. Why had he set aside his betrothal?

She could hardly breathe for wanting to know. 'I expect he is halfway back to the manor by now.'

'Aye.' Gentle fingers moved up and down her ribcage. 'Elise, I almost forgot, I bought you a gift in Paris.'

'Oh?'

Easing back, Gawain opened his scrip and pulled out a small roll of silver silk, tied up with a white ribbon.

When Elise took it from him her fingers were thumbs. Giving him a curious glance, she tugged at the ribbon and caught the glitter of gold. 'A chain?' she murmured, holding it up. 'You are giving me a gold chain?'

His lips twitched. 'Never fear, it's not strong enough to constrain you,' he murmured. 'It's for your pendant. It will be safe on a proper chain.'

Touched that he understood how much the enamel daisy meant to her, she closed her fingers over his gift. 'Thank you, Gawain.' Her voice was husky.

'Let me help you put it on.'

Elise pulled out her pendant and the old cord was swiftly removed. She ran her fingertips over the chain. 'It's beautiful, thank you.'

'My pleasure.' His eyes danced. 'I hoped you would like it because there's something important

I wish to ask you.' A tiny smile lifted the corner of his mouth. 'Elise, will you marry me? Will you share your life with me?'

Her mouth went dry. She could barely answer. 'I might.'

An eyebrow lifted. 'Might?'

Lifting up on her toes, she kissed his chin. Gawain loved her. He must love her, for Gawain, that most honourable, most chivalrous of men, had done the unthinkable. He had gone to the King and asked to be released from his betrothal agreement. He wouldn't have done that if he didn't love her. Gawain was a man of action and his actions spoke for him. He had torn the town apart looking for her last year; he had taken them to live in La Rue du Cloître in order to protect them; he had given her a manor so that she and Pearl would never go hungry. He had bought her a gold chain for her pendant.

'Gawain, if you love me, I shall consider it.'

His eyes gleamed. 'I need you. And, yes, I most certainly do love you. Elise, say yes. You know you love me.'

She shook her head. 'Do I?'

'You know you do. Besides, we have to marry. Think of Pearl—if we marry, she can be legitimised.'

'Gawain, I am not your match. You need an heiress, someone trained to be wife to a count.'

He shrugged. 'You have your manor. Practise on that.' His grip tightened. 'Be warned, Elise, I'll not let you refuse me. To my mind, you've had exactly the right training.'

'How so?'

He lowered his mouth to within an inch of hers. 'You have spent many years in a convent. You have learned the virtues of control and self-denial. You are patient and loyal to your friends. You are a wonderful seamstress. Oh, and you sing quite well…'

He smiled and the warmth of his mouth was temptation himself, but Elise didn't give in to it. Not yet. She longed to marry him, but she had to know that Gawain understood that the difference in their upbringing might cause difficulties. Their road would not always be easy.

'Elise, half the noblewomen of Christendom are trained in convents. You've had exactly the right training. And I've seen you as Blanchefleur. You have poise and elegance as well as beauty. I have no doubt that you could deal with a thousand importunate retainers if need be.' He dipped closer and their lips touched.

He sounded very sure. Elise's heart swelled. She

ran her forefinger lightly down his nose, cupped his cheek with her palm and smiled into his eyes. 'Yes, I will marry you.'

His breath caught and he bent to kiss her. The kiss drew out. Their tongues played and their breath became flurried. Rain pattered on to the pavilion. *'Merci à Dieu.'* He kissed her cheek. 'Beloved.' He kissed her neck. 'I missed you in Paris.' He nibbled at her ear and drew back as though looking for her response. 'As I missed you last year.'

Elise's throat was tight. 'I missed you too, Gawain.'

He lifted his head and it bumped the canvas. A stream of water cascaded through the tear in the back. Laughing, he pulled her aside. 'One moment.' Fastening the door flap, he delved into the coffer and draw out the blanket. 'We shall sit over here and wait out the storm.'

She arched an eyebrow at him. 'Sit? My lord, you disappoint me.'

A large hand reached for her and she was pulled unceremoniously on to the blanket and shifted on to his lap. 'We've work to do, before we can sit,' he murmured.

'Work?'

A glint in his eyes, Gawain turned her head.

Long fingers found a hairpin and pulled it out. A shiver of pure delight ran through her. 'This veil is soaked, beloved. You'll catch a chill. It has to come off.'

'Very well.' She let him remove her veil, but when she felt his fingers at her side lacings she covered his hand with hers and shook her head. 'Your sword belt must be very uncomfortable, my lord.'

He tossed the sword aside, and then it was his turn again. 'Your gown.' He shook his head.

She grinned. 'Too wet?'

'Far too wet.'

A brief, breathless flurry later, and a few stolen kisses, Elise was sitting on his lap in her shift. Gawain's hands were on her breasts, gently stroking, smiling each time he teased a moan from her. There was another exchange of kisses so heated they were breathless when they drew apart. Cheeks on fire, Elise ran her palm over his tunic and tugged at it. She frowned. 'Damp, definitely damp. I cannot allow the man I love to die of the lung fever.'

Dark, grey-flecked eyes looked deep into hers. 'Love?'

Flushing, she nodded. 'I love you, Gawain.'

His tunic vanished. Somehow they were lying

on the blanket and Gawain was stroking her shift up and out of the way. He moved over her and she felt him ease into her body.

'Beloved.' He closed his eyes and his groan of pleasure made Elise feel as though she might melt. 'Is that all right? I'm not rushing you?' His face changed and she felt him freeze. 'It's not too soon after Pearl?'

'No, no.'

'Not hurting?'

'Not hurting. Heaven,' Elise managed. She curved her hands round his buttocks and held him to her. She was tingling all over, alive as she hadn't been in months.

Gawain still had his boots on. He hadn't stopped to remove his hose. She'd planned to play with him a little, to tease him as he had teased her when he'd fondled her breasts, but her body was more than ready. And she understood his impatience, she felt the same. She pressed her body against his and gripped him hard, finding the rhythm that she remembered so well.

Her gasps mingled with his and the rhythm quickened. 'I love you, Gawain.'

'Love, love,' he muttered, running his tongue around her ear.

Elise was heedless of the knights a few yards

away, heedless of the lightning flickering outside, heedless of everything save the warmth of Gawain's breath against her skin and the feel of him inside her again.

He groaned into her ear, 'Beloved, I love you.'

'I love you,' Elise gasped her response and the purple pavilion faded in an explosion of joy.

* * * * *

MILLS & BOON®

Why shop at millsandboon.co.uk?

Each year, thousands of romance readers find their perfect read at millsandboon.co.uk. That's because we're passionate about bringing you the very best romantic fiction. Here are some of the advantages of shopping at www.millsandboon.co.uk:

* **Get new books first**—you'll be able to buy your favourite books one month before they hit the shops

* **Get exclusive discounts**—you'll also be able to buy our specially created monthly collections, with up to 50% off the RRP

* **Find your favourite authors**—latest news, interviews and new releases for all your favourite authors and series on our website, plus ideas for what to try next

* **Join in**—once you've bought your favourite books, don't forget to register with us to rate, review and join in the discussions

Visit **www.millsandboon.co.uk**
for all this and more today!